Mouthwatering Praise for Nancy Coco's Mysteries

Death Bee Comes Her
"Personable characters and lots of honey lore."
—*Kirkus Reviews*

"Sprinkled with delightful notes on honey and its various uses, this debut novel in the Oregon Honeycomb Mystery series is a fun introduction to a new cozy series. Everett, the Havana Brown cat, is an animal delight, often proving to be smarter than the humans around him."
—*Criminal Element*

"The author writes a captivating story with interesting characters. Naturally, Everett [the cat] contributes to the solution. A charming read."
—**Reviewingtheevidence.com**

"This warm-hearted book is fast-paced, with realistic dialogue and a captivating plot."
—*Mystery and Suspense Magazine*

Have Yourself a Fudgy Little Christmas
"Two nasty murders, charming surviving characters, plenty of Christmas cheer, and enough fudge recipes for a major sugar rush."
—*Kirkus Reviews*

Forever Fudge
"Nancy Coco paints us a pretty picture of this charming island setting where the main mode of transportation is a horse-drawn vehicle. She also gives us a delicious mystery complete with doses of her homemade fudge . . . a perfect read!"
—*Wonder Women Sixty*

Oh, Fudge!
"*Oh, Fudge!* is a charming cozy, the sixth in the Candy-Coated Mystery series. But be warned: there's a candy recipe at the end of each chapter, so don't read this one when you're hungry!"
—*Suspense Magazine*

Oh Say Can You Fudge
"Beautiful Mackinac Island provides the setting for a puzzling series of crimes. Now that Allie McMurphy has

taken over her grandparents' hotel and fudge shop, life on Mackinac is good, although her little dog, Mal, does tend to nose out trouble. . . . Allie's third offers plenty of plausible suspects and mouthwatering fudge recipes."
—*Kirkus Reviews*

"WOW. This is a great book. I loved the series from the beginning, and this book just makes me love it even more. Nancy Coco draws the reader in and makes you feel like you are part of the story."
—**Bookschellves.com**

To Fudge or Not to Fudge
"*To Fudge or Not to Fudge* is a superbly crafted, classic, culinary cozy mystery. If you enjoy them as much as I do, you are in for a real treat."
—**Examiner.com** (5 stars)

"We LOVED it! This mystery is a vacation between the pages of a book. If you've never been to Mackinac Island, you will long to visit, and if you have, the story will help you to recall all of your wonderful memories."
—*Melissa's Mochas, Mysteries and Meows*

"A five-star delicious mystery that has great characters, a good plot, and a surprise ending. If you like a good mystery with more than one suspect and a surprise ending, then rush out to get this book and read it, but be sure you have the time, since once you start, you won't want to put it down."
—**Mystery Reading Nook**

"A charming and funny culinary mystery that parodies reality-show competitions and is led by a sweet heroine, eccentric but likable characters, and a skillfully crafted plot that speeds toward an unpredictable conclusion. Allie stands out as a likable and engaging character. Delectable fudge recipes are interspersed throughout the novel."
—*Kings River Life*

All Fudged Up
"A sweet treat with memorable characters, a charming locale, and satisfying mystery."
—**Barbara Allan**, author of the Trash 'n' Treasures Mystery Series

Also by Nancy Coco

The Oregon Honeycomb Mystery Series

Death Bee Comes Her

A Matter of Hive and Death

The Candy-Coated Mystery Series

All Fudged Up

To Fudge or Not to Fudge

Oh Say Can You Fudge

All I Want for Christmas Is Fudge

All You Need Is Fudge

Oh, Fudge!

Deck the Halls with Fudge

Forever Fudge

Fudge Bites

Have Yourself a Fudgy Little Christmas

HERE COMES THE
FUDGE

A Candy-Coated Mystery

Nancy
Coco

KENSINGTON
PUBLISHING CORP.

www.kensingtonbooks.com

This book is dedicated to Gracie Lou, aka Little Dog, for thirteen years of inspiration, love, and companionship. You inspired the character Mal and will always be with us in story. I miss you.

White Chocolate Caramel Fudge

Ingredients:
24 ounces white chocolate
14 ounces sweetened condensed milk
4 tablespoons butter
1 tablespoon vanilla
½ cup caramel sauce

Directions:
In a double boiler, slowly melt white chocolate over medium heat. Be careful, it burns easily. Add sweetened condensed milk and butter. Stir until melted and combined. Remove from heat and add vanilla. Stir until combined. Heat caramel sauce for twenty seconds until easy to spoon and drizzle.

Pour fudge into a parchment-lined 8 x 8-inch pan. Drizzle caramel sauce on top. Use a knife to swirl the caramel into the fudge. Chill until thickened. Cut into one-inch squares and enjoy! Can be stored in an airtight container in the refrigerator or freezer. Makes 32 servings.

Chapter 1

Thursday

"It's bad luck to walk under a ladder."

I stopped short and looked up to see Peter Ramfield salute me with a paintbrush. Waving back at him, I stepped off the sidewalk in front of the McMurphy Hotel and Fudge Shop to get a view of the new color. "Is it bad luck for you or me?" I asked.

"I think it's best if we don't find out either way," he said.

"That's probably true," I called up. Lately I've had my fair share of bad luck and didn't want to cause it for anyone else.

At least now the McMurphy was remodeled and back to its glory. The historic committee had agreed I could go back to the original butter yellow color with pale blue trim. The old girl looked quite lovely decked out in her new colors.

"How's it looking?" Mike Hangleford called from his place on the scaffold beside Peter.

"Looks great!" I said and did a thumbs-up motion. Mike's company had won the bid to paint the exterior of the building.

Winter retreated slowly on the island and this spring had been cold. The temperatures were only now reasonable for outdoor painting. The guys were pros, painting quick enough to take advantage of the warmth and make the McMurphy whole again.

It was the last week of May on Mackinac Island and we were far enough north to still get frost. I wore a spring jacket over a hooded sweatshirt and a turtleneck made of cotton and sprigged with flowers. The sun shone warmly in a bright blue sky, but the wind was cool off the lake as it brushed up against the flowers on Main Street.

Still, it was warm enough to paint. That was what I told myself anyway. The early bird pricing was also attractive.

Technically we had less than one week until the tourist season started. Main Street officially opened to tourists the first week of June, but I had chosen to be open year-round. During the dark, deep winter months of January, February, and March, I had only one, maybe two guests a week. Often they were contractors working on the interiors of the stately Victorian cottages. The homes were called "cottages" and considered vacation homes, even though they were huge, sometimes three-story mansions with gingerbread accents and wraparound porches.

"Hold the door!" my best friend, Jenn, called as I went to open it. She hurried around the scaffolding. "Thanks! Isn't it gorgeous out?" Her face glowed, her cheeks rosy from the wind.

"Yes," I said. "I'm so glad the weather is finally warming up—especially with the summer season starting next week." We both walked into the McMurphy's lobby. My bichon-poodle pup, Mal, greeted us with a joyous bark, followed by a run and slide. She loved sliding and hitting my legs with her head first.

Reaching down, I picked her up and scratched her behind the ears. Mella, my calico cat, opened one eye and gave the dog a disapproving look from her curled-up position on top of one of the wing-backed chairs near the fireplace.

"I've got the most amazing good news," Jenn said. "I booked the Wilkins wedding." Jenn was not only my best friend, but was a business partner, building her event-planning operation out of my office.

"Wonderful," I said. "When is it?"

"They want to be married the second week of June," she said as she opened an app on her cell phone.

"Wait, isn't your wedding next week?" I had to point out the obvious. "How are you going to have time to plan hers and yours? What about your honeymoon?"

"The Wilkins wedding is the event of the year and I am not turning down the opportunity to build my brand. Besides, they want to use your new rooftop deck. Think of the view and the pictures. It'll be the best publicity of the year. People will start booking the entire hotel for the wedding party. You're only a carriage ride away from historic St. Anne's Church and the beach."

"But your wedding is a once-in-a-lifetime event," I said. "You should be concentrating on that."

"That's what I have you for," she said with a wave of her beautifully manicured hand. The one-carat, princess-cut diamond on her finger sparkled in the light.

"I'm your maid of honor, so it's my responsibility to let you know that I don't want work to overshadow your big day." We walked through the pink-and-white-striped lobby of the McMurphy to the back corner, where the reception desk was.

Frances Devaney, my general manager for the hotel, sat behind the desk working on her computer. "I have to agree with Allie," Frances said. "As a new bride myself, I can tell you that your wedding day is more stressful than you think. Seriously, it's very different from planning someone else's."

"Pooh," Jenn said. "I have everything about my day under control." She raised her hand, counting on her fingers. "My dress is coming in this week from Chicago and I have an appointment with Sara Grant for final alterations. Sandy Everheart is making the cake, which is a salted honey, orange blossom cake with honey and orange buttercream frosting. She's going to make a chocolate carriage with a bride-and-groom figure for the top. Then the rest will be decorated with real flowers that mimic my bouquet. Which I've ordered already. Terra Reeves is going to cater the reception, which will take place on your rooftop deck, and set up as an informal buffet. We're having ham and scalloped potatoes, which are Shane's favorite. Bruce Miller will deejay and we'll dance the night away with family and friends."

I shook my head and smiled at the dreamy, determined look on her face. "You know as well as I do that even the best-planned events can take wrong turns along the way."

"Pish," she said and leaned on the reception desk. "I have back-up plans for my back-up plans. It'll be perfect and I'll have plenty of time to work on the wedding of the year."

"Where are you two going for your honeymoon?" Frances asked. Frances was seventy-three years old and had gotten married last summer to my handyman, Douglas Devaney. The two had delayed their honeymoon until after the tourist season. "The Bahamas are great. Quite a bit more sun and warmth than here, although I do love our beaches."

Frances was five foot four at one time and had shrunk an inch or two as she aged. She had short brown hair and wide brown eyes. Today she wore a long, red sweater over a yellow blouse and a yellow and red skirt that covered her knees. Her makeup was always perfectly done. I had seen pictures of her in the '60s and her hair had been a short bouffant. It still was well styled and you would guess she was in her early sixties.

"Shane and I are meeting for dinner at six to make our final choice," Jenn said. "I want to see Paris in the springtime. He's more practical and thinks we should go to Quebec instead." She sighed.

"Quebec is lovely in the spring," Frances said. "You can save money for a house."

"Oh, we don't have to save," Jenn said. "That's where I went this morning. We bought the old Carver cottage near Turtle Park."

"You bought a house?" I asked. "How did you swing that?"

"The Carver cottage has been abandoned for a decade at least," Frances said. "I heard it was on the auction block."

"Yes," Jenn said. "We got it for ten grand. It needs a new roof, new windows, new floors, new plumbing, upgraded electrical, and other minor upgrades. The basics like the roof, plumbing, and electrical will be done before the wedding so that we can move in and finish the rest ourselves. Shane and I are excited about doing a lot of the work."

"I didn't know Shane was into construction," I said. Shane Carpenter was the crime scene investigator for Mackinac County, which included Mackinac Island and St. Ignace, which was a ferry ride away on the Upper Peninsula of Michigan.

"He put himself through college roofing homes," Jenn said. "I'm going to do the decorating. Anything we can't do ourselves will be done by Shane's friends."

"Sounds like fun," I said. "But are you sure you aren't doing too much?"

"Have you ever known me not to accomplish what I set out to do?" Jenn asked.

"No," I said with a smile. "But you've never been the bride before, either." I put Mal down so she could settle into her dog bed beside Frances. "Just don't be afraid to ask for help. You have friends who are willing to pitch in."

"I know," Jenn said. "That's why I love you guys. Okay, I've got to scoot. I promised to set up a cake tasting for Jessica Booth. She and Max, and the families are all in Chicago. Good thing I know some great cake shops in Chicago."

"Wait, the Wilkinses aren't local?" I asked.

"No, silly, that's why we're going to rent the entire McMurphy for the wedding weekend."

"But don't you want to be there for the cake tasting?" I asked.

"That's why we have airplanes," Jenn said. "Which reminds me, I have to call Sophie to schedule flights up and back for myself and the family. Got to run!" She hurried up the stairs behind the reception desk.

The McMurphy's lobby took up the entire first floor of the building. At the front of the building, in the right-hand corner, was the fudge shop. I had walled it off in glass so that guests could watch the fudge making and my pets would be safely outside the kitchen.

Across from the fudge shop was a small, cozy sitting area with free Wi-Fi, a fireplace. and open views to Main Street. Behind the sitting area was Frances's station, which included the reception desk and mailbox cubbies for the guest rooms. Across from that was another seating area with winged-back chairs, two comfy couches, and the all-day coffee bar.

Finally, there were two sweeping staircases to the upper floors on either side of the lobby and in the center of the back wall was an old-fashioned, open elevator for guests who couldn't walk up the stairs.

"That girl has too much energy," Frances said with a shake of her head. "But it's great that she is going to fill the McMurphy with wedding guests."

"I know two weeks out is the middle of June, but it's been so cold this year. I hope it's not too chilly for the reception on the rooftop deck."

"We have the tower heaters," Frances pointed out. "That was a good investment, by the way. Along with the white tent top in case of rain."

"Those were for Jenn's reception," I said. "But if she keeps reserving the rooftop for her events, they will pay for themselves by the end of the season."

"I don't know where she gets her energy, but I'm glad she's back."

"Me, too," I said. "Her time in Chicago nearly broke my heart."

"We have Shane to thank for her return." Frances looked

down through her brown cat-eye glasses at her computer screen.

I agreed. Last fall Jenn had an opportunity to work for one of the most prestigious event planners in Chicago and we had all let her go. But by Christmas she had missed us and realized she couldn't be away from Shane. So she had come back and proposed her own event planning business, to be run out of the McMurphy. I had agreed immediately, of course. Shane, on the other hand, had taken his time to welcome her back. But when he did, he did it with an engagement ring.

The dead of winter isn't the best time to start an event planning business on Mackinac Island because it's really isolated, so Jenn had gone back to Chicago until April to finish out her contract. It was great to see her so happy— even if she was making me wear a blush pink brides-maid's dress.

It was nearly nine p.m. and I was getting ready for bed when my phone blew up with a flurry of text messages. I heard the whoosh beep, whoosh beep, whoosh beep as the messages came through. It was not a good sound. I put down my hairbrush and picked up the phone, but before I could read the messages, the phone rang. It was Jenn.

"Jenn, what's going on?" I sat down on the edge of my bed. Mal looked up at me from the floor while Mella leaped onto the bed and eased over to me.

"Shane didn't show up for dinner," she said. Her tone was one part angry and another part worried. "I sent him text messages, but he didn't answer. I called and it went to his voice mail."

"Where are you?"

"I'm in front of the Nag's Head Bar and Grill," she said. "We were supposed to meet here at seven. I waited until eight to call him. I mean, sometimes he can get caught up in his work at the lab. But he's never been this late."

"Did you call his office?"

"Yes," she said and blew out a long breath. "He left at five. The ferry company says he was on the five-thirty ferry. So he's here, but I don't know where. I'm worried."

"I'll get dressed and meet you down there," I said. "Call Rex and see if he might know what's going on. I'll text you his cell number so you don't have to go through the police dispatch."

"Thanks," Jenn said. "I'm sorry, I know you like to go to bed early."

"Don't worry, just stay where you are and I'll meet you." I pulled on a pair of jeans and a thick, long, pull-over sweater. Mal followed me around, wagging her stump tail hard. "Oh, you think you're going out?"

She was totally going out with me. When it came to my friends and my fur babies, I would drop everything to make them happy. I put on her halter and leash. She grabbed her leash with her mouth and followed me out of the apartment, down the stairs, and out through the lobby.

Luckily I remembered to snag my jacket on the way out of the lobby. We stepped outside, and a brisk wind rushed off the lake, forcing me to zip my jacket quickly and pull my gloves from my pockets. Mal followed along beside me, carrying her leash. We were a block away from the bar when Mal spotted Jenn and sprinted toward her.

"Mal!" Jenn called her name and picked her up and scratched her behind the ears.

"I thought you could use a couple of friendly faces," I said. "Did Rex know anything?"

"No," Jenn said and I could see the dark shadows of worry on her face from the light given off by the bar. "He said it had only been a couple of hours and he was certain there was nothing to worry about."

"But you're worried," I said.

"Shane's never done this," she said. "Never. And then to not pick up my calls or even send me a text . . . Something is wrong."

"I agree," I said and put my arm through hers. "But it's freezing out here. Let's go grab a coffee at the Lucky Bean and make a plan."

"Okay," Jenn said, sounding a little bit comforted by my and Mal's presence. "I'm glad you came. I didn't know what to do. I couldn't just go home and wait. What if he's lying in a street somewhere hurt?"

I gently guided her toward Market Street and the Lucky Bean, which was across from the police station. She clung to Mal like a lifeline. My pup loved the attention and I was glad I'd brought her. "I know Rex downplayed your concern, but don't think he's not looking for Shane, too."

The streets were dark, lit by only a handful of replica gaslights that now burned electricity. A horse-drawn carriage went by, the hooves clipping at a slow, steady state. Mackinac Island banned all motor vehicles except for the fire truck and ambulance. It meant that most people got around by horse-drawn carriage, bicycle, or walking. I liked the fact that life moved at a slower pace here. It drew people to vacation on the island and enjoy a step back in time.

We got to the mouth of the alley that ran between Main and Market streets. Mal sniffed the air, barked, and leaped out of Jenn's arms.

"Mal!" we both called at the same time as she took off, dragging her leash down the alley away from the McMurphy. We hurried after her. The alley was dark and filled with the trash bins and back-door decks of the apartments and shops that lined Main Street.

"I can't see her," Jenn said.

I pulled out my phone and hit the flashlight app. It lit a few feet in front of us. I heard Mal bark. We moved swiftly in her direction. Mal stopped and barked again. My flashlight caught the shadow of a man wearing a short coat. His back was to us and when he turned we recognized him.

"Shane!" Jenn and I said at the same time.

Shane turned back and the light from my phone glinted off something metal in his hand. Something dark dripped from what looked like a hunting knife. I stopped cold when I saw a heap at Shane's feet.

"Shane?" Jenn slowed as her brain registered the scene.

"Call nine-one-one," Shane said, his voice sounding shaky. "There's been a murder."

Chapter 2

"Shane?" Jenn said.

"Stand back," he said. His hand shook. "This is an active crime scene."

"Nine-one-one, what is your emergency?"

"Charlene," I said, keeping my eye on Shane. "There's been an incident. We're in the alley between Huron Street Pub and Grill and the Lilac Bed and Breakfast. Please send the police and the ambulance."

"I've notified them both," Charlene said. "Allie, did you find another dead body?"

"I'm not sure," I said. Jenn opened her mouth and I put up my hand like a stop sign. "There's a lot of blood."

"Well, thankfully you are close to the police station. You should be able to hear sirens."

"I do," I said and took Jenn's hand and gently pulled her to my side.

Rex ran down the alley. He was wearing workout gear, but had his gun in his hand. Officer Brown was not far behind him, wearing his on-duty uniform and riding a bicycle. Behind him came the ambulance. The siren stopped and the lights of one of the few motor vehicles allowed on the island lit up the scene.

"What is going on?" Rex asked as he stopped between us and Shane.

"We came out to look for Shane," I said and glanced at Jenn, who covered her mouth with her hand in horror.

"Looks like you found him," Rex said and pointed his gun. "Shane, put up your hands and drop the weapon."

Shane raised his hands in the air.

"Slowly," Rex ordered.

Officer Brown ditched the bike and had his gun pointed at Shane. My heart pounded in my chest. "Do it," Officer Brown said.

Shane nodded and slowly bent his knees, keeping his left hand up, and placed the knife on the ground a foot away from the person who was still bleeding.

"Now, stand up slowly," Rex said, his expression grim. "Do you have any other weapons on you?"

"No," Shane said.

"Take careful slow steps toward me and out of the scene," Rex said and put his handgun in the back waistband of his running sweats. Rex was about five foot ten and had a shaved head, broad shoulders under the sweatshirt he wore. I always thought he had that action hero sort of look to him.

Jenn and I held our breath as Shane took slow careful steps toward Rex. He stepped in a straight line. We were all highly aware that Officer Brown still held a gun on Shane. Jenn had tears running down her cheeks. Mal sat beside Rex and appeared to be waiting to see if he needed any help.

Shane got to within a stride's distance from Rex, who said, "Get on the ground." His tone was very serious. Shane immediately did as requested. He was slow and determined in his actions. "Put your hands behind your back," Rex said.

Shane followed through. Rex nodded toward Officer Brown, who put away his gun and cuffed Shane. Then he pulled him to his feet. Once Shane was cuffed, EMT George Marron hurried to the person lying in a pool of their own blood, his kit in hand. George was tall with copper skin and high cheekbones. He wore his hair traditionally long and in a single braid down his back.

We waited while George felt for a pulse. He looked up toward Rex. "He's dead."

"How long?" Rex asked.

"I'm not an ME." George stood and carefully retraced his steps out of the crime scene. That's when we heard a moan.

Adrenaline rushed through me. George whipped around, but the dead man didn't move. Rex swept his flashlight over the scene and we all gasped when he discovered someone sitting with their back against the building. They had long hair and wore jeans and a sweatshirt.

George hurried toward them. Rex went with him. "Bring a gurney," George shouted. The second EMT went running back to the ambulance and brought back the wheeled gurney. I'd never seen this EMT. He was young, maybe twenty-two, with short blond hair and a thin physique.

Rex hit his radio. "Dispatch, we're going to need a medevac."

I inhaled sharply. I'd never heard him call for off-island help before.

George and the new guy quickly rolled the person onto the gurney and took them into the ambulance.

"Where are they going to meet a helicopter?" I asked.

"They have to go to the airport," Rex said. "Lucky for that woman, George is excellent with stab wounds."

"Woman?" Jenn parroted. "Who? Do we know her?"

"Was the knife Shane was holding what stabbed her?" I asked.

The ambulance took off, leaving us in darkness once again except for Rex's flashlight.

Officers Megan Lasko and Tim Jones showed up on their bikes.

"Seal off the block," Rex ordered. "Call in the crime scene unit."

"How?" Megan asked. "Shane's here."

"John Kingsma, over in Cheboygan," Shane said. "He's the next best CSI."

Megan turned and looked at Shane, then nodded. "I'll make the call." Then she walked past Jenn and me and greeted us with a quiet nod as she went back to the mouth of the alley.

Officer Jones walked in a single line to the opposite side of the alley and strung up crime scene tape. In the dark, his movements were a circle of flashlight light bobbing up and down as he walked the tape across and then headed back our way.

"ME's on his way," Officer Lasko said. "I've strung crime scene tape at the mouth of the alley."

"Keep watch over it until the medical examiner gets here," Rex ordered. "Ladies, please follow me to the police station and refrain from speaking. I'd like to interview you separately," he said as he moved to Officer Brown and took hold of Shane by the forearm. "Brown, stay here and guard the scene. I'll send a couple of other officers to help until the ME gets here."

"Yes, sir," Charles Brown said.

Jenn and I followed Rex and Shane to the admin building. The silence was deafening, only broken by a few small sobs from Jenn. Shane didn't say a word as he walked in step with Rex.

We arrived at the police station and waited in the lobby while Rex took Shane away. Nearly an hour later, I looked at the time on my phone. It read two a.m. Mal slept quietly in my lap and I wondered how Shane was doing.

Rex stuck his head out into the lobby. "Jenn, could you come with me, please?" I picked up Mal and stood with Jenn. "Just Jenn right now, Allie."

With a sigh I sat back down. Mal sat on my lap, alert to any changes that may be coming next. Another ten minutes went by and Rex walked Jenn out, along with Officer Phyllis Davis.

"What's going on?" I asked, standing again.

"Allie, could you come with me, please?" Rex said. "Davis, see that Jenn gets home safely."

I put Mal down and she picked up her leash and followed me through the door. Rex took me to the smaller interview room and waved toward the chair opposite him. I took it. Rex sat, too, and Mal jumped up into his lap. "Mal, get down," I said. "Come here." I patted my lap and she reluctantly got down and got in my lap. "Rex?"

"This will be a quick interview to get your statement," he reassured me. "Can you tell me what happened?"

I recounted the story and that we followed Mal and found Shane.

"Did you happen to see anyone else in the alley?"

"No," I said. "But I didn't really look after seeing Shane or I would have mentioned seeing the woman who moaned by the building. I turned and called nine-one-one. Surely Shane would never hurt anyone."

"But you saw him holding the knife, right?"

"Yes," I said. "But that's all I saw. It would be pure speculation if I said his holding the knife meant anything at all."

"After you saw him, what did he do?" Rex asked.

"He said to call nine-one-one, and to stay back as he was standing in a crime scene," I said. "Or something very close to that. I can't remember exactly; it was a shocking sight, but I'm pretty sure that's what he said because I called nine-one-one right after that."

"Did he make any move to run away?" Rex asked.

"No, he stood perfectly still," I said.

"Did you feel like you were in danger at any point?"

"No." I shook my head. "No, we were all sort of frozen. It was hard not to go and help him."

"All right, that's all I needed," Rex said. "You and Mal can go home, but I may be calling on you again, and don't forget to let me know if you remember anything else."

"Okay," I said and stood, picking up Mal.

We both walked to the door and he held it open for me. As I passed by him, he said, "And Allie, please don't meddle in this case. Okay?"

I studied his handsome face and gorgeous blue eyes. "You know I don't stay out of things if my friends are involved."

He cocked his head to the left and narrowed his eyes. "Allie."

"Have a good night, Rex." I walked quickly down the hall and out into the cold spring night.

When I arrived home it was nearly time for me to get up and start making fudge. I took the wrought-iron stairs that went up to the fourth-floor owner's apartment and let myself inside. The lights were all on and Jenn was pacing the kitchen floor. The kitchen was galley style. The entire place still smelled fresh with the replaced cabinets, appliances, and new wood floors.

"Oh good, you're home," Jenn said and rushed to me. "What happened? What did Rex say?"

I gave her a quick hug and then bent down to release Mal from her leash and halter. "He asked me standard questions, like did I see Shane kill the victim and what did I see and what happened next." I straightened. "I imagine they were the same questions he asked you."

"Yes, most likely they were the same," Jenn said and wrapped her arms around herself. "He wouldn't let me see Shane. I have no idea what happened. Why didn't Shane meet me for dinner? What was he doing in the alley? Who was the victim? Who was that woman who was also stabbed? What happened?"

"I know," I said and hugged her again, but she was restless from adrenaline. "I'm going to make us some tea."

"That would be great," she said and walked around to the opposite side of the kitchen island that served as a breakfast bar and paced back and forth in front of it. "What can we do? Should we call a lawyer for Shane?"

"Any lawyer wouldn't get here until the planes or the ferries are running," I said. "I'm sure Shane is smart enough not to say anything until he has a lawyer. He's probably just hanging out in an interview room."

"I hate this," Jenn said.

"Me, too," I took two mugs from the cupboard beside the stove. "Earl Grey?"

"Yes, please," she said. "I really don't think I'm going to sleep tonight at all."

"Me, either," I said as I put tea bags in the mugs, poured in the boiling water, and turned to place one in front of her. "But you need to stop pacing. I don't want you to wear a hole in my new floors."

She sighed and half sat on one of the barstools. "My mind is racing," she said.

"Mine, too." I sipped the tea. I wasn't going to tell her that Rex had tried to get me not to investigate. He'd tried and failed a few times before. You would think he would give up and just let me work with him, but Rex was a sucker for the rule book.

"Did you get a glimpse of the victim or the injured person at all?" Jenn asked me.

"No, it was too dark, and then, when the ambulance came, all I could do was try to keep you still and watch Shane as he carefully stepped away from the scene and then was cuffed."

"It about broke me to see those guns pointed at Shane," she said in a half whisper. "To see them make him get on the ground and cuff him."

I reached over the wide island and rubbed her arm. "That was pretty scary."

"You see it on cop shows, but when it's live and someone you love . . ."

"Do you want some breakfast?" I asked and straightened.

Meow. At the sound of the word *breakfast*, Mella hopped up on the counter and rubbed against me.

"I don't think I can eat," Jenn said, her expression looking far away.

I picked up Mella, put her on the floor, and opened the cupboard where I kept her dry cat food and poured some in her bowl. Mal was suddenly beside me, sitting pretty and looking up at me with sweet eyes. I put kibble in her bowl and set it on the ground on the opposite side of me. Unlike most people who had to feed their pets in different rooms or they would fight over each other's food, I had trained my pets to eat only out of their bowl. Of course, once the bowls were empty and I left the kitchen, I suspected they each checked out the other's bowls.

"Do you think they'll arrest him?" Jenn's voice was shaky.

"That would be absurd," I said and moved around the kitchen island, took her arm, and walked her to my new blue velvet Chesterfield couch. "Shane is our crime scene investigator, and a very good one. If he were to kill someone, it would be very difficult to prove. Don't you think? I mean, he's smart enough to know what the police look for when they investigate and he would take precautions."

"Right," she said and sat down on the couch. I sat beside her. "That's right," she said. "Shane is too smart to just stab someone and wait for the police to come . . . unless it was in self-defense." She turned her head and looked at me with an emotion I couldn't label in her gaze. "What if it was self-defense? What if the victim wasn't a victim at all? What if he attacked that woman and Shane and then got in a scuffle with Shane and he stabbed the dead guy?"

"We can't try to imagine what did or did not happen," I said and put my arm around her shoulders. "We just have to sit and wait."

"I hate waiting," she said. "And who was the woman? What was Shane doing with a woman in a dark alley?

"First off, Shane most likely heard a scream and came to her rescue. Secondly, I don't know a single person who likes waiting," I said. "But there truly is nothing more we can do until we hear from Shane or Rex." I patted her knee and stood. "I'm going to take a shower and get ready to make fudge."

She glanced at her phone. "Wow, I didn't realize how close it was to your time to get up. Are you sure you don't want to get at least an hour or two of sleep?"

"I can grab some sleep after the fudge is made and Frances comes in to work," I said. "Without an assistant, I need to make all the fudge and get online sales in the mail before noon."

"You should put up a sign for a new assistant," Jenn said. "You really shouldn't be doing it all alone."

"It's what I signed up for when I took over the family business," I said. "But you're right. I'm still sad that Sandy Everheart got a better offer at the New Grander Hotel, but I need to list the job in the *Town Crier* before it's too late and all the summer workers are snatched up."

"Oh, you should put an ad in at the culinary school in Chicago. I'm sure some of the students there would love a candy making internship for the summer," Jenn said.

"Great idea," I said and put my half-empty teacup in

the kitchen sink. Mal was curled up in her doggie bed fast asleep and Mella slept on top of the cat tree in the corner of the living area nearest the windows. "I'm off to take a shower. Why don't you try to get some sleep? Shane is going to need you well rested when he gets out of jail."

"Ugh, that's so weird to hear." She frowned and stood. "Shane in jail instead of investigating a crime. I'm pretty sure I won't sleep, but you're right, I should try."

Decadent Salted Caramel Pretzel Brownies

Ingredients:

Crust:
1½ cups crushed pretzels
¼ cup brown sugar
½ cup melted butter

Brownies:
12 ounces butter (melted)
1¾ cup brown sugar
3 eggs
1⅓ cup baking cocoa
1 teaspoon vanilla
⅓ cup caramel topping
Himalayan Pink Salt

Directions:

Mix crust ingredients in a medium bowl until combined. Scoop into an 8 x 8-inch parchment-lined pan and bake at 350 degrees F for 8 minutes. Remove.

In a medium-sized heavy saucepan, melt butter. Remove from heat, add sugar, and stir. Add eggs one at a time and stir until combined. (Don't over stir the eggs.) Add baking cocoa and vanilla. Mix until well combined. Pour over the top of the crust and bake at 350 degrees F for 30–35 minutes until a toothpick poked in the center comes out moist but not gooey. Remove from heat. Let cool completely (if possible). Then warm the caramel by microwaving for 10–20 seconds until easy to drizzle. Drizzle caramel over brownies. Sprinkle salt on top for decoration. Slice and enjoy. Makes 16 2-inch squares

Chapter 3
Friday

Jenn told me that Shane didn't get out of police custody until four o'clock in the afternoon. It had been a crazy day. I managed to run on pure adrenaline and worry, finishing my fudge orders early, filling the fudge shop glass-fronted display case, cleaning the fudge shop kitchen, shipping the boxes, and walking my pup. We had ten guests check in and one check out. After lunch I managed an hour nap before getting up and working in the office on the ads for a new assistant candy maker.

Now, I made lasagna in my kitchen while Jenn sat on the couch drinking a big glass of wine.

"So they didn't charge Shane after all?" I asked as I put the lasagna in the oven and set the timer for forty-five minutes.

"Rex told me that there wasn't enough evidence," Jenn said. "Because he didn't do it, right? He wouldn't do it.

He would never attack two people, kill one outright, and then stay at the scene."

"What does Shane have to say?" I asked. "I presume you've been in touch. In fact, I sort of figured he'd come here first." Jenn planned on continuing to live with me until the house they bought was habitable.

"He did call me to let me know he was out and not charged," Jenn said and took a sip of wine. "But he won't talk about what happened."

"Not even a little?"

"Nope," she said, her expression unhappy.

I grabbed my smaller glass of wine and took the chair across from the couch. Mal jumped up in my lap. Mella was already in Jenn's.

"So, what did he tell you?" I asked.

She took a large swallow and stared at the contents of her glass for a moment. "He said he loved me and he wasn't going to tell me anything so you and I wouldn't get involved."

"Did you ask him about who the woman was?"

"Darn right I did," Jenn said.

"What did he say?"

"He said it was none of my business. I got so mad I hung up on him." Jenn frowned. "I haven't talked to him since."

"If it helps, Rex isn't talking to me about the case, either," I said.

"Well, Shane had better bring me into the case or there might not be a wedding," she said.

"Don't say that. You're just scared right now," I said. "I would be, too. Do we even know who the male victim is?"

"All I've heard is that identities were pending family notification," Jenn said. "That was a few hours ago."

"I think it's because with Shane out of the picture, we have to go to Cheboygan for information," I said. "Plus, they medevaced the woman there as well."

"I wish I lived in Cheboygan," she said.

"Is Shane going home on the late shuttle tonight?"

"No," Jenn said. "That's one thing I did get out of him. Rex asked him to stay on the island until further notice. He's going to stay with his buddy, Scott Vaden. Scott lives near the airport. Seems they went to school together."

"That's good," I said. "I was worried he was going to stay at your house even though it doesn't have power yet. When you're under suspicion it's good to have someone around to keep an eye on you should something else happen and you need an alibi."

"Yes," Jenn agreed. "We learned that the hard way."

"But he never explained why he stood you up for your dinner date?"

"He refused to talk about it," she said and got up to pour herself more wine.

"Well, don't give up on him yet," I said. "I bet we can still figure out what happened. Mackinac is a small island. Someone has to know something."

"I don't know how I can keep planning my wedding, not knowing if Shane is even going to be there." She hugged her waist with her left arm, the wineglass in her right hand.

"Don't you worry about it," I said. "I'm going to take care of the details from now on. You can concentrate on the Wilkins wedding."

"And our investigation," she said.

"Yes," I agreed. "And our investigation."

* * *

After dinner, and after the dishes were washed, I went into my bedroom and called Liz McElroy. Liz and her grandfather Angus ran the *Town Crier* newspaper. If anyone knew what was going on, it would be Liz.

"Allie," she said. "What's up?"

"Hi, Liz," I said and closed my bedroom door. "I saw the article you wrote on the latest murder on the island."

"Leave it to you to discover yet another dead body," she said. "Is there anything you can tell me?"

"I was hoping there was something *you* could tell *me*," I replied. "Any word on who the victim is or the name of the woman?"

"Well, it's not official and you haven't heard it from me, but the dead man is believed to be Christopher Harris, the local pharmacist. All of his family is in Florida right now for his grandmother's funeral. It's probably why they are waiting to let the family know."

"Christopher Harris, the local pharmacist," I parroted. "I don't think I know him. I don't really use prescription drugs."

"Oh, you know him," she said. "Tall, lanky, with dark brown eyes and sandy hair. He's about thirty-five and hangs around with Rex and the others who grew up here."

"I'm sure I'd know him if I saw a picture," I agreed. "What about the woman?"

"What woman?" Liz asked.

"There was a woman in the alleyway," I said. "She was badly hurt and they life-flighted her to Cheboygan."

"Interesting," Liz said. "Why did I not know that?"

"Was it not listed in the police blotter?" I asked.

"I didn't see it in there," Liz said. "I'm going to contact the station right now to find out why it wasn't listed. Thanks for the tip."

"If you find out anything, let me know, okay?" I asked.

"You bet," she said and hung up.

Mal scratched at the door, and I opened it and picked her up.

"Did you learn anything?" Jenn asked.

"I learned that the police blotter didn't mention the woman," I said. "Why not? How were they able to keep that quiet?"

"There's something going on," Liz said. "We need to find out what."

"It's late," I said. "I got so little sleep last night. I'm going to turn in, but I promise you, tomorrow I'm going to figure out what is going on."

"Not if I do first," Jenn said. "Not if I do first."

Chapter 4

Saturday

The next morning I was up at five a.m. to make the fudge. One thing about living on Mackinac Island was that the sun rose early and set late because we were so far north. Frances came in by eight a.m. and refreshed the coffee in the coffee bar.

Frances stuck her head into the fudge shop area. "Good morning," she said. "Douglas is in the back fixing that lighting problem we had late last night."

"Great, I'll be out in a moment for our morning staff meeting," I said. Then I sliced up the last batch for the online orders, boxed them up, and took off my hairnet and apron. Frances sat at her station behind the registration desk working on her computer. Mal got out of her doggie bed beside Frances and greeted me. Mella opened an eye but didn't move from her place in the window, soaking up sunshine. It was supposed to be warmer today, in the high sixties, which made the window pretty comfy for a kitty.

I poured myself some coffee and Douglas met me at the reception desk.

"Good morning," he said with a nod.

"Good morning, team," I said. "What all is scheduled for today?" Frances let me in on which guests were coming in and which guests were leaving. We still weren't running at full capacity.

"Let's see if we can incentivize people to write some good reviews online," I said. "That way people will know we are up and running."

"What would you suggest?" Frances asked.

"We could give a pound of fudge, or we could offer a twenty percent discount on their next stay over five days," I said.

"Great idea," Frances said. "I can design some flyers and send out some emails."

"Where's Jenn this morning?" Douglas asked. "It's not like her not to be down here plotting and planning things."

"Let's give her some time," I said. "She wasn't feeling happy when we went to bed last night."

"Is Shane not talking about what happened?" Frances asked.

"How'd you guess?" I asked.

"I figured he and Rex would tighten ranks to keep you guys from investigating this."

"They have," I said. "And Jenn is definitely not happy about it. She was talking last night as if the wedding would be postponed."

"Oh dear," Frances said.

"We need to keep an eye on her," I said. "I've never seen her so down. She feels like Shane doesn't trust her, and then finding out a woman was also involved and Shane won't talk about it is like a knife to the gut. No pun intended."

"We'll see what we can do," Frances said.

"In the meantime, I'm going to do some work in the basement," Mr. Devaney said. "Frances had a great idea for adding flower boxes on the outside of the windows to keep the crowds from pressing their noses on the glass."

"I'm hoping it means less window cleaning," she said.

"Sounds good to me," I said. "I'm ready for flowers to bloom."

My phone rang and I pulled it out of my pocket as I made my way to the fudge shop to label and mail the on-line packages. "Hello?"

"Allie, I know who the woman is," Liz said on the other end of the line.

I closed the glass door behind me so that everyone in the lobby couldn't hear. "Who?"

"It's Becky Langford," she said.

"I don't recognize the name," I said and drew my eyebrows together. "Does she live on Mackinac?"

"She grew up here, but I think she moved away after she and Shane broke up."

"Wait, she's Shane's ex-girlfriend?" My mind spun at the possibility that Shane had been late to dinner because he met with his ex.

"Oh no," Liz said. "Becky was Shane's old fiancée."

That stopped me in my tracks. "Shane had a fiancée?"

"Yes. Those two were hot and heavy starting in high school. They even went to the same college, and Shane proposed to her after he got the job in the county Criminal Investigation Unit. Becky said yes, and the whole island was buzzing. Becky's folks have a lot of money."

"So, what happened?"

"Mike Hangleford happened," Liz said. "There was a rumor that Becky had an affair with Mike. Anyway, Becky sent Shane a Dear John letter, breaking up with him. Then she packed her bags and moved to Oregon. We haven't seen her since. So no, you don't know her."

"What do you think she's doing back on Mackinac?" I asked.

"I can speculate," Liz said. "Maybe she heard Shane was getting married and wanted to see him one more time."

"Why?"

"Nostalgia, maybe," Liz said. "Or maybe she wanted to see if the sparks were still there. You know, take him back before he says 'I do.'"

"Yeah, I know a little bit about that," I muttered. Rex and I had gone on one date when his second wife, Melonie, decided she wanted him back. She'd asked Rex if she could stay with him because she had a stalker. He'd rescued her, certain she wouldn't be on the island long. But she made it through the winter on the island. So last month Rex demanded she move out of his second bedroom and find her own place.

She wasn't happy about it, and she let me know whenever she saw me.

Rex hadn't said anything about dating again. But the fact that Melonie was still on the island put a damper on romance for me.

"Does Jenn know about Becky?" Liz asked.

"I don't know," I said. "She's never talked about her.

Listen, thanks, Liz, for the tip. Keep me posted when you learn anything and I'll do the same." I hung up, made the labels, and prepped my fudge boxes for shipping. Then packed them into my totes and stepped out of the fudge shop. "I'm going to the shipping office," I said to Frances. "If you see Jenn, can you tell her to set aside some time to meet with me today?"

"Sure will," Frances said.

The bells on the door jangled as I stepped out into the street. The wind off the lake was brisk. Mal barked from the other side of the door. I'm certain she was upset I didn't bring her with me, but I didn't plan to be gone that long.

"Hey, Allie," Mrs. Tunisian called to me from across the street. She was dressed in a workout outfit and a puffy vest. Her gray hair was covered by a knitted cap with a large pom-pom on top.

"Hi, Mrs. Tunisian," I said and waited to ensure she crossed the street safely. Once she had her eyes on me, she wouldn't pay attention to the road. She almost got run over by a carriage a couple of weeks ago, when the horses had returned to the island.

"So, I hear you found another body," she said with a glint in her eyes. "What are we doing? How are we investigating?"

"Oh, I hadn't thought about it yet," I fibbed and crossed my fingers behind my back. "I still don't know who the victim was."

"I can help you with that," she said and leaned in close. "He was Christopher Harris, the pharmacist."

"Any idea who would want to kill Christopher?" I asked.

"Maybe for the drugs," she said. "People love to hold up pharmacists when they need their drugs."

"But that's never happened on the island before, has it?" I asked.

"There's a lot of things that haven't happened on the island before," she said and winked at me. "I'll see what I can find out about Christopher. I'll be in touch." She waved at me and walked quickly away.

I shook my head and took my boxes to the shipping store. Then I stopped by the police station.

"How can I help you?" Officer Travers asked from behind the front desk.

"Is Rex around, er, Officer Manning?" I asked.

"He's in a meeting," Officer Travers said. "Do you want to leave a message?"

"No," I said. "I'll text him." I went through the door and stopped beside it to write it. **Hi, Rex,** I texted. **Anything new on the murder case? How is Becky doing? Have you any updates**? That should get his attention.

My phone rang. It was him.

"Hi Rex," I answered the phone. "Where are you?"

"How did you know Becky's name?" he asked.

"You should know by now I have my sources," I said. "Did you tell Shane he couldn't talk to us about what happened? Why was he with his ex-fiancée? What happened?"

"Right," he said and blew out a long breath. "I'm at the Lucky Bean. I'll pick up drinks if you meet me there. What would you like?"

"Small hot cocoa," I said and hit END. Then turned on my heel. The Lucky Bean was right across the street from the police station. I opened the door as he stepped out. "Good timing." He sent me a crooked smile and handed me my cocoa. "Let's walk along the beach."

It was cold and the sun had gone down, so the beach was completely abandoned. We walked and sipped in silence for a while, listening to the waves.

"I wish I'd brought Mal out," I said. "She would like this walk."

"She's a clever pup," Rex said. He was silent for a moment. Then, without looking at me, he said, "I don't suppose you're going to leave this alone."

"Leave what alone?" I pretended not to know what he meant, but we both knew I was lying. "The fact that Melonie has moved out of your place but still gives me the stink eye when she sees me? The fact that you didn't tell me that she moved out and it takes me finding a dead body to get your attention?"

He was quiet for a moment. "My timing has always sucked."

"Trent isn't coming back this summer," I said. "Paige told me. She's in charge of all the island properties."

"So, you're only left with me?" he asked with a twinkle in his eye.

"I'm not desperate, if that's what you mean." I sipped my coffee.

"I've been giving you space," he said. "You had a lot going on with the rebuilding of the McMurphy and losing your fudge-making assistant."

"A girl needs friends, too," I said.

He stopped and looked at me. His gaze was warm and caused a tingle down my spine. "I've been tagged as Shane's best man."

"I'm Jenn's maid of honor."

"So, will you be my plus-one?"

"For the wedding?" I was confused. "Isn't that assumed?"

He shrugged. "Just thought I'd make it clear that it was a date."

"But that's next week, if they're still getting married and you don't lock Shane up."

"I'm not going to lock Shane up," he said.

"I know, let's do something crazy and work together on this one," I said.

"I'm tempted," he said and brushed a hair away from my face. "But it's not legal and I don't want to jeopardize the case."

"Yep," I said. "You are a man who never strays from his truth. How is it you've been divorced twice?"

"Ouch." He turned away and continued walking.

"Look," I said and touched his arm. "I'm sorry, that was low. I just want to make sure nothing gets in the way of Jenn's wedding and long-term happiness."

"And what about Christopher Harris? Don't you want to see him get justice? The only way to do that is to do things by the book."

"Okay," I said and put my arm down and continued walking.

"Okay, what?"

"You win," I said. "I'm not going to argue this with you. We're both too stubborn to see each other's side."

He touched my shoulder. "Just . . . just be safe if you're not going to listen. Okay? Every time you get caught up in one of your investigations, I lose more hair."

"You shave your head."

"See? No hair left."

We both had a chuckle and he reached down and took my hand. We walked back toward Main Street hand in hand, listening to the waves, content with the now.

Chapter 5

Sunday

I had finished making fudge the next morning when I got a text from Mrs. Tunisian: **Bring a plate of fudge to the senior center. We have news on the murder investigation.**

I texted back that I was on my way. I stepped out of the fudge shop with totes of fudge to be shipped and a plate of fudge for the seniors. Frances was at her station checking out a guest. I piled my totes on the settee next to the front door and grabbed my coat. Mal was there, wagging her stub tail furiously. "Yes, I'll take you today," I said. I put on her halter and her leash. "We're going to the senior center after the shipping office," I said to Frances.

"Stay safe," she said and waved me out as she gathered the information for the couple's next visit.

We were lucky; most people loved to schedule their next visit as they were leaving. Of course my new discount of 20 percent off for five nights didn't hurt either. In fact, it was working like a charm.

Mal behaved herself quite nicely as we walked down Main Street and then stood in line at the shipping store. Next we walked up toward the senior center. The new building was designed to represent the original native huts that once dotted the landscape, only made with modern materials. It had ramp access for wheelchairs and walkers.

Inside was trimmed with entirely honey-colored wood, warmed with a beeswax rub. There was space for a large kitchen. A small stage area and round tables for meals and the regular bingo night.

Mrs. Vissor met us at the door. "Oh, Allie, Carol said you were coming and bringing fudge. Thank you." She took the plate from my hands. "I'll be sure to leave some for everyone else." Her eyes had a twinkle of mischief in them.

I took off my coat and hung it on the coatrack and walked toward the group of seniors in the far corner, plotting how to help me solve Christopher's murder. "Hi, guys, what's up?"

Mal jumped straight into Mr. Faber's lap. The old man doted on my doggie and she knew she would be welcome.

"Well, we've gathered everything we could find out about Christopher the day he died," Mrs. Tunisian said. She pointed to a whiteboard behind her. "Here's our unofficial timeline. Mrs. Albertson saw Christopher on his regular run that morning at five thirty a.m. We know he usually runs around the island every day—eight miles in about fifty-five minutes. Right on time, Mrs. Gooseman saw him finishing his run and checking his watch around six. He went home, and thirty minutes later, Mr. Beecher saw him entering the back of the pharmacy dressed in a navy suit, a white shirt, and brown shoes."

"That's pretty specific," I said.

"Do you know what he was wearing when he died?" Mrs. Tunisian asked me.

I winced. "It was dark and I don't remember."

"You would remember this suit," Mrs. Albertson said. "I had to go pick up my prescription and he had his lab coat over it, but still the man was lovely."

"What time did you pick up your prescription?" I asked.

"I went at nine a.m.," she said.

"We seniors tend to be early. We only have so much energy and we like to do everything we can before we peter out," Irene Hammerstein said.

"The next time one of us saw Christopher was at noon," Mrs. Albertson said. "My friend Agnes saw him at Tim's New York Deli for lunch. She stopped and asked him how he was. She also asked him if he was dating someone. He said yes, but it was too new to talk about just yet. But yes, he was dating someone new. Someone special."

"The next time he was seen by a senior was at three p.m. at the pharmacy. Macy Williams said he was filling her prescription when a very pretty girl came in," Irene continued.

"Was it Becky Langford?" I asked.

"Oh, is Becky back on the island?" Mrs. Abernathy asked.

"Not at the moment," I said. "But she was earlier."

"Wait, is Becky the woman who was stabbed in the alley?" Mrs. Tunisian asked.

"Let's get back to the timeline," I said. "Did Christopher leave the pharmacy early?"

"No," Irene said as she shook her head. "He wouldn't make anyone wait for their prescriptions."

"Did anyone see him at the pharmacy the rest of the day?" I asked

"Barbara," she said.

"Mrs. Vissor?" I asked.

"Yes, she was shopping at the pharmacy and chatting with Christopher until six p.m., when he closed up."

"Isn't the pharmacy open until nine?" I asked.

"Not on Tuesdays and Thursdays," Carol said. "They are closed Sundays altogether. I suppose you wouldn't know. You're too young to have as many prescriptions as we seniors do."

"Okay, so he closed up at six p.m. And for the sake of argument, he left with Becky," I said. "Then where did he go?"

"They were next seen by Flo Johnson going into Mackinac's Little Gallery," Irma Gooseman said.

"That sounds like a date," Carol said. "Don't you go into an art gallery on a date?"

"It could have been," I said.

"That would give Shane motive," Mrs. Albertson said.

"It's a weak motive," I said. "He's engaged to Jenn. They are getting married next week."

"If the police have to grab at straws, they will grab at his motive no matter how weak," Irma said. "They have in the past, you know."

"Yes, I do know from experience," I agreed. "I need to check into Becky's background. Maybe she was dating someone else. Perhaps someone in Cheboygan or Mackinaw City, depending on where she's living now."

"I heard through the grapevine she lives in Cheboygan but was planning a move to New York City for a new job," Mrs. Albertson stated.

"Then why go on a date when you're leaving?" I wondered.

"Maybe she wanted him to go with her," Carol said. "They could have had a disagreement and Christopher snapped, stabbed her, and she killed him in self-defense."

"Well, that could be," I said and drummed my fingers on my chin. "Then Shane found them just before we got there. But that still doesn't explain why he didn't show up for dinner with Jenn. They had a date at eight at the Nag's Head Bar and Grill. Shane never showed. We went out looking for him at eleven p.m. Where was he all that time?"

"You should ask him," Agnes said.

"Jenn tried," I replied. "He won't tell us anything. It's driving a wedge between Jenn and Shane."

"Then we're investigating the wrong person," Carol said. "We should do a timeline on Shane."

"All I know is, he was on the five thirty ferry from St. Ignace," I said and glanced at my watch. "Oh, I've got to go." I snapped a picture of their timeline with my cell phone. "I'm in charge of all the errands for Jenn's wedding." I gave each of them a hug and a kiss on the cheek and hurried off.

The table favors had arrived at the dock and would soon be portered to the McMurphy. It was my job to look them over to ensure none were broken and to assemble them. Frances had promised to help with the assembly.

The weather was cool, but the first lilacs had started to bloom. In a few weeks it would be the start of the Lilac Festival on the island, celebrated annually in June.

I went into the back of the McMurphy, took off my jacket, and hung it up on one of the hooks near the door. Mal rushed over to get me to take off her leash, wagging her stump tail and begging for me to pick her up. I pulled off her leash, picked her up and rubbed her belly as she put her head on my shoulder. I walked into the lobby to find Mella curled up next to Frances, who was working on the accounting.

"Did the boxes of favors come?" I asked. "I got a notice they were delivered."

"They are over by the coffee bar," Frances said. "How'd it go at the senior center?"

"It went well." I walked over to the four boxes. "Irene Hammerstein and Mrs. Tunisian, had a whole timeline of most of Christopher Harris's day."

"Well, that's good," she said.

"But what we don't have is Shane's timeline to see where they crossed paths and why. And we both know Shane isn't talking." I picked up a box cutter and opened the first box. There would be 150 people at Jenn's wedding. She had picked a beautiful pyramid-shaped glass terrarium. Terrariums had been popular in Victorian times, and because we were on Mackinac Island, Jenn wanted an elegant Victorian wedding. I inspected all the boxes.

"How are the favors?" Frances asked.

"Looks like they all arrived intact," I said. "Did they deliver the succulents?"

"They did," Frances said. "I put them upstairs in your office. They will get better sun there."

"And the matrix for the bottom of the terrarium?

"Came just after the succulents. We have bags of potting soil, bark, moss, river rocks, and charcoal. Also the little toadstools came. They are so cute and match her colors of blush pink and champagne."

I loved the idea of the little terrariums. But I also knew the work it would take to get them assembled. I grabbed a box and put it in the elevator. Then another and another, until all the boxes were in the elevator, and then I pushed the button for the third floor. The elevator didn't go up to the fourth floor because that was the owner's floor and I didn't want guests to mistakenly go up there. If they had to take the stairs, we could let them know the fourth floor was off limits.

I carried the boxes up the last flight of stairs. My office was next to my apartment at the top of the stairs. I pulled the boxes into the office and found Jenn inside. "Hey, girl, how's the planning on the Wilkins wedding going?"

"Pretty well," she said. "They want a beachy wedding because the reception is on the rooftop with views of the beach. The ceremony will be on the beach and then they will all ride in carriages around the island and stop here for the rooftop reception. I have fifteen carriages ready. The style is so cute. I have these little bottles with sand and Petoskey stones and a tiny succulent inside to look like beach grass. A cork and a raffia ribbon around the top and voilà! What do you think?" She showed me her mock-up.

"Cute," I said.

"What's in the boxes?" she asked. I heard Mal rush up the stairs and into the office before she jumped into Jenn's lap.

"These are the terrariums for your table favors," I said. "We have the dirt, the stones, the charcoal and bark and tiny air ferns, along with some cute little toadstools in your colors. So, I've got all the things. Want to help me put the first one together so I know how to make the rest?"

"Sure thing," she said with a glint of excitement. It was the first excitement I'd seen in her all day.

We spent a nice hour side by side creating wedding favors. Me with the terrariums and Jenn with her succulents in glass bottles.

"You know what?" I said. "I bet those would be cute with a message in the bottle along with the plant. You know . . . message in a bottle."

"That would be cute," Jenn said. "I'll make a note to talk with Jessica about it."

"Jessica and Max Wilkins," I said. "That makes for a nice couple."

"It sure does," Jenn agreed.

"Like Shane and Jenn Carpenter," I said.

"If we get married," she said with a deep sigh.

"Okay." I stopped what I was doing. "How are you? I've been waiting for you to talk to me about it, but you haven't. Still, you have to talk to someone, and who better than your best friend?"

She sat back and put her hands in her lap. "I . . . I don't know what is going on with Shane." Her voice shook and tears sparkled in her eyes.

"Okay, let's take a break on this for a while. Come on, come with me. Let's get you some tea and we'll talk."

She let me take her by the elbow and gently guide her out of her chair and into my apartment. Mal and Mella were happy to follow us. Mella disappeared to her favorite box in the closet and Mal went to her puppy bed and turned three times before lying down. Jenn sat down at the breakfast bar of my open kitchen and put her head in her hands.

I let her gather her thoughts for a moment and put on the kettle, picked up two mugs and a selection of teas. I placed the mugs in front of her and me and got some honey and some milk. The kettle whistled, and still Jenn hadn't said anything. I made us both tea and gestured for her to put in honey or milk.

"Let's sit on the couch. Maybe that will help," I said.

Jenn sat and held her hands wrapped around her mug. "Shane still isn't speaking to me."

"Why not? What happened?"

"I asked him what happened and he said he wouldn't tell me. Then I went to the store and found out from Sherry Watson that the woman was Shane's ex-fiancée. I asked him, again, what he was doing in an alley with her. I tried not to sound upset, but it's upsetting." She frowned. "That's when he got up and walked away."

"I don't understand why he wouldn't talk to you," I said.

"Neither do I," she said as a tear ran down her check and splashed on her hand. "I mean, he told me he had a fiancée, but she had been out of his life for three or four years. Why did she come back now? Why was he found in the alley with her and Christopher?"

"I don't know," I said. "But I'm going to find out."

"Please don't," she said. "Shane told me to leave it alone. He said he wouldn't marry me if you or I put ourselves in danger over this."

"Why would he say such a thing?"

"I don't know," she said. "He knows we work well on our investigations. He needs help. He's the number one suspect. The wedding really will be off if he goes to jail."

"Then we need to have a plan," I said.

"A plan?"

"Yes," I was firm. "A plan that he won't find out about. A plan where we find Christopher's killer without letting him know."

"Good luck with that," she said and tilted her head against her right hand, the mug in her left. "Shane knows everything Rex knows. Those two are tight."

"Well, then, we'll just have to keep Rex from knowing what we're doing." I held out my right pinky. "Pinkie swear only you and I will know. We'll tell everyone we're not investigating."

"Pinkie swear," she said and we hooked pinkies and lifted them up in the air.

After all, what could possibly go wrong?

Peanut Butter and Chocolate Fudge

Ingredients:
12 ounces dark chocolate chips
14 ounces sweetened condensed milk
1 cup mini marshmallows
¾ cup peanut butter
1 tablespoon vanilla

Directions:
In a heavy saucepan, mix chocolate, milk, marshmallows, and peanut butter. Heat over medium heat, stirring constantly until it is completely melted. Remove from heat and add vanilla. Stir until combined.

Pour into parchment-lined 8 x 8-inch pan. Chill until set. Cut into one-inch pieces. Store in an airtight container in the refrigerator or freezer. Makes 32. Enjoy!

Chapter 6

I checked on Mr. Devaney, who was in the basement of the McMurphy. When I remodeled the hotel I had the contractors put drywall on the walls and ceiling and install really good lighting before painting it all white. There once was a door to a secret tunnel that moved under the alley and linked to the hotel behind me. But I had it plastered shut and drywalled over it.

"Wow, the place is nice and bright," I said as I stepped down into the basement. How do you like it?"

"It's better," Douglas said. "I can finally see what I'm working on."

"The trellis looks gorgeous," I said.

"Jenn showed me one in a wedding book that she liked," he said. "It was easy to copy because she didn't want an arch but a rectangular one." He had painted it white and the basement smelled of fresh paint. He had the single window cracked so air could flow in. It was a casement window, but it did the trick.

"I'm supposed to take it to the florist when I'm finished so they can place flowers in it. She wants blush pink and champagne roses and other flowers so it will look like it was taken from a garden." I touched a spot he hadn't painted yet. "It's going to be so pretty."

"I'm glad they're using Arch Rock for their wedding," he said. "It's a nice natural limestone arch in the park. It's better than the beach. Should be a lot fewer gulls and such there."

"Jenn thought about the beach, but the Wilkinses are doing that and she didn't want the same area. Besides, this will be just as nice or nicer," I said. "The trestle is so nice. I bet we can keep it after Jenn's wedding and offer it to other couples who are getting married to rent as part of their wedding package."

"Huh, so you're doing wedding packages now?"

"Yes," I said. "Depending on the size of the wedding they can rent out the entire hotel, have their wedding and reception on the rooftop, house their guests, and we will offer a champagne breakfast for everyone the next morning."

"Are you going to cook that?" Douglas asked, looking a trifle worried.

"Oh no," I said. "I've got enough on my hands making fudge. Terra Reeves is a great caterer who will work with us. Anyway, the newlyweds will have their room comped if they take the entire hotel for the weekend. We will also offer other services as they crop up and we see how this new addition to our seasonal guests works out."

"You sure are making the McMurphy a destination place," he said. "Not sure that's a good thing."

I laughed. Douglas was a tad bit of a curmudgeon, always worrying about what could happen. "It will be great," I said. "We have the entire month of June booked and we are starting to book out to October."

"Huh," he said and scratched his head. "Guess destination weddings are still a thing."

"They sure are," I said and patted him on the back. "Great work." I headed up the stairs to the lobby, and Mal met me at the top. I picked up my pup. It was nearly six in the evening and Frances was closing up for the day. We rarely got guests after six on Sunday, so I let her go home. We had hooked up a buzzer system in case late guests did arrive.

"How's Jenn doing?" Frances asked.

"She's hanging in there," I said and Frances raised an eyebrow at me to let me know she knew I was lying. "She's worried about Shane and the wedding."

"And well she should be," Frances said. "I understand Shane is still the leading suspect in the murder of Christopher and the stabbing of Becky."

"We all know Shane would never do that," I said.

"Never say never," Frances said. "Shane's not talking and that's not a good sign."

I sighed. "I know."

"Have you gotten much further on the investigation?"

"No," I said. "We were looking for someone who might want Christopher dead, but everyone seems to agree that he was a great guy and they couldn't imagine anyone wanting to harm him."

"I know his mother," Frances said as she put a jacket on over her long skirt and flowery shirt. "Joan is a joy. She must be hurting. I'm going to go home and make her food, then go visit."

"Oh, good idea," I said. "Can I go with you? I can bring her some fudge or cookies."

"Depends. Is this a sympathy visit or are you investigating?" she asked me. I could never lie to Frances. She had that look like my mom got when she wanted a truthful answer.

I took a step toward her and lowered my voice. "No, I'm not going to Joan's home to investigate, but that doesn't mean I won't listen if someone says something of interest. Besides, I don't want to cause more trouble for Jenn. Shane and Rex have been adamant on shutting us down on this one. If I show up asking questions, Shane might react adversely."

"Well, I don't blame them," she said. "It would be horrible if the killer got their hands on either of you. The last thing the blushing bride needs is to have stitches or bruises on her big day because she got involved with a killer."

"You know we're careful," I protested.

"I also have watched you both get into some deep water. It wouldn't do for her maid of honor to have bruises or stitches or anything broken, either. Think of the pictures."

I laughed. "That's the worst excuse ever, 'think of the pictures.' You know they have photo editing now and can take anything out of a picture."

"Not the video," she continued.

"Well, then, I'll be sure to stay extra safe," I said. "Now, I just checked on Douglas and he looks like he might be about an hour from completing his painting for the day. I'm going to make some cookies. Call me when you're ready to go over or I'll go myself."

"I'll call you," Frances said. "Somebody has to keep you out of trouble."

"Thanks," I said and took Mal upstairs to the apartment with me. I loved baking as much as I loved fudge making. I'd chosen cookies because they were easy to freeze and also easy to offer the visitors who came to sit with the grieving mother.

The perennial favorites were peanut butter cookies with chocolate chips in them. I whipped up a quick batch and ate a salad and soup for dinner. Frances texted me that she was there. So I fed my fur babies, grabbed the wrapped-up cookies, and locked the door behind me.

"Let's go," Frances said. "I don't think anyone should show up at her house after eight p.m."

I glanced at the time on my phone. "It's seven fifteen," I said. "I think we have plenty of time."

I grabbed my coat and we went out the back. Christopher's mom lived on the other side of St. Anne's Church from the McMurphy on a road behind the church facing east. The house was another beautiful bungalow. The lawn was surrounded by a picket fence and filled in with flowers. The house itself was a pale blue-white with sky blue shutters. I found it quaint and pretty.

Frances knocked on the door. Carol answered. "Hi, ladies, come on in. Let me take the food. You can put your coats on the side chair here. Joan is in the living room."

"I'll take my cookies with you," I said, seeing that it would be difficult to hold both Frances's thirteen-inch casserole dish and my overflowing plate of cookies.

Frances took off her jacket and held the cookies so I could take mine off, and then she went into the living room to greet Joan while I followed Carol into the kitchen.

The interior of the house was as lovely as the exterior.

Painted pale green throughout, it was calming. The kitchen was in the back and quite small, but filled with storage space because it had cabinets that reached to the ceiling.

"Have you come to investigate?" Carol asked.

"No," I said. "I came to offer my condolences."

"But you are investigating," Carol said. "I've got my network trying to track down what Shane was doing after he arrived on the island."

"I appreciate that," I said. "But we should really be here for Joan right now."

Carol winked at me. "Okay, we'll keep this under wraps."

"Thanks." I walked out of the kitchen. The cozy living room was filled with women come to console one of their own who had lost her baby. Christopher Harris was a well-loved man. It seemed the seniors adored him. I went and gave Joan a hug and an air kiss. "I'm so sorry for your loss."

She patted my hand. "Thank you." But her eyes seemed glassy, as if she wasn't thinking, only reacting. Joan Harris was pretty, with shoulder-length, blond hair. She wore a black dress and slippers on her feet. Her fingernails were well manicured, but she wore no makeup. I imagined she would have cried it off if she did put any on. Tears rolled unstopped down her cheeks. The ladies chatted around her, trying to talk about books they've read and the upcoming Lilac Festival. I stood behind Frances's chair, leaving the seats to women older than me out of respect.

"Isn't that right, Allie?" someone asked.

I blinked. "Excuse me, could you repeat that?"

"I was saying that the police will hunt down and catch

the person who did this horrible thing," Mrs. Albertson said.

"Yes, they will," I agreed.

"And Allie will make sure they do," Carol said.

Everyone looked at me.

"I'm sorry," I said. "I don't have any authority to do that."

"But clearly you do," Mrs. Schmidt said. "You've made sure in all the other cases."

"Please don't stop now," Joan said, tears rolling down her cheeks. Mrs. Emry handed her a tissue. "Someone needs to pay for what they did to my poor baby boy."

"I heard now that Christopher is gone we're all going to have to go to mail-order prescriptions. The drugstore will have to shut down," Mrs. Albertson said.

"Lucy, that's probably a little premature," Frances said. "David Peele is the owner and he also has a pharmacy in Mackinaw City. I'm sure he'll have his pharmacist there come work here for at least two days a week."

"That makes good business sense," I said with a nod.

There was a knock on the door and Carol answered it. It was Liz McElroy. She handed Carol a dish of food and took off her coat. The first thing she did was give Joan a hug and a kiss on the cheek. "How are you holding up?"

"I'm okay," Joan said and blew her nose on the handkerchief she was handed. "The ladies are sitting with me to keep me company." Her eyes still were glazed, as if she hadn't really processed what the meaning of her son being murdered truly meant. No grandchildren and no one to care for her in her old age. Joan was widowed five years earlier and Christopher was her only child.

"Good, good," Liz said. Her dark curly hair was a bit

wild from the wind. She wore jeans and a plaid shirt and her favorite lightweight hiking boots. She came and stood beside me. "How are you?" she asked in a low tone.

"I'm good," I said.

"We need to talk later," Liz said, her eyes sparkling with curiosity.

We stayed for about thirty minutes and then Frances stood to leave. We said our goodbyes, put on our coats, and walked out into the twilight. Liz came with us.

"Well, that was sad," Liz said. "I didn't want to ask, but someone needs to write Christopher's obituary for the paper."

"The place was too full of people to talk about obituaries," Frances said to Liz. "Or ask questions about Christopher," she said to me.

I felt fully chastised. The visit was supposed to be about Joan, not me and my curiosity. "In my defense, it will bring her closure when we catch the killer," I said.

"So you are investigating," Liz said. "Do you have any theories? What was it like to find the body? Did you help Becky?"

"My goodness, you are full of questions," Frances said to Liz.

Liz grinned. "I should be. It's my job. Say, Allie, come with me to get some hot cocoa."

"Hot cocoa?" I asked. "I just had that the other night. Couldn't we get something more spring like?"

"Still cold out, though," she said and shrugged. "We could get tea or coffee or a hot toddy." She blew on her hands and rubbed them together.

"I guess the wind off the lake is a bit chilly," I said. "Let's walk Frances to the McMurphy first, then go."

"It's a deal," Liz said.

"I don't need to be walked like some little child," Frances protested.

I took a hold of her arm and put it in the crook of mine. "We know that, but there's a killer on the loose and it's better to be safe than sorry. Besides, Douglas would never forgive me if you walked home alone."

Frances made a face but allowed us to walk her.

"Not a lot of gossip going on at Joan's house," I said.

"There's not a lot of information about what happened to Christopher," Liz said. "The police are really keeping this quiet."

"They must not think the killer is a threat to anyone else," Frances said. She glanced at me. "They must think it really was Shane who did it."

"Oh, come on," I protested. "We all know that Shane would never snap and start stabbing people."

"So Christopher was stabbed to death?" Liz asked.

It was my turn to give her a look. "That wasn't announced in the police press release?"

"No," Liz said. "They listed the cause of death as not yet known but believed to be homicide. How do you know he was stabbed to death?"

"It's just a guess on my part," I backpedaled. "When we found Shane—"

"Who's 'we'?" Liz asked.

"I'm assuming this is all on the record," I replied.

"It is," Liz said.

"Then I don't think I should say anything more," I said. "Rex is going to kill me for telling you as much as I did."

"Look," Liz cajoled. "It's all got to come out sometime."

"Later is better than sooner in this case," I said. "Go bug the police if you want to know more."

Liz's mouth flattened in disappointment. "I thought we were friends."

"We are," I said. "But I've been told in very blunt terms to stay out of this one."

"I know you're not," she said. "I've been talking to Carol Tunisian."

"Well, then, quote her," I said and waved my hand as if to say *go ahead*. "She knows everything anyway."

"I wanted a second source," Liz said. "Carol can tend to embellish things."

"Now that's true," Frances said as we arrived at the McMurphy. All the lights were on and a feeling of satisfied warmth at how beautiful the place looked spread through me. I loved my family's hotel and fudge shop. It was nice to bring it back to its original condition. Thankfully, I'd had help from family photos and the historical society archives.

Douglas waited by the fire, Mal in his lap and Mella curled up on the top of the wing-backed chair he occupied. He stood when we entered and let Mal down. She ran toward us and stopped short a few feet away so she could slide over the wood floors and hit me in the shins.

"How was Joan?" Douglas asked as he kissed Frances.

"She seems out of it," she said. "But I suspect it's still a shock. She's not as hardy as Maggs."

"I'm glad I went," I said. "Most of the ladies were there."

"Shall we go home and get some dinner of our own?" Douglas asked Frances.

"Certainly," she said and looked at Liz and me. "Don't do anything stupid."

"We won't," we both said at the same time.

We watched Douglas and Frances leave. "Do you still want that cocoa?" I asked Liz.

"Sure," she said.

"Want to come up to my place and get it? I do make a mean homemade cocoa."

"I suppose that means we can talk freely," Liz said and followed me up the stairs. I unlocked my apartment and Mal and Mella squeezed by us to be the first ones inside. Mella went to her closet, while Mal danced around Liz's feet.

I grabbed a saucepan and made cocoa while Liz sat on a barstool across from the kitchen island.

"This place looks great," she said. "I love the paint colors."

"Thanks. I like soft colors," I said. "It keeps the place feeling light and bright."

"I always wondered what it would be like to live in a brand-new home," Liz said. "I inherited the cottage from my parents, who inherited it from my grandparents. It's why my grandfather Angus lives there with me."

"How is Angus doing?" I asked. He'd gotten sick last fall and was in a nursing home in Cheboygan throughout the winter.

"He's much better," Liz said and leaned her elbows on my soapstone island top. "In fact, he came home yesterday. It will be good for him to be here for the season. He loves the hustle and bustle of the tourists and the clip-clop of the horses as they come and go."

"I'm glad he's doing better," I said. "That's great news." I stirred the cocoa in the saucepan to heat it gently. "Listen, I need to place an ad for a new assistant fudge maker. Can I do that tomorrow?"

"For this week's paper?"

"Yes," I said. "I need them asap so that they don't all get snatched up by the other fudge shops on the island."

"Sure," Liz said. "Are you going to tell me what you know about Christopher's death?"

"I'm sure Carol told you everything," I said.

"She does like to spin a tale," Liz said. "She embellished with a full moon and a ghoulish Shane standing over Christopher with a knife in his hand that was dripping blood."

I had a sudden flashback to finding Shane in the alley. Carol's embellishments weren't too far off. I turned off the stove, grabbed two mugs, and set them on the island. Then I poured cocoa from the pan into each mug, added marshmallows, gave the first mug to Liz, and picked up my own. "Let's sit in the living area."

"Your new couch is pretty comfy," she said as she sat with her cocoa in hand. Mella jumped up to sit between Liz and me.

"I like the velvet covering," I said and ran my free hand along the nap of the back of the couch. "It's also easy to clean, which is a good thing because I have pets."

"How is Shane?" she asked and sipped her cocoa.

"I'm not sure," I said and wrapped my hands around my warm mug. "He's not talking."

"He never was much of a talker," Liz said. "Not shy, just keeps his opinions to himself."

"He's not even talking to Jenn much right now," I said. "And their wedding is next weekend."

"That's not good," Liz said. "As her bridesmaid, I'm concerned."

"Me, too." I nodded my agreement. "So, what are you going to write for the paper?"

"I need to talk with Rex," she said. "I don't have enough details yet to go into depth. But you will give me the whole story once a killer is arrested, right?"

"Sure," I said. "Now, let's talk bridesmaids. Do you need to get your dress fitted? I've got an appointment for Jenn to get a final fitting at Sara Grant's house. Because we are the only bridesmaids, we need to look really elegant. Victorian elegance is her theme, you know."

"I'm surprised she's doing it at the Arch and not in a church then," Liz said.

"Jenn loves the color of the natural stone arch and wanted it as a backdrop for her ceremony. Douglas is making a gorgeous rectangular trellis. We're going to decorate it with blush-colored flowers."

"When is the fitting?" Liz asked.

"Tomorrow at two p.m. Shall I put you down as well?"

"Might as well," Liz said. "Then we can see what we look like all together."

For our bridesmaid dresses, we both got to pick out the style of pink or blush knee-length dress we wanted. Then the seamstress had created long, sheer overskirts made of the same lace as the skirt of Jenn's ball gown. The overskirts were full length. Then we were to wear a nude shoe. The idea was that we could use the dresses for events after the wedding. The long overskirts made them match for the wedding. I personally loved the idea of a sheer floor-length skirt over my dress. It certainly took a simple blush dress to another level. We finished our cocoa as Mal curled up in a ball between us sleeping.

"I should get going," Liz said and stood. "I've got a police officer to interview."

I glanced at my watch. It was ten-thirty. "Kind of late for that, isn't it?"

"As Grandpa Agnus likes to say, 'Got to keep him on his toes,'" Liz said and gave me a quick hug. "I'll keep you posted on what I find out."

"Thanks," I said and walked her to the back door of my apartment. "Rex and Shane are trying to keep me out of trouble."

Liz laughed. "As if anyone could."

Chapter 7

Monday

I was up at five a.m. the next morning making fudge. I had a heavy load of online orders, plus, with the ferries running regularly now, we had more tourists coming, so I liked to keep my fudge shop display cabinet full. It was a good strategy because most days I sold out.

I thought a long time about why Shane might have missed his dinner with Jenn and how he ended up in that alley. I would have guessed that Becky texted him and asked him to meet her. That would make sense, but the fact that he hadn't texted Jenn that he would be late meant that theory was probably untrue.

It seemed the only way to crack the case would be to figure out what Shane did from the time he left the ferry. So I would start with the ferry crew. The first ferry came in at ten a.m.

Frances and Douglas got to the McMurphy at eight

a.m. I had a few hours to pack my fudge and prepare my questions.

I had my questions ready and had finished packaging up my online orders when Frances stuck her head into the shop. "Good morning," she said. "Looks like you have a lot of online orders."

"It's record-setting," I said. "And that's something, considering that Christmas is high season for fudge."

"We have a cart in the basement if you want to use it," Frances said. "I don't see how you're going to carry all those boxes without one."

"I was going to make trips," I said. "But a cart would be perfect."

"I'll have Douglas go down and get it." She went to Douglas, who was at the coffee bar making them both a cup. I watched him nod and go down to the basement. He came back with a nice foldable cart, brought it to me, and unfolded it.

"Do you need help loading it?" he asked.

"The cart? No, no thanks. How's the arbor going?"

"It's done," he said. "I'm going to take it to the florist's. They're going to put the flowers on it twenty-four hours ahead of time and then bring it to the park the day of the wedding."

"Sounds great, thanks," I said.

Mal barked and I glanced up to see what she was look-ing at. It was Jenn, coming down the left-hand steps. She was dressed in jeans and a boatneck sweater. Mal went running. Jenn picked her up and gave her pets.

"Good morning, Jenn," Frances said.

"Hey all," Jenn said. She was strangely okay, consid-ering her fiancé wasn't speaking to her.

I loaded the cartons and called to her. "Jenn." She

came over and stood in the doorway. "What's on your plate today?"

"I've got a lot of people to check up on for the Wilkins wedding," she said. "They decided to go with a cake from the Grander Hotel."

"That's good," I said. "It helps when we can give business to locals. Don't forget we have fittings at two p.m. today."

"Oh right," Jenn said absently. She made a note on her smartwatch. "Thanks for the reminder."

"Hey," I said and caught her arm. "Are you okay?"

"I'm fine." She grimaced. "Trying to pretend it's going to be all right. I mean, it is going to be all right, isn't it?"

"Yes, it is," I said and patted her arm.

"I've got to run over to Tallulah's Gifts and More. She's got some gorgeous beachy centerpieces that light up to put on the tables."

"Okay," I said. "Has Shane said anything more to you about that night?"

"No," she said, her mouth forming a thin line. "He seems to want to pretend it never happened."

"Don't worry," I said and patted her arm again. "We're going to figure this out before Rex arrests him and ruins your wedding."

"I can't even think about the nightmare that would be." She hugged herself and rubbed her forearms.

"I won't let that happen and Rex won't, either," I said. "Don't you worry."

"I keep trying to push worrying thoughts away," Jenn said. "Shane and I are going to meet for dinner again. This time at our renovation cottage. I'm going to pick up dinner from the Irish Steakhouse and he's going to bring lanterns and a blanket."

"Sounds like fun," I said.

"It's a good thing there's a fireplace because we don't have heat yet and the nights are still a bit cool."

"Yes, I think thirty-four degrees Fahrenheit would be chilly to have dinner in," I said, putting on my jacket and grabbing the cart handle. "Well, everyone, I'm off to shipping. Frances, how many guests do we have coming in today?"

"We have five," she said. "I've got them all on the second floor."

"Thanks!" I said and pulled the cart out the door while Jenn held it open for me. She went her way on Main toward the fort and I went in the opposite direction to the shipping store. I was texting Rex to see if there were any updates when I ran smack into a well-muscled chest. "Oops, sorry," I said and removed my hand from it.

It was the very handsome Harry Winston. "You do have a habit of running into me," he said as his eyes sparkled.

The heat of a blush reached my cheeks. "I guess I shouldn't text and walk at the same time," I said. "How long have you been back on the island?" Harry had left after Christmas to help his parents move to Florida.

"I got in on Friday," he said. "I've been opening up the bed and breakfast, airing it out and looking at what needs to be done first."

"I was in that boat last year when my Papa Liam passed on and I had to open the McMurphy all by myself. Then I took on the challenge of a remodel. It was tough, but I got it done before the June first season opening."

"So you think I'll be fine," he stated.

"I do," I said with a smile.

"I've seen your remodel and it's impressive," he said. "Why don't you come by the bed and breakfast and take a look at mine. I'd like to get another hotelier's take on what else needs to be done."

"Sure, what time?" I asked.

"Say four-thirty today?"

"I have a dress fitting for my best friend Jenn's wedding, but that's earlier in the afternoon. You met Jenn, right?"

"Yeah," he said. "Gorgeous girl, long straight hair and legs for miles."

"That's her," I said, trying not to be jealous. "She's marrying Shane Carpenter."

"The CSU guy," he said. "Right?"

"Very good," I said. "I've got to get these packages to the shipping store before the morning mail flight goes out. See you at four-thirty?"

"See you, then," he said and walked away. He wore jeans that hugged his backside and a black T-shirt that showed off his muscles. It was chilly enough that I needed a jacket, but he seemed to be perfectly comfortable.

I turned back toward the shipping office before I ran into someone else. My thoughts went to this time last year, when Papa Liam died and I was left on my own to make the McMurphy work. I'd been so proud to get approved to bring the lobby back to its original Victorian look. After this fall's fiasco, I was able to save what I'd done in the lobby, but the third and fourth floors had to be completely rebuilt.

By the time I arrived, the shipping store was bustling with people who were dropping off and picking up packages. I waited in line until I got to Sandy Seacrest. "Hi Sandy, you look busy," I said.

"It's the first week of the season," she said. "Historically one of our busier times." She spotted all my boxes of fudge. "Looks like this is your busy time as well." Sandy was an older woman with white hair and turquoise streaks. She was a librarian and bought the shipping store after she retired for something to keep her busy.

"I think word is spreading about our fudge," I said as I placed the boxes on the counter.

Watching her put labels on the boxes and mark them in, I wondered if she might know something about Shane. Sometimes if you ask new people questions, you get better answers, or at least clearer ones. "Did you hear about Christopher Harris?"

"I did. Such a shame," she said. "He was a very nice guy. The world needs all the nice guys it can get these days."

"Was he connected to Shane at all?" I asked. "I mean, they probably knew each other, but was it more than a passing acquaintance?"

"They were in the same grade," Sandy said and tucked her hair behind her ears. "But while Christopher lived on the island and went to the island public school, Shane went to St. Ignace. They were in all the same sports, so I think it would be fair to say they had a friendly rivalry."

"But nothing adverse," I said.

"No, everyone around here gets along for the most part," she said.

Of course, my experience was different because I'd seen some pretty terrible murders in the last year. One would think the tourists would be the ones doing it, but so far it was mostly islanders.

I shook away my thoughts, paid for the shipping, and dragged my cart out the door. Ahead of me, walking down the sidewalk, I saw Shane. Maybe if I got him alone, he'd let something slip. I hurried to catch up with him. "Hi, Shane," I said as I got close to him.

He glanced at me. "Allie, how are you?"

"I'm good; big orders today and then Jenn, Liz, and I are getting our final dress fittings this afternoon. How are things with you? Are you on a case? I mean, you're usually in St. Ignace on a workday."

"I'm on suspension," he said. "Until they find whoever killed Christopher Harris." He kept walking, and I walked with him.

"Even though you did nothing wrong?" I asked.

He peered at me through his thick glasses with their black frame. "How do you know I'm not guilty?"

"Because you aren't," I said firmly. "What I don't understand is what happened that night. Why did you skip dinner with Jenn?"

"You tried to slip that one in, didn't you?" He shook his head at me. "I'm not going to talk about it."

"But not talking about it is hurting Jenn," I said. "I can't imagine you want to hurt her."

"Hurting Jenn is the last thing I ever wanted to do. Which is why I'm not talking about it. I don't want to put her in harm's way."

"Who would harm her? The actual killer? Do you know who that is?"

He frowned at me. "Don't you think if I knew who the killer was, they'd already be in jail?"

"Of course," I said and tried to change tactics. "Look," I stopped him by putting my hand on his arm. "I figure you were walking by the alley and heard Becky screaming. So you rushed down and shouted at the killer, who dropped the knife . . ."

He rolled his eyes.

"Okay, he didn't drop the knife. You wrenched it from him and he ran off before you could stop him."

"Sounds like a fairy tale," he said.

"Was the killer wearing a mask or a hoodie?" I asked. "Is that why you didn't know who they were? Were they short, tall, fat, thin? Could it have been a woman? Did they seem young or old?"

"I'm not going to tell you, Allie," he said. "Let Rex handle it."

"Right, because he wants to indict you for the murder of Christopher and for the assault on Becky," I said.

"He doesn't have anything but circumstantial evidence," Shane said.

"Becky was your ex-fiancée, wasn't she?" I said. "Did you come to her rescue?"

"I don't want to talk about Becky. I'm marrying Jenn." He turned to go, but I stepped out in front of him.

"Let me help you," I said. "I'm pretty good at helping, you know."

"Then help Jenn put together our wedding, okay?" He stormed off and I stood there for a moment, watching him go.

He moved away from the administration building, which meant he had either just come from the police department and seeing Rex or he was out looking for the killer. Did he suspect who did it and was trying to find concrete evidence? If so, why didn't he let me help?

Chapter 8

Liz met me at the McMurphy at one forty-five in the afternoon. She was dressed in jeans, a T-shirt with a flannel shirt over it, and hiking boots.

"I'm wearing a sundress," I said. "So I can get in and out of it quickly for the fitting."

"Well, I only wear dresses on important occasions, like my friend Jenn's wedding. I prefer jeans," Liz said.

We both gathered up the long dress bags that held our dresses.

"We'll be back in an hour or so," I told Frances.

"Go, have fun," she said. "We'll look after the McMurphy."

"Have you seen Jenn?" Liz asked me.

"This morning," I said. "She had a lot of errands to run for the Wilkins wedding."

"She's nuts worrying about planning someone else's wedding with hers so close," Liz said.

"I think it keeps her busy so she doesn't worry," I said. "So, did you get any more information about the murder for your column?"

"Rex is pretty tight-lipped about this one," Liz said. "I think because Shane's involved. The police like to keep things close to their vest when it involves one of their own."

"I suppose that's true," I said. We went four blocks east and two blocks north and stopped in front of a tiny cottage with a sign on the front porch offering fittings and alterations. "This is it."

Liz went to knock on the open screen door as we heard Sara call out.

"Come on in, ladies," she said quite clearly, considering that when we made our way inside she had her mouth full of pins. She took out the pins. "Well, what do you think?" She waved her hand toward Jenn, who stood on a small ottoman dressed in a magnificent ball gown with an illusion neckline and lace sleeves. Her waist looked so tiny.

"You look gorgeous," I said.

"A knockout," Liz said.

"I hope so," Jenn said. "The color is champagne, so I don't want to look like a huge marshmallow coming down the aisle."

The top was lace on illusion material so it looked like she was brushed with lace on her bust and arms, which flowed into a corseted waist.

"This is definitely a Victorian era dress," Sara said. "It's such a pleasure to work with it."

"It fits like a glove," I said, staring at the vision that was Jenn.

"All that's left is the hem," Sara said. "Why don't you two ladies take your dresses and go into those curtained dressing areas in the back? Slip on the dress and the shoes you're going to wear and we can see what I have to do."

Liz and I changed quickly into our dresses, mine blush and hers pink. Then we attached the lace corsets with full, see-through lace skirts that landed at the floor. I slipped my feet into nude pumps and stepped out to admire myself in the mirror.

"I'm just glad we didn't have to wear a bustle," Liz muttered as she came out and put on her nude pumps. "Can you imagine me in a bustle?"

I was taken aback by Liz in a gown. She had quite a figure and looked like a lost Gibson Girl with her curly hair piled on top of her head in a messy bun. "You look amazing," I said. "You should wear dresses more often."

"Naw," she said. "I'm not a fan of all the rigmarole that happens when you wear a dress. I mean, how exactly do you get around in these without showing off something you don't want other people to see?"

"You have to act like a lady," I said lovingly. "I know you can do that."

"Yes, but why?"

We both laughed and walked into the main room. Sara was putting in a final pin on Jenn's dress. The lace of our sheer maxi skirts and corsets matched the lace on the large ball gown.

"What a wonderful complement those dresses are to your gown," Sara said. "Come here, ladies." She pulled us into the center of the room, positioning us on either side of Jenn. "Look in the mirror. So pretty!"

We did indeed complement Jenn and I was glad. The idea that Shane could go to jail and Jenn not get to have her wedding made me even more determined to figure out who committed this heinous crime and how I could bring them to justice.

After the fitting I went down to the docks to see if anyone there could tell me where Shane went after he got off the ferry that fateful day. I knocked on the manager's door at the first dock. "Come in."

"Hi," I said to Bill Blast.

"Hey, Allie. What brings you to the docks?"

"I was wondering if I could ask a favor," I said.

"Depends on the favor," he said and leaned back in his chair. Bill was a bald man with a square body. He had hazel eyes and wore a plaid shirt and jeans. My guess would be he was in his mid-fifties.

I took the seat in front of his desk. "I was wondering if I could talk to your staff," I said. "I know they have work to do, but I need to know if any of them saw Shane get off the boat the night Christopher died."

"Well, we have a record of him buying a ticket and using it," Bill said. "I already told Rex that."

"I was hoping to find out if anyone saw what direction Shane went when he got off the boat," I said and sent him a look that meant I was saying "please."

"I suppose it wouldn't hurt for you to ask," Bill said. "Lacey, Jared, Ethan, and Brandon were working that shift. You're in luck; they are working right now." He glanced at his watch. "They should be docking soon. I'll give you five minutes, but you can't delay our schedule."

"Thanks!" I jumped up. "I promise, no delays."

"Okay," he said and went back to his work. "You can go." He waved me off.

"I'll bring you some fudge," I said.

"I like peanut butter," he replied.

I walked out of the dock office and glanced at the time. It was four o'clock. I had half an hour before I was to go to Harry's bed and breakfast. I should have plenty of time. Five minutes later the ferry came in. It slowly edged toward the dock and the workers carefully jumped out and tied the boat in place. They lowered the gangplank and people started to walk off. It was a light crowd because it was cold on the island and most people didn't come this late unless they lived here or were going fishing in the morning.

I found Lacey first. She stood near the gangplank and helped people who were unsteady on their feet to safely make it to the dock. The boat shifted with the waves and people liked the helping hand.

"Hi, Lacey," I said. "How are you?"

"Allie, what brings you to the docks?"

"I asked Bill if I could get a moment of your time and he said yes." I pulled out my phone and hit RECORD.

"What can I do for you?" she asked.

"Bill said you were part of the crew working the night Christopher Harris died."

"Yeah, sad that happened. He was a nice guy and easy on the eyes." Lacey was in her twenties, born and raised on the island. "He was always kind to my grandmother."

"I was wondering if you saw which direction Shane Carpenter went when he got off the ferry."

"Oh, hmmm." Lacey helped a gray-haired woman safely to the dock. "I don't really pay attention once they get off the ferry. I'm usually focused on the next part of my job. You know, helping to check the boat over for safety and such before the next round of passengers board."

"Oh okay," I said.

"But I did see him when we got off work," she said.

"Wow, where?" I asked.

"The crew and I went to the Boar's Head for drinks after, and he was there."

"What time was that?"

"Around seven," she said. "Give or take."

"That was close to the eight o'clock dinner date he had set with Jenn," I said. "Was he alone?"

"No, he was with someone. They were wearing a hoodie and jeans. I couldn't see the face, but they were about my height and thin." She shrugged. "It could have been a guy or a girl. It's hard to tell because they were sitting down."

"That's very helpful, thanks," I said. "I'll let you get back to your job."

Next I interviewed Ethan, Jared, and Brandon. They all told me the same story. They saw Shane in the back corner of the bar, talking to someone. None of them could identify who the person was.

I left the docks thinking I should head into the Boar's Head to see who had been working that night and if they knew who Shane was talking to.

Justin Alders was working the bar when I entered. The place was about half full of regulars who had finished their shifts for the day, interspersed with construction workers who stopped in for a drink before they took the ferry home.

"Hi, Allie," Justin said. "I don't see you in here very often. What can I get you to drink?"

"Oh, I'm not here for a drink," I said. "I've got a four

thirty appointment, but I wanted to pop in to ask you a question."

"Sure, what is it?" Justin worked full time at the Boar's Head. If anyone knew who worked that night, it would be him.

"The night Christopher Harris was murdered, Shane Carpenter was seen here in the far corner," I said.

"True," he said. "I was here, tending bar."

"I was told he was with someone. Do you know who that was?"

"Ah, the real question," he said and shrugged. "The police were in here earlier asking the same thing."

"Do you know?"

"I didn't recognize them," he said. "Sorry."

"Do you know if the person was male or female?"

"It was a girl," Terry Tarrant said from the barstool next to me. "I saw her go into the ladies' room."

"Okay, thanks," I said. "Did you recognize her?"

"Maybe," Terry said and took a swig of his beer.

"Justin, pour this man another round on me," I said and dug some money out of my pocket.

"Thanks," Terry said and saluted me with his current mug of beer. "I thought she looked like Annie Hawthorne."

"I don't think I've heard that name before," I said as I paid the tab.

"She's from St. Ignace. She's not a regular on the island," Terry said. "So you won't know her from the town hall meetings or anything like that."

"How do you know her?" I asked.

"She's my neighbor," Terry said.

"Oh, you live in St. Ignace?"

"Yep," he said and took a swig from his new glass of

beer. "I work here, that's why I'm a regular. Ain't that right, Justin?"

"Yep," Justin said as he wiped a glass with a bar towel.

"Annie Hawthorne," I repeated. "Thanks for the intel." I glanced at my phone, which said I had ten minutes to get to Harry's bed and breakfast before I was late.

I arrived with two minutes to spare. Nothing like a power walk up and down the Mackinac Island hills to get your blood pumping. I stopped and ran my hand over my hair to ensure I didn't look like a wild thing, then knocked on the door.

The bed and breakfast was a huge Victorian cottage. The paint on the outside was peeling and faded, but it looked as if it once was painted three colors. Most of the gingerbread cutouts were still intact.

The door opened and Harry's face lit up. "You came!"

Now who could resist those broad shoulders and that gorgeous jawline? He kind of reminded me of the guy who played Thor in the movies.

"I came," I said.

He motioned his strong arm to welcome me inside. "Come on in and take a look at the place."

I stepped in, brushing past him and fully aware of the smell of his spicy cologne. Inside there were stairs going up on the right side, a large hall in the center, and to the left was a parlor that had a bay window that curved out onto the porch, which ran the length of the front and wrapped around the side.

"Very nice," I said, studying all the wood trim and paneling that was chair-rail height. The floors appeared to be newly sanded and refinished. I marveled at the bright blue tones of the parlor. Running my hand along the wall nearest me, I asked, "Is this the original color scheme?"

"Yes," he said. "I'm glad you can tell. I got the specs on the original house paints from the historical society. I was able to match them at the hardware store."

"Thank goodness for color matching," I said. "The Victorians sure did like their bright colors."

"They layered them so elegantly," he said. "I painted the ceiling a soft white to highlight the blue. What do you think of the chandelier?"

I stood under the magnificent crystal chandelier and studied it. "This is gorgeous. Where did you find it?"

"In the attic, of all places," he said. "I cleaned it up and put in new wiring and put it back in the parlor. It was a labor of love, actually."

"I can only imagine," I said. There must have been dozens of crystals. Something like that stored in an attic meant years of dirt and took careful washing. There wasn't a speck of dust on it now.

"And in here is the dining area," he said and waved me into the three-toned, green room. All the rooms were bare; he still had some paint cloths on the floor. "I know it's empty, but imagine five little café tables with four chairs each."

"Will you have a buffet?" I asked. "When I do offer a hot breakfast we do it buffet style."

"Yes," he said. "I plan on a large hot breakfast for my guests."

"How many guests will the B and B hold?" I asked.

"There are six bedrooms," he said. "I'm living in the carriage house above the old horse stalls and carriage area."

"Are you going to have horses?" I asked.

"No," he said. "But I do have a lovely carriage in the outbuildings so my guests can view up close the type of transportation used in the Victorian era."

"Oh good," I said. "I can't imagine what it would be like living over the top of horses."

"That's really old world, isn't it?" he asked. Then he put his hand on the small of my back and guided me to the den across the hall. "This is where I'm going to offer a library. I put in all the bookcases floor to ceiling and this great library ladder to help them reach the top books."

"This is marvelous," I said. "It looks very much like you know what you're doing. Is the entire inside finished?"

"Except for the touch-ups and the first-floor furniture," he said. "It's just the outside that needs painting. I've got a call in with Mike Hangleford. He's going to send out a crew as soon as they finish with the McMurphy."

"Oh, I do recommend him," I said. "His crew has been great working with us at the McMurphy."

"I saw that," he said. "It's why I called him. Good thing I did, too, because I got the last opening. They are swamped for the rest of the season."

"Well, I'm sure they'll make your old girl look as good as new."

"Oh, and I have an elevator here." He pointed out where it was tucked beside the stairs and across from the dining room. "Let's go up."

I stepped into the elevator with him. It was a small box and rattled a bit on the way to the third floor. "It only goes three floors?"

"Yes," he said. "The fourth floor was the attic, but I remodeled it into a suite, so I will rent it only to people who can climb the stairs."

I peeked into each of the five bedrooms. He had them decorated with various flower and sailing themes and antique furniture to match. "The Victorians loved their bright colors," I repeated.

"Is it too much?" he asked.

"No, no," I reassured him. "People like the Victorian flavor when they come here. They expect it. Plus, in a bed and breakfast they want to feel as if they've gone back in time. Do you know your price point?"

"I'm charging one hundred fifty dollars per night with discounts for multiple nights," he said. "The suite is two hundred fifty dollars per night."

"Can I see it?"

"Sure," he said and motioned toward the staircase. "Right this way." The attic had originally been set up for maids to use, with wood floors and dormer windows. Harry had turned it into a gorgeous suite complete with an en suite bath that had a jetted tub. The decor was tasteful and modern.

"Why did you change up the decor?" I asked.

"I wanted to do an A/B test to see which decor visitors wanted," he said. "This one is more expensive, but also more modern. All the rooms have free Wi-Fi and streaming televisions."

"Most people will be out in the state parks or shopping," I said. "They rarely use the televisions except to look at weather reports."

"I figured, but televisions are expected, like irons and ironing boards and a coffee bar," he said.

I headed downstairs. There was something a bit tension making about being in a room alone with him and a bed. When I reached the bottom I turned and smiled at him. "This is great! Thanks for sharing it with me. We're doing a promotion for anyone who plans a wedding with Jenn. They can buy out the entire McMurphy to house their family for what evens out to seventy-nine dollars per room per night. You might want to think about doing the same for smaller affairs."

He reached over the top of me to open the front door. The movement put me dangerously near him. "I don't know about that," he said and we walked out onto the porch. "It sounds like a great deal, but I can imagine all the shenanigans that would happen when a single family takes over the building. Think family Christmas or Thanks-giving arguments."

I laughed. "I hadn't thought of that."

He stuck his hands into his pockets and shrugged. "I have a big family. Don't get me wrong, I love them all, but they can be a handful when left to their own devices."

"How many brothers and sisters do you have?" I had to ask.

"I'll tell you over dinner if you want to grab a bite," he said.

A glance at my watch told me it was early; around five-thirty in the afternoon. "It's a little early."

"I can wait until eight if you have things to do," he said.

"I do owe you a dinner." I tapped my cheek. "As long as I'm buying . . ."

"Done!" he said. "I'll pick you up at eight."

"See you then," I said and gave him a quick hug, then went on my way. I vowed not to look back, but it was a very hard vow to keep.

Chocolate Almond Butter Crunch Bars

Ingredients:
1 cup honey
1 cup sugar
1½ cups dark chocolate chips
1½ cups almond butter
4 cups crisp rice cereal

Directions:
   Use a medium saucepan to combine the honey, sugar, chocolate chips, and almond butter. Heat on medium heat and stir until melted.

   Add the crisp rice cereal and stir to coat. Place in a heavily buttered 8 x 8-in. pan. Chill until set. Slice into 2-inch squares. Store in an airtight container. Makes 16. Enjoy!

Chapter 9

"Do you know who Annie Hawthorne is?" I asked Jenn and Frances as I approached them chatting at the reception desk.

"I have no idea," Jenn said. "Why?" Today she wore a black jumpsuit and heels.

"Annie lives in St. Ignace," Frances said and put on her red reading glasses. She typed on her computer. "Her family runs a building contractor shop." She turned her screen toward us and we saw the building contractor website. There was an older man, a younger man, and a young woman who was very thin and, if dressed right, could look very androgynous.

"As best I can tell, she's the last person to see Shane that night before we found him in the alley," I said.

"Shane was with a contractor?" Jenn asked.

"At the Boar's Head bar around seven p.m.," I said.

"He must have wanted some advice or to hire someone to help with the cottage remodel," Frances said.

"That still wouldn't explain his standing me up for dinner or why he was in that alley," Jenn said and put her hands on her hips.

"But it's a start," I pointed out. "The people I talked to said she was wearing a dark hoodie and jeans. They couldn't tell if she was a woman or a man, but Terry said it was Annie. I'm going to talk to her."

"I wish Shane would just tell us what happened that night," Jenn said. "Then we wouldn't have to sneak around behind his back."

The bells over the door rang out and Rex walked in. "Behind whose back?"

"Shane's," I said. "Did you know he met with Annie Hawthorne that night?"

"I'm not going to talk with you about an ongoing investigation," Rex said. "But I did want to talk to you about the fundraiser for the police and firemen's ball."

"A ball?" Jenn perked up.

"It's a lot of fun," Frances said, "and raises money for the police and firemen, along with the EMTs. Are you bringing us tickets?"

"Yes," Rex said and pulled out a batch. "Are you in for selling fifty?"

"How much are they?" I asked.

"One hundred fifty dollars per person," he said. "Two hundred fifty dollars per couple. It pays for the ball and helps us earn a good profit."

"We'll take fifty," Frances said.

"There's also a silent raffle and I was wondering if you wanted to offer a McMurphy basket. Maybe a two-night stay and some fudge?"

"I can do that," I said.

"I'll put together a smaller basket," Jenn said, "to advertise my event planning business."

"Great," Rex said and wrote us down in his notebook. "Thanks, ladies."

I walked him to the door. "Rex, why don't I remember a policemen's ball last year?"

"We usually hold it in April, but this year the committee decided to try the end of June instead."

"Oh, huh," I said. "Thanks for stopping by and giving us tickets to sell. I'll make a great basket. Is a value of around five hundred dollars good?"

"That would be perfect," he said. "We can usually get a thousand dollars over value in these auctions."

"Great," I said as he opened the door and left. "So, Frances, why am I just now learning of this ball? I could have planned for a really big giveaway."

"It completely slipped my mind this year," she said. "What with remodeling the McMurphy and everything else going on."

"Is it elaborate?" Jenn asked. "How elaborate?"

"The ladies like to wear elbow-length gloves," Frances said. "The theme is usually Victorian."

"Oh, so there are a lot of ball gowns," Jenn said and rubbed her hands together. "Goody, I just love a ball gown."

"I guess I have some shopping to do," I said. Then glanced at my phone. "Goodness, look at the time. Frances, you and Douglas should go home. Jenn, can you watch the McMurphy for me tonight?"

"Oh no," she said. "I have a dinner with Shane scheduled and trust me, no one is backing out of it this time."

"Oh right," I said and tapped my chin.

"Why?" Jenn asked. "Where were you going?"

"I was going to dinner with Harry Winston," I said. "To pay him back for his help over Christmas."

"Harry Winston? The Adonis-looking guy with the remodeled bed and breakfast? That Harry Winston?"

"Yeesss," I said, sounding suddenly unsure. "Should I not?"

"I thought you were finally getting together with Rex," Jenn said.

"Well, I don't know about that," I said. "Listen, Frances, can you watch the front desk for a few minutes? I'm going to run to Doud's to pick up some stuff. If we can't go out, we'll just dine in. I'll make my lasagna, open a bottle of red wine, make a salad, and bam! Dinner is served."

"Brilliant," Frances said. "Go on, then, scoot. Douglas and I will wait until you return."

"Thanks," I said and grabbed my purse, then strode out of the hotel. I had no idea why Jenn was so set on me dating Rex. I mean, we did hold hands, but he hadn't called me or invited me out since that day when we got interrupted last month. I wasn't going to sit on my hands and wait for him.

Besides, I did owe Harry a meal. This was only paying my debt.

"I have good news and bad news," I said as I met Harry in the lobby. "I'll start with the bad news. I have to stay here tonight. I couldn't find anyone to watch the reservation desk, so I'm sort of on call. You see, we have a buzzer that rings in my apartment should someone come in late and need something or want to be checked in."

"Well, that's too bad," he said and looked a little heartbroken. He wore a very nice dress shirt in blue that made his eyes sparkle, dress slacks, and dress shoes. He smelled of rich cologne and pure male.

"But I have good news," I said as I took his hand and led him toward the stairs.

"What?" He raised his right eyebrow.

"I've made dinner, so we can dine in at my place," I said.

"Sounds like a great solution," he said.

He followed me up to the fourth floor. "This is my floor," I explained. "Over here is my and Jenn's office— Jenn's my roommate until her wedding next week. And this," I got out my key, "is my apartment. Beware—my fur babies like to greet people at the door."

I heard a joyful bark as I opened the door. Mal jumped up on me for pets, then went straight to Harry. She wagged her little stump tail and put her front paws on his leg. "This is Mal," I said. "She's a year old. And this older lady is Caramella, Mella for short." I scratched Mella's calico head and behind her ears.

Harry stepped inside and I closed the door behind him. "Well, hello there," he said to Mal and squatted down to get closer to her height. He gave her a good rubdown. "Do you know any tricks?"

"All kinds," I said. "Her favorite is up."

"I saw that," he said. "Sit." Mal sat. "Can you do down?" She lay down. "How about roll over?" he asked. Mal rolled and then got up and ran to him so he could pet her and tell her she was wonderful. "She's so cute."

"Thanks," I said.

He rose. "It smells delicious in here." He stepped over to the couch and greeted Mella. Then he took a seat on one of my barstools.

"It's my favorite lasagna," I said. "I went to CIA—the Culinary Institute of America. I majored in candy making because, well, that's the family business, and I always planned on being here. But I minored in Italian food in case I ever had to do a side gig at a restaurant to pay my bills."

"Well, you have my mouth watering," he said and sent me a look that put a little sizzle down my spine.

"Wine?" I said quickly. "I have a nice bold cabernet sauvignon."

"Sounds great."

I poured us both wine, then took the lasagna out of the oven to set up. It needed fifteen minutes out of the oven to settle into its flavors. I grabbed my wineglass and moved to the living room. "Come have a seat."

"The place looks brand-new," he said. "Did you re-model?"

"I kind of had to," I said. Then I explained about the roof deck and why the McMurphy needed to be rebuilt.

"That sounds like a lot of work. You wouldn't even know it," he said. "Here's to good work."

"To good work," I agreed and we tapped glasses and took a sip.

The next morning I woke up tired, but with a smile on my face. Harry was great company. We talked for hours about our businesses, our families, and our hopes and dreams. I put two empty wine bottles in the trash. Jenn came home around eleven p.m. and joined us for an hour and then went to bed, which was Harry's cue to leave.

He left me with a kiss on the cheek and a promise to spend more time together.

"So," Jenn said as she came into the kitchen and grabbed a cup of coffee. "Late start today, huh?" She wiggled her eyebrows at me.

"Hush," I said. "I get to have some fun in life."

"He's a cute guy," she said and leaned against the counter. "What about Rex?"

"Oh my gosh, I completely forgot about him," I said in a false, Southern belle accent. "Whatever will I do?"

"Oh, I touched a nerve," Jenn said.

I sighed. "I can't not have relationships just because Rex might commit to ours. I mean, after two failed marriages he is a little gun-shy."

"But Harry doesn't seem gun-shy." She sipped her coffee.

"I like him, okay? We have a lot in common." I leaned on the counter across from her. "How was your dinner with Shane last night? Did he tell you why he missed your last dinner date?"

Her mouth became a thin line of disappointment. "No. He said I had to trust him that he would have shown up if he could," she said. "He promised me that he would always show up if he could."

"What does that mean?" I asked. "Was he kidnapped or something?"

"He asked me to leave it alone," she said. "But it sure put a damper on our wedding plans."

"Did he at least tell you why he met with Annie Hawthorne that night?"

"He did," she replied. "Remember I told you that he wanted our cottage to have basic remodeling done before the wedding, so he was bringing in a contractor to do some rewiring and plumbing? The other stuff like painting and flooring and such we can do while living there."

"It's probably a good idea," I said. "The house was built in the 1910s. So one-hundred-year-old wiring and plumbing needs upgrading."

"It was done in the sixties," she said. "So not quite one hundred years old, but still needing upgrades. We want to be able to have Wi-Fi and a modern washer and dryer set."

"Makes sense," I said and glanced at my phone. "Oh shoot, it's nearly eight and I have to get to work making fudge. What's on your plate today?"

"I'm spending the day with the Wilkins bride. This morning we're ordering flowers," she said. "And after lunch we're visiting the Grander to see about a groom's cake."

"You are a busy woman," I said.

"Almost as busy as you," she said. "I'm going to ask Frances to give me some of those police and firemen's ball tickets. I may be able to sell a few while I'm out and about today."

"That would be great," I said. Then I patted Mal on the head and went downstairs to make fudge. I had fed my fur babies first thing and Mal and I went on a short, brisk walk before I'd come back upstairs for coffee. So I knew my babies were taken care of. Mal loved to go down with me when I went to the shop to make fudge. We were usually alone, but I was so late today that Frances was already at her perch behind the registration desk.

"Good morning," she said. "Did you oversleep?"

"A little," I replied. "I get to give myself some grace every once in a while. Besides, I shipped all the online orders yesterday. We have two today, so I'll cut them from the fudge in the display cabinets once I make it."

Frances held up her hands. "I was simply asking to make sure you weren't sick."

"Oh, she's not sick," Jenn said, behind me. "She had a date last night."

I sent her a look as Mal greeted Frances, got her pets, and then went to her doggie bed beside the registration desk.

"We'll discuss later," Frances said.

Rolling my eyes, I said, "I'm off to make fudge."

The rest of the morning went quickly. It usually took me four hours to make the fudge to fill the cabinet. Today was no exception. I picked flavors that matched my online orders: peanut butter and dark chocolate, rum raisin, and cashew milk chocolate. Then it was a simple chocolate fudge, a bright strawberry fudge, and a piña colada fudge.

Around lunch, I had a few people walk in off the street to watch me make fudge and then get a taste. I sold a few of the five-pound boxes and a three-pound box. Once I packaged up my online orders and cut a box of samples, I left the fudge shop to relieve Frances so she could go to lunch with Douglas.

I also had some final checkouts of guests who had asked for extensions. Checkout time was eleven a.m., but we did allow for late checkouts.

Carol Tunisian walked in. Mal ran and slid to greet her. Carol laughed with delight and picked her up. Getting picked up was Mal's favorite thing in the whole world. She would live in my arms if she could.

"How do you get any work done with this cutie around?" Carol asked.

"I have to pretend I don't see her," I said. "And even then I give in more times than I should."

She petted Mal and gave her a kiss before putting her down in her bed. "So, I heard something I thought you might like to know."

I leaned on the top of the desk. "What?"

"I heard that Shane has made some enemies," she said.

"Really? Like who?"

"Well, the people he's helped put away, of course. One of them was Peter Ramfield,"

"Wait, Peter was working with Mike on painting the McMurphy," I said. "I had no idea he had been in prison."

"Mike likes to help guys get back on their feet when they get out of prison," Carol said.

"So you think Peter might have done something to frame Shane?" I asked.

"I heard Peter stopped Shane when he came out of the Boar's Head that night. He asked him to walk with him and the two went up a side street."

"Why would he want to talk to Shane?" I asked.

"That's the key question," Carol said. "Maybe he had proof that Shane made a mistake. A mistake that got him jail time. Seems like that would be something Shane wouldn't want people to know. Might be why he's not talking to you or Jenn about that night."

"Hmmm," I said. "That's a good theory. I'll see if I can't find out more. Please let me know if anyone saw Shane or Peter after that meeting, okay?"

"Will do," she said and snitched a couple of pieces of sampler fudge from the open box on the reception desk. Popping it in her mouth, she chewed and smiled. "Good fudge."

"Thanks," I said. "The samples are for the senior center. I was going to take them down and ask questions. But you've given me something better to pursue. So, do you want to take the fudge to the center for me?"

"It will be my pleasure," she said and swiped the box from the registration counter and tucked it under her arm. "See ya."

"I will be asking the others at the center if they got the fudge," I said as she headed out the door.

Carol waved at me and was gone in a flash.

The news about Peter put a whole new spin on things. Surely if Shane made a mistake he would own up to it, not hide it. We all made mistakes. While I couldn't talk to Shane about it, I certainly could talk to Peter.

Frances and Douglas came back from lunch and I put Mal on her leash, gathered up my shipping boxes, and headed out the back door. I stopped so Mal could do her business in her favorite patch of grass on the other side of the alley.

"Well, good afternoon, Allie."

I turned to see Mr. Beecher walking toward us. He always wore dress slacks, a waistcoat, and a suit coat. Today's suit was brown tweed. With his white hair and white mustache, he reminded me of the snowman in the *Rudolph the Red-Nosed Reindeer* television special. "Hi, Mr. Beecher."

Mal finished fast and ran to the old man. She jumped up and he reached into his pocket and pulled out a small treat for her. Mal liked that he always had treats. Mr. Beecher was one of her favorite people.

"A fine afternoon, isn't it?" he asked as he straightened up from patting Mal on the head and giving her the treat.

"It is warmer today than yesterday," I said. "I didn't

get out my jacket. Only a sweater today. Summer is coming."

"It's your second tourist season. How are you doing? Do you feel more ready for it this time?"

"I don't know if *more ready* are the words I would use, but I certainly have better support this time. I've made lots of good friends in the last year—including you."

"I understand your Mal found another body," he said.

"She seems to be able to root them out, doesn't she?" I said. "Listen, do you know Peter Ramfield?"

"He was one of the painters who finished the outside of the McMurphy, right?"

"Yes. Carol told me he might have a grudge against Shane Carpenter. Shane's evidence helped put him in jail."

"I imagine he might have a grudge against Shane," Mr. Beecher said. "Peter went to jail for five years over a felony theft conviction in St. Ignace. He did his time and has been a model citizen ever since."

"So I shouldn't worry about him being around the Mc-Murphy?"

Mr. Beecher shook his head. "I don't think so. I heard he has a new fiancée and is settling down in St. Ignace. Nothing like a good woman to get a man's mind straight."

"Do you think it would be safe for me to ask him some questions?"

"I don't see why not," Mr. Beecher said. "Like I said, Peter seems to have come out of the whole experience a better man."

"Thanks, I said. "Have a great day." I waved and he tipped his bowler hat to me as he started down the opposite way in the alley. "Well, Mal, we have to ship this fudge first. Then we can go see if we can't hunt Peter down. He might be painting Harry's place already. We'll look there first."

Mike and Peter had finished painting the McMurphy the day before. Harry told me they were going to squeeze his place in, which meant there was a good chance they were over there now.

With only two packages, we were in and out of the shipping store quickly. Harry's place was a few blocks away from the store, so we strolled over there. The wind off the lake rippled my wavy hair. I tried tucking it back behind my ear. It smelled of spring and rain. I glanced up at the sky. Clouds were forming on the horizon.

"We'd better hurry," I told Mal. "If it starts to rain they will pack up the painting and be gone before we can talk to them."

We power walked our way to Harry's place and, sure enough, Peter and Mike were up on ladders painting the main exterior a lovely blue gray. There were swatches of white on the trim and red on the accents of the trim.

"Hi, guys," I said and waved up. "This is looking good."

"Thanks, Allie!" Mike said and climbed down from his ladder. "We love these traditional red, white, and blue cottages."

"So, blue with white trim and red accents?" I waved at the white and red swatches.

"Yes," Mike said. "We painted swatches to get Harry's opinion on the shades. The red, white, and blue were his suggestions."

"Smart," I said.

"What brings you out this way?" Mike asked. "Is there a problem with the McMurphy job?"

"Oh no, no problem, the McMurphy is her lovely self again," I said. "Thanks so much. Mal and I were just out selling tickets to the policemen's ball. Have you or Peter purchased tickets already?"

"I haven't," Mike said. "How much are they?"

"One hundred fifty dollars for a single and two hundred fifty for a couple. I'm sure your wife would love to go, and all profits go directly to the police and fire departments."

"I'll take a ticket for two," he said and reached into his pocket for his wallet.

"Fantastic," I said and pulled off a couple's ticket. The tickets were inside envelopes that were labeled single or double. I took his money and handed him his envelope. "Thanks. Oh, do you mind if I talk to Peter for a few minutes?"

"Sure, no problem," Mike said and put the envelope with the tickets in his back pocket. "Just don't steal him for too long."

"Thanks," I said and went over to where Peter was painting the far side of the house. "Hi, Peter," I said and waved.

"Allie," he said from the top of the ladder. "How are you?"

"I'm good," I said. Mal barked that she was good as well. "Can I talk to you for a minute?"

"Sure." He climbed down and then hopped off the ladder. "Mind if I take a swig of water?"

"No, go ahead," I said.

He picked up a nearby water bottle and took a big gulp. Then he wiped his forehead on his sleeve. "What can I do for you?"

"Oh, I was wondering if you heard about Christopher Harris's death," I said.

"Sure. The whole island is buzzing," he said. "I didn't know the guy personally, but I feel bad for his family."

"Do you remember talking to Shane Carpenter the night Christopher died?"

"Why do you ask? Is Shane the killer? I heard he had something to do with it."

"Oh," I said. "No, I'm convinced he isn't the killer, but he's not talking. Anyway, I was told you and Shane were seen talking that night. You caught him on the corner of Main Street and Astor. Then you both went into the pub."

"Oh yeah," he said and took another swig. "I heard Shane was getting married to your friend Jenn and I wanted to ask him for some advice when it comes to fi-ancées." He blushed. "I'm not the best at relationships and I wanted to know how he was handling all the wedding hoopla."

"I see," I said. "Do you know how long you two talked?"

"I'd say about half an hour," he said. "I bought us drinks and he only had one. Said he wasn't feeling so good, and I asked him if he wanted me to walk with him. He must have been drinking a lot before I met him because he seemed to stumble a bit. He asked me to take him to his new cottage. I did and that was that."

"Where'd you go afterward?"

"Is this an investigation?" he asked, mopping his forehead again.

"No, no," I reassured him. "I'm just trying to retrace Shane's steps."

"I went back to the pub," he said. "It was snooker night."

"Thanks." I touched his forearm. "This was really helpful. Say, do you want to buy tickets to the policemen's ball? It's a great place to bring a fiancée."

"Sure," he said and got out his wallet. "How much?"

"One hundred fifty for a single, two hundred fifty for a double."

"I'd better take the double," he said. "Don't want to mess things up with my lady before the wedding."

We exchanged money and the ticket. Mal sniffed his paint-covered work boots and barked.

"Oh Mal, I know I promised you a walk and I've stopped to talk," I said. "Come on, then. Let's finish and go home. I've got work to do on Jenn's wedding."

"Thanks for the tickets," Peter said and he climbed up the ladder.

"Looks like a storm is brewing," I said. "Stay safe!"

"We always do," Peter said and picked up his paint sprayer, pulled a mask over his nose and mouth, and proceeded with spraying blue paint.

So, Shane had gotten drunk and Peter left him at the cottage. Seemed a little out of character for Shane but might explain why he missed dinner with Jenn. Also why he might be too embarrassed to own up to it.

So how did he come to be in that alley that night? What did he see that made him pick up the murder weapon with no gloves on?

Chapter 10

"You're back later than I thought," Frances said as I unhooked Mal from her halter and leash.

"I sold four tickets," I said triumphantly as I handed her the cash. "Doubles to Mike and Peter, and I ran into Suzy Olds and Tracy Birk. They each bought doubles, too."

"Wonderful," Frances said.

"I also learned a bit more about Shane's whereabouts the night Christopher was murdered."

"Is it good news or bad?"

I explained to her what Peter told me. "I'm going to talk to Jenn to see if she knows why Shane might get so drunk he had to be walked back to the cottage."

"Good call," Frances said. "Oh, by the way. We've had everyone check out today. We don't have guests coming in until Thursday for Jenn's wedding."

"That leaves us two days with no guests to spruce things up," I said. "We can do a spring cleaning."

"Things will pick up when the season gets going," Frances said. "They always do."

"I'm not going to worry. We have our discount offer and, like I said, it's a good chance to air out the rooms and do some deep cleaning. I'll go get started."

"You make a good innkeeper," Frances said.

"Yes, well, if we do get any walk-ins, please tell them we have availability. Even the best innkeepers need a steady income stream."

"Will do," she said and went back to her computer.

Later that afternoon Jenn walked into the office carrying a gorgeous bouquet of fresh-cut flowers in a vase.

"Those are beautiful," I said. "Did the florist give them to you for inspiration?"

"Nope," Jenn said and grinned as she set them on my desktop. "These are for you."

"For me? Who would send me flowers?"

"Read the card," Jenn advised.

I was so surprised. I loved getting flowers, but Trent had been the only to buy me flowers and we had broken up months ago. I grabbed the card and opened it and read: *Thanks for dinner last night. Thinking of you, Harry.*

"It's from Harry," I said and smelled the lovely fragrance from them.

"So, the date went very well, then." Jenn waggled her eyebrows at me.

"This was very sweet," I said. "I'm going to text him." I opened up my phone and texted Harry a nice thank-you.

"He sure knows how to make you blush," Jenn teased.

"I love flowers," I said. My phone chimed with a text. I glanced down. It was Harry, telling me that I was welcome and he hoped I would have dinner with him in two days. "He wants to go to dinner again in two days," I said. "Do you think that's too soon? I mean, we do have guests coming in for your wedding. Oh wait, that would be Thursday, and we're doing the bachelorette party. I guess I have to say no."

"The question is, do you want to say no?" Jenn asked.

"Of course I do; I've planned a super fun girl's night that evening. I'll ask if we can do it another time."

"So next week, stop and take a break and enjoy some time with a beautiful man," Jenn said.

"You know, you're right, I should. Wait, Rex asked me to be his plus-one at your wedding."

"You are my maid of honor and he is the best man," Jenn said with a twinkle in her eye. "Do you want me to ask Harry to come?"

"Oh, um, can I say no?"

She laughed. "Of course you can say no. What are you going to do?"

"I don't know," I said and studied the beautiful bouquet. "Rex isn't exactly buying me flowers and Melonie is still on the island, trying to get him to see her as marriage material—er, remarriage material." I leaned back. "I have a question. Would you feel any different about Shane if he had two divorces behind him?"

Jenn sat on the edge of my desk. "I might," she said. "It's hard to separate the man from the failed marriages. Was it bad luck? Was he bad at picking wives? I'm not sure, but it seems the odds might go up of you being ex-wife number three."

"It doesn't help that Rex has been dragging his feet for

a year," I said. "It's on-again, off-again. Why couldn't I have just married my high school sweetheart and spent my whole life with him, like my parents? None of this weird dating stuff."

"Did you have a high school sweetheart?" Jenn asked and crossed her arms.

"No," I said and frowned. "You know I didn't have time for that. All my time was spent preparing to enter the Culinary Institute."

"Just be honest with Harry. Tell him you're going to my wedding with Rex."

I sighed. "I had such a good time with Harry last night. I like him, too."

"Then tell him that, too," she said. "Honesty is the best policy in relationships."

"Speaking about that, has Shane told you what happened yet?"

"No." Jenn shook her head. "He said it was for my own protection, but frankly, I think he's embarrassed about the whole thing."

"What if I told you that he not only had drinks with Annie Hawthorn that night, but also Peter Ramfield? In fact, Peter told me that they talked for about thirty minutes and Shane became really drunk. So Peter asked to walk him to the cottage so he could lie down for a while and sober up."

Jenn's eyebrows pulled together. "Shane never gets drunk. Is Peter certain that's what happened?"

"Very certain," I said. "So he walked Shane to your cottage and left him there. It would explain why Shane stood you up. Did you check the cottage that night?"

"I did," Jenn said and pursed her lips. "The cottage was the first place I went, but I didn't see him. Of course there was no power and I was using a flashlight, but it seems like if he were there, I would have seen him."

"You probably just missed him," I said.

"Hmph," she said. "Then how did he end up in that alley with a knife in his hand?"

"I'm going to keep digging, but I'm thinking only Shane knows, and possibly Rex, if Shane told him."

Jenn shook her head. "It's all so weird."

"I know," I said and stood and hugged her. "But we're going to get to the bottom of this and finish the plans for your wedding. Don't forget, tomorrow we have hair appointments."

"I didn't forget," she assured me. "We're doing the hair and makeup consultation. I am so glad Emma didn't mind us doing one."

"She's doing it for free, right? How'd you manage that?" I asked.

"I'm sending her all the ladies in the Wilkins wedding," Jenn said. "Unlike my two bridesmaids, Jessica has nine."

"Wow, I don't think I know nine women who would want to be in my wedding," I said. "That is, if I were getting married."

"If you had married Trent, I'm sure they would have come up with nine bridesmaids for you to make everything look grand."

"Right," I said. "I'm afraid that ship has sailed."

"Have you seen Paige?" she asked. Paige Jessop was Trent's sister and she had taken over management of all the businesses on the island the Jessops owned. There were a lot.

"No," I said. "I heard she was on the island, but I've been busy and so, most likely, is she."

"We should invite her for girls' night," Jenn said. "I invited her to the wedding. She sent back her RSVP with a plus-one."

"Really?" I said. In the year I'd known Paige, I'd never seen her dating anyone. I figured whoever her boyfriend was, he lived in Chicago, where her family and now Trent resided full time.

"Yes," Jenn said. "I can't wait to see who she's dating."

"Let's talk bachelorette party," I said. "I've invited Sandy Everheart, Liz, Sophie, Mary Emry, Frances . . . and now Paige. Is there anyone else you'd like there?"

"No, I think eight is enough," she said.

"I booked the back room of the Boar's Head," I said. "They will supply an open bar and a buffet of sliders, nachos, quesadillas, and other bar foods. Then there will be cake."

"Yes, we have to have cake," Jenn said. "What kind of cake?"

"Your favorite, '' I said.

"Lemon?"

"Yes," I said.

"From Suzy's Cakes?"

"Yes," I said. "There will also be a few games and some fun surprises."

"Sounds fabulous," Her eyes twinkled with delight.

"I thought I'd schedule it the night before the wedding, but I changed it to two nights before," I said. "To give us all time to recover so our skin looks better for the pictures."

"Smart woman!" Jenn said. "I'm going to suggest that for all my clients. Let the men look all hung over. Just one thing," she said.

"What?"

"No strippers, right? The last thing I want is some half-naked man I don't know sitting in my lap."

"Aw, now you're killing all the fun," I said with a wink.

"Allie . . ."

"You don't get to dictate what happens at your bachelorette party," I said. "That's for the maid of honor to do."

"Your parents are coming for the wedding, aren't they?" she asked.

I sighed. "Yes, they are coming. My mom can't wait to meet your mom."

"My mom wanted to come in the Sunday before the wedding, to," she made air quotes with her fingers, "help. But I told her no, that you had it under control and she and Daddy should just fly in the Friday before."

"So the night before? That seems restrictive," I said.

Jenn laughed. "That's exactly what Mom said, so we compromised and she'll be here tomorrow."

"Oh, so she'll be here the bachelorette party night," I said. "Should I invite her?"

"Oh no," Jenn said. "No one wants their mom at their bachelorette party. Trust me, having Frances come is hard enough."

"Fine," I said. "What about a tea party on Friday? That way all the women family members can meet and we can invite some of our favorite seniors from the senior center."

"Now that's a great idea," Jenn said. She tapped her fingers on her mouth. "That means I need to take time off from work from Thursday until Monday. Our honeymoon will be after the season so I can keep my business going.

That said, I'll need to rearrange my planning schedule to accommodate the tea, but I'm all in!"

"Great!" I exclaimed.

"Wait, how are you going to manage all this and your fudge business and the hotel and investigating?"

I shrugged. "I'll figure out a way. I always do. Maybe by then Becky will be out of the medically induced coma and will help shed some light on the whole thing. Then I can let the investigation go."

"Now that's a happy thought," Jenn said.

As an only child, I wasn't used to big family to-dos. My parents had a tendency to stay out of their own family events. Jenn was also an only child, but she had a big extended family and loved being part of all the noise and business of it. I guess that made her more of an extrovert and me more of an introvert. That might be why we worked so well together.

Chapter 11

Wednesday

The next morning I was up at four a.m. I'd placed a notice on my website that online orders would not happen between Thursday and Monday for Jenn's wedding. The last thing I needed was to get up before dawn to make fudge with all the people and events happening. I took my duties as maid of honor quite seriously. I didn't want anything to screw up Jenny's wedding.

What I hadn't accounted for was that the minute I put up the days I wasn't shipping, more orders piled up, as if people were stockpiling to get themselves through the days without it. That meant I was working double time to meet the demand.

I wondered if anyone had seen my ad for an assistant in the paper. So far, the sign in the window hadn't brought in a soul looking for a job. It made me wonder if

I needed to go farther and put up ads at local colleges. Maybe I could catch students who wanted a summer gig.

It was nearly nine a.m. by the time I had all the online orders filled and the cabinet stocked with enough fudge for a weekday. Frances and Douglas were working. So I packed up my online fudge and put Mal in her halter and leash.

"Going to the shipper's," I said. "Do you need anything while I'm out?"

"No, we're good," Frances said.

"Come on, Mal, let's go." We went out the back so that Mal could make a stop at her favorite patch of grass. Then I stopped by the shipping store, said hi to Sandy Seacrest, and put in my orders.

"That's a lot more than usual," Sandy said. "Are you having a sale?"

"No, but I am closing this weekend for Jenn's wedding festivities. My announcement resulted in a larger number of sales."

"Well, that's one way to do it," Sandy said. "Is Jenn's wedding still on?"

"Sure, why wouldn't it be?"

"I thought the police hauled Shane in today. Word is they're getting ready to make an arrest."

"That's not good," I said and frowned. "Thanks for the tip."

Mal and I hurried out. It wasn't far to the police station. The big white building was located on Market Street. One block up from Main. I opened the door and stormed up to the reception desk. "Is Rex in?"

"He's busy right now," the young Officer Hatch informed me.

"You don't understand, Officer Hatch. Rex Manning will see me. Just give him a quick call."

"I'm sorry, but he's in an interview," Officer Hatch informed me.

"If you don't give him a call, I will," I said and pulled out my phone.

"Hold on," he said and picked up the phone, then punched in a number. "Officer Manning, there's a woman out here asking about you. She has a dog. Yes, sir; of course, sir." Officer Hatch hung up the phone. "He said to have a seat and he'll be right out."

I sat down on one of the uncomfortable plastic chairs that were pushed against the wall. Mal jumped up in my lap. I kept my phone out and debated whether I should text Jenn or not. I decided to wait and see what Rex said before I did that. I didn't want to worry her when she was busy finalizing plans for the Wilkins wedding.

It was going to be a good event for the McMurphy. The family had bought out the whole inn for five days. They'd arrive the Wednesday after Jenn got married. If she got married. I tried not to worry too much about that.

The door opened and Rex walked out. He wore his Michigan State Police uniform, perfectly pressed and tailored to his wide shoulders. "Allie, let's go outside," he said and took my elbow.

I held Mal and went out with him. "I heard you have Shane in custody," I said. "What happened? Why would you do that? His wedding is just days away."

"Becky is awake," he said. "We've got some new information from her and we want to go over Shane's statement."

"Becky's awake? What did she say? Does she know who attacked her?"

"I can't disclose information concerning an ongoing investigation," he said and put his hands on his hips. "You know that. And don't go bugging Becky, She's still in Cheboygan and in critical condition."

I squeezed Mal. "She's not saying Shane did it, is she? Because I don't believe it."

"Allie," he said, "stay out of it. Please. "

"I can't if it means you're going to arrest Shane or ruin the wedding," I said.

Rex lifted his hat and ran a hand over his bare head before putting it back on. "I'm fully aware of the wedding. I'm the best man, darn it. I wouldn't do anything that wasn't by the book and you know it."

"Just because you can't doesn't mean I can't."

"Allie, I'm warning you—"

"Haven't you learned yet that warning me only makes me want to look harder?"

"Don't you have a hair appointment to go to?" he asked.

"How do you know that? And it's not for a couple of hours."

"I know because Jenn tells Shane and Shane tells me," he said. "Trust me, Shane wanted to come in the moment Becky woke up. This is all for the best."

"Whose best?"

"Christopher's best and Becky's best," he said. "Justice for the victim. Do you ever think about that?"

"I do think about it," I said. "That's why I try so hard to find the real killer. No one wants the wrong person to go to jail while the real killer is loose."

"Listen, I've got to go back inside," he said. "You don't need to stay. I promise not to do anything rash."

"Fine," I said.

"Good," he said. Then he petted Mal and looked me in the eye as if he wanted to say something more, but then his gaze went flat and he didn't say a word as he went back inside.

I called Jenn and started back toward Main Street.

"Allie," Jenn said. "What's up?"

"Rex has Shane back down in interrogation," I said.

"Why would he do that?"

"Becky woke up. They wouldn't tell me what she said, but whatever it was, they want to hear Shane's story again."

"I'll call him," she said.

"I don't think they'll let him keep his phone," I pointed out.

"Then I'm calling the lawyer," she said.

"That might be a good idea," I said. "Keep me posted. I'll understand if you want to skip the hair consultation."

"Let's keep it for now," she said. "I might need a distraction. Listen, I'm going to call the lawyer. See you soon?"

"Okay." I hung up. And Mal and I walked quickly back toward the McMurphy. Mrs. Tunisian and Mrs. Schmidt met us on the corner of Main Street.

"Allie, we heard that Shane has been arrested," Carol said.

"I just talked to Rex," I said. "He said that Shane was only in for questioning. It seems Becky woke up, and now they want to understand what happened from her point of view."

"How terrible for Jenn," Mrs. Schmidt said. "Is she okay? Will they postpone the wedding?"

"No postponement yet," I said. "Jenn is calling in a lawyer."

"Someone needs to go to Cheboygan to talk to Becky," Carol said. "Maybe she remembers things wrong."

"I'm not sure we know what she remembers or doesn't remember," I said. "What I do know is that I'm pretty sure there will be a guard outside her door. So the trip would be wasted. Listen, ladies, I'm holding a tea Friday to celebrate Jenn. You're invited. I'll be sending out email notifications to all the ladies from the senior center and others. It will be a nice tea and time to congratulate Jenn and meet her mom and Shane's mom. I hope you can come."

"Oh, honey, we'll be there," Carol said with a hand to my arm.

"We wouldn't miss it for the world," Mrs. Schmidt chimed in. "Do keep us posted on Shane's whereabouts. We'd hate to see Jenn left standing at the altar. That girl is too wonderful for that."

"I agree," I said, and Mal and I moved on to the Mc-Murphy. We went in the front and the bells jangled as we stepped inside. It was warm from the light that filled the front windows. I took Mal off her leash and harness and she went running for her water bowl.

"Did you hear the news?" I asked Frances.

"That they took Shane in for questioning?" Frances said. "Yes."

"News travels fast on a small island," I said.

"I also heard you went straight to Rex about it," she said. "You know that doesn't help, right?"

"I had to try," I said.

"They aren't arresting him, are they?" Frances asked. "Some people think they are."

"Rex said it was only an interview again. It seems

Becky woke up," I said. "I so badly want to go see her, but she's in Cheboygan."

"They questioned her, right?"

"I believe so," I said.

"You don't know what she said?" Frances asked.

"No. Rex wouldn't tell me," I said. "I tell you what, this is getting nerve-racking. I told him he can't arrest Shane and make him leave Jenn at the altar. He assured me that he was doing his best. I just don't understand what the motive might have been. I mean, Shane loves Jenn. Becky might have been his fiancée years ago, but he loves Jenn now. He wouldn't do anything to jeopardize that."

"I agree," Frances said.

"Anyway, I've decided to have a tea here, Friday, for just the ladies. I would like you to come. I want to get all the ladies together, including my mom, Jenn's mom, and Shane's mom, and most of the senior ladies. That way we can all have a nice prewedding meetup."

"That's a wonderful idea," Frances said. "Who's going to cater?"

"I took Thursday, Friday, Saturday, and Sunday off from fudge making," I said. "So I will be happy to make some tea cakes and little finger foods. There won't be more than twenty or thirty coming. So the batches will be small. We can hold it in the lobby because the family bought out the McMurphy."

"I love the idea," Frances said. "But I think you should cater it. You're going to be too busy to cook. That said, I tell you what, I'll make the tea. I have several nice teapots at home. We can brew different types and label them so the ladies can choose their own. Do you want to put out tables?"

"I was thinking bar-height tables, maybe five or so. That way the ladies can mingle."

"But the older women can't stand terribly long," Frances pointed out. "It might be better to have tables."

"I guess you're right," I said. "Well, then, eight tables of five people each it is. That way if we have anybody wander in, we'll have room. And I guess I agree on the caterer. Oh, I'll get Sandy Everheart to make us chocolate sculptures for the centerpieces, and we can surround them with flowers in Jenn's wedding colors."

"Sounds perfect," Frances said.

"I need to go upstairs to make some calls," I said.

As I hurried up the stairs, Frances called out, "Allie, your parents are here."

"Mom, Dad," I said as I came down the stairs to greet them with hugs. "You're a day early."

"Your mother wanted to be here to help in any way we can," Dad said as he rolled in their suitcases.

I gave them each a hug as Frances came to greet them.

"Stephen, Ann," Frances said. "Welcome. Your room hasn't been cleaned yet. Let me put your suitcases in storage."

"Oh, don't worry," Dad said. "I know where the storage closet is." He took the suitcases and Frances walked with him.

Mom grabbed my arm. "I heard that Shane might be arrested before the wedding can happen. What are you doing about that?"

"I'm doing my best to help," I said to my mom. "But Shane isn't talking. He doesn't want to worry Jenn and he definitely doesn't want my help."

"Well, you're helping anyway, right?" Mom said as she brushed the hair out of her eyes.

"Yes, Mom, I'm doing what I can." I glanced at the time. "Oops, I've got to go. We have hair and makeup appointments. Talk to you later."

"Definitely," Mom said. "Don't forget, I want to hear all about how you're working toward finding that killer."

Jenn, Liz, and I showed up at Emma's for our hair and makeup consultation. We were sipping wine and watching Jenn getting her hair done into a Gibson Girl–like bun.

"Did you bring your veil?" Emma asked. "We can pin it in and see how you like it."

"I've got it," I said. The veil was lace and would touch the ground, but wouldn't be as long as the train on the dress. The lace on it matched the lace on the dress. I unrolled it from its tissue paper and showed it to Emma. "This gets attached to the back of the bun. Then we have a silk orange blossom headband to mimic Queen Victoria's." I handed the veil to Liz and pulled out the floral headband. Jenn had had an artist friend construct it from silk flowers.

"Oh, these are beautiful," Emma said. She carefully placed the headband to frame Jenn's face. Then pinned the veil to the back. "Now, stand up and have a look." She waved to her full-length mirror in her hair studio, a small room off the side of her home. It was at once welcoming and cozy.

"It's perfect," Jenn said as she studied herself in the mirror. She stopped for a moment and her eyes filled up with tears. "Shane is going to be all right, isn't he? I feel terrible playing dress-up while he's in the police station being questioned."

"It's okay," I said and hugged her as best I could without harming her hair or veil. "Rex is Shane's best man. He's going to do his best to keep Shane safe."

"Come here," Emma said. "Let's take off your veil and headpiece." She worked quickly to take them off and I rolled the veil carefully back into its tissue container, then placed the silk headpiece in the box. "Now sit," Emma said, pointing to one of the comfy chairs. "Have a nice glass of wine. It's going to be okay."

"I'm sure Shane wants you to go on with the wedding plans," I said as I climbed into the stylist chair. My wavy, frizzy hair was going to be hard to capture and tame into a bun, but I would let Emma worry about that. "The last time I talked to him, he said he wasn't going to let anything get in the way of your wedding."

"It's just so terrible," Jenn said. "To think a man was murdered and a poor woman stabbed and nearly died."

"I truly believe Shane came to their rescue," I said.

Liz checked her phone. "It's going to be all right. The police haven't put out a press conference notice. That means that what Rex said was true. They're only talking to Shane right now." She handed Jenn a tissue. "Come on, wipe away those tears and enjoy this. It's the only time you'll get to be a bride. You should enjoy every minute of it."

"Surely we'll do this when you and Allie get married," Jenn said and dabbed at her eyes.

Liz laughed. "That's so far in the future, you won't even remember this day. I'm not dating anyone right now. Allie . . . how is your love life?"

I felt the heat of a blush rush up my cheeks as everyone looked at me expectantly. "I'm not sure," I said.

"She got flowers after making dinner for a very handsome man named Harry Winston," Jenn said.

"Oh, is he the start-up millionaire who bought the Strauses' old bed and breakfast?" Liz asked. "I have to admit he is some nice eye candy."

"I made him dinner is all," I said. "I'm Rex's date for the wedding."

"Does handsome Harry know that?" Liz teased me and sipped her wine.

"It didn't come up," I said nervously. "But I'm sure it will."

"What about Rex? Does he know you made dinner for Harry?" Liz leaned forward, seeming to be having too much fun with this interrogation.

"I don't have to tell Rex everything I do," I said. Emma pulled my hair, trying to tame it. "Ouch!"

"Sorry," Emma said. "Your hair is very thick."

"That should make it easier to poof out, right?" I asked.

"One would think," Emma said, a frown on her face.

"Anyway, Rex and I can't seem to be at the same place at the same time," I said. "And Melonie is still on the island and she has her cap set on remarrying Rex. I don't like fighting over men."

"Did you tell Rex that?" Liz asked.

"What? No," I said and frowned. "Relationships are hard."

"They sure are," Jenn said. "But so worth it."

"I heard that Shane was once engaged to Becky," Liz said.

"Yes," Jenn said. "He told me that she chose moving to New York over marrying him. I, on the other hand, am not going anywhere."

"But Becky was back on the island," Liz said. "I understand she was staying at the Parson's Bed and Breakfast. Does anyone know why she came back?"

"No clue," I said. "But I do know she was out on a date with Christopher that fateful night. So she's not interested in Shane."

"But she had more than Shane for a suitor the last time she was on the island," Liz said.

"How do you know?" I asked.

Liz smiled. "I'm a reporter. I pay attention to that kind of thing. Christopher wasn't the first guy she dated since she got back."

"Who else was she seeing?" I asked.

"I heard she had a torrid affair with one of the locals," Liz said. "Then dumped him for Christopher."

"Well, there you go," I said. "We have motive."

"You think her affair got Christopher killed?" Jenn asked. "Do we know who she had the affair with?"

"I heard the man was married," Liz said. "He wanted to leave his family for her, but she wouldn't be a home-wrecker."

"I think that ship has sailed," I said. "The minute she had the affair she became a home-wrecker."

"I don't think she looked at it that way," Liz said.

"Okay, Allie, how is this for your hair?" Emma gave me a handheld mirror. I looked at my reflection in shock. She had managed to tame my mane into a gorgeous pouf of a Gibson Girl bun.

"Wow," I said.

"Wow," said Jenn and Liz at the same time.

"I guess we have a winner," Emma said. "One tip to help me get this right the day of the wedding: Don't wash your hair for twenty-four hours before. Otherwise it will be slick and soft and fall out of the bun."

"Noted," I said and got up to let Liz take the chair.

We talked and laughed for another hour as Emma tamed Liz's curls and then showed us all what the make-up should look like. We left the salon a little buzzed on wine and looking like three Gibson Girls in modern clothing.

Jenn hadn't talked about Shane's possible arrest again, but I knew it wasn't far from her mind. We walked home after leaving Liz at the corner where she lived.

"I know you're worried," I said to Jenn.

"I don't know how not to be worried." Jenn glanced at her phone. "Shane has been at the police station all day. I don't know what that means."

"All it means is that Rex is being thorough," I said. "My parents arrived this morning. When are your parents coming in?"

"They are supposed to be here tomorrow," Jenn said. "My mother sees everything. I don't know how I'm going to keep my worry from her."

"Maybe you shouldn't," I suggested. "Your mom is really cool. She loves you so much that I bet she'll help you keep your mind focused."

"Maybe," Jenn said. "She's never been on the island, so I can spend the day taking them all around to see the sights."

"There you go," I said. "That's a great idea. Then we have the bachelorette party that night, the tea for the older ladies on Friday, and the wedding Saturday."

"I'd feel better if Shane never had to go into the police station again," Jenn said. "Which is ridiculous, I guess, because he works for them."

"Somebody knows something. I'll keep trying to figure this out. In the meantime you can help me entertain my parents. You know my mom is hypercritical at times. Let's divert her attention to your lovely wedding."

"I love your mom." Jenn brightened. "I'll be happy to divert her for you." She put her arm through mine. "We ladies need to stick together. With all the relatives coming, it's going to take a lot of work to keep everyone entertained. I say we have a bonfire and marshmallow roast tonight near the marina."

"Now that's something I can get into," I said. Anything to keep Jenn busy while Shane was in police custody.

Chapter 12

Rex let Shane go in time for the bonfire and marsh-mallow roast with my parents and Frances and Douglas, Jenn, and Liz. The marina was quiet. It was still a bit chilly for people to go boating. At best a few brave souls had opened their boats for the season, taking off the winter proofing and bringing them in from dry dock.

The waves splashed against the rock wall of the marina in a gentle rhythm, sending up sprays of lake water to perfume the air. Here the beach was sacrificed for docks and deeper water to allow the boats to shelter and people to get back and forth. The sound of gulls screeching overhead and the fire crackling in the firepit were comforting. The sun had gone down and it was cold, but we sat in our deck chairs huddled under blankets while our marshmallows roasted on long sticks.

It reminded me of my summers as a kid. I missed Papa

Liam and Grammy Alice at times like this. But it was nice to have Mom and Dad here, chatting away, making Jenn and Liz laugh.

"Allie, you're a million miles away," Mom said from across the fire. The flames threw shadows across her face. My mother was beautiful in the way that well-bred women were. Her hair was pulled back and perfectly styled for the breeze that came off the lake. Her makeup was natural and enhanced her large eyes and toned jawline. I always felt just a little less around her. I had no idea how to be so put together. Heaven knows my mother tried hard enough when I was growing up, but clothes didn't always fit right on me, and I had a tendency to get them dirty while I was in the kitchen making desserts or outside running around with my friends.

"I was just thinking how nice this is," I said and pulled my brown marshmallow from the flame. "It's been a long time since we were all here having a bonfire."

"It certainly has," Dad said. "We'll have to make a concerted effort to come out more often. Right, dear?"

"Certainly," Mom said, but she didn't sound all that sure. The whole reason I had inherited the McMurphy and not my father was that my mother didn't like island living. She'd grown up here and couldn't get away from the small-town atmosphere quick enough. After they married Mom convinced my father to move to the suburbs of Detroit. I'd grown up there, amid the hustle and bustle of a large city. Unlike my mother, I loved the island and was happy to make it my home.

"Dad, you should get a boat," I said. "Then you could sail up to the island."

"That's quite a distance, dear," Mom said and pulled her perfectly roasted marshmallow from her stick.

"You know what they say about boats," my father said. "The best day in a man's life is the day he gets his boat—not including his wedding day and the birth of his children—and the second best day?"

"Is the day he sells his boat," I finished for him. Dad liked boating, but as a busy architect he hadn't been sailing in years and was now content to let someone else do the work.

"How's that fine boy, Trent Jessop?" Mom asked. "You haven't talked about him in months."

I felt the heat of a blush rush over me that she would bring up my love life in front of Shane and my friends. "Mom, I told you Trent's father turned over the majority of their holdings to him. He's living in Chicago now. His sister, Paige, is looking after their Mackinac Island properties."

"Ah, so you chased another good man away," she said and popped the marshmallow delicately into her mouth.

Dad cleared his throat and changed the subject. "So, Jenn. I'm looking forward to meeting your parents. What does your father do?"

The conversation returned to the genial laughter of friends. When the fire had burned down too far to keep us warm, we put it out, packed up, and walked back to the McMurphy. I stepped beside Shane in the back of the group.

"So, how are you holding up?" I asked him.

"I'm fine."

"I don't believe that," I said. "How are you really?"

He turned his head in my direction, his thick glasses glinting in the streetlight. "I spent the day going over all I remember about that day. It wasn't fun, but I got through it."

"I understand Becky woke up from her coma. Did she have anything pertinent to add?"

"Not that I'm aware of," Shane said. "Rex keeps his information close to his chest."

"He's not blaming you, is he?"

"He's—"

"Hey, baby," Jenn interrupted and put her arm through his. "Let's sneak off for some quiet time." She kissed his cheek. "My parents come in tomorrow and from then on, we won't have any peace."

"Sounds good to me," Shane said. "See you, Allie."

"Have fun, guys." I followed my parents into the Mc-Murphy. Frances had put them in the third-floor suite. I had two rooms in my apartment, but Jenn currently shared it with me, so there wasn't space for my parents.

I walked them upstairs. "Thanks for coming," I said. "Jenn is glad you're here. She's been worried about Shane."

"I heard you found the boy standing over a dead man," Dad said. "Has he told you why?"

"He's not talking to us about it," I said. "Doesn't want the investigation to be tainted."

"But you are looking into it, right?" Mom asked again when we arrived on the third floor. The hotel was empty except for my parents. Jenn had bought it out for the week to let her family come to stay whenever they wanted. Shane's family was staying in St. Ignace.

"I am," I said and waited while Dad unlocked the door with the key cards I had installed.

"These key cards take away the charm of an actual key," he said as he opened the door. Inside was a two-room suite. There was a couch and TV area and then the bathroom and then the bedroom. Dad and I had created the suites on the new third floor so that we could offer more space for larger families.

I sat down on the flowered couch. Mom joined me and Dad took the striped side chair. All three were overstuffed and comfy. "The key cards are safer," I replied.

"You certainly can use some safety measures," Mom said and took off her shoes.

"Dad, did you get to check out the rooftop deck?" I asked.

"Yes, Douglas took me up there this afternoon. It's nice. You can see a lot of the lake."

"Jenn's reception will be up there," I said. "She's working on booking more weddings and wants to show people that she believes in the space so much, she used it for her own."

"When do her parents get in, dear?" Mom asked.

"Tomorrow," I said. "They've never been on the island, so Jenn has planned a full day of playing tourist. You can join them if you'd like."

"We just might," Dad said. "It's been years since we've acted like tourists."

"I can't wait to meet them," Mom said. "They did a good job raising Jenn."

"They certainly did," I said. "Tomorrow's my last day of fudge making for the shop until next Monday. I took the time off to focus on Jenn's wedding."

"What a wonderful idea!" Mom gave me the first compliment of the night and it lifted my spirits.

"Unfortunately, that means I'll be in the kitchen part of the day tomorrow. I want to fill the cabinet with enough for the wedding guests."

"I saw you're looking for a fudge making assistant for the season," Dad said.

"Yes, I have an ad out, but no one has applied. Why? Do you know someone?"

"One of my buddies back home has a set of twins. They're graduating culinary school next week and I was thinking they might want to come to the island."

"Twins?" I said. "I don't know if I can afford to pay two assistants."

"They could both work half-time. It would be like only paying for one but getting two."

I thought about it. "Sure, why not? Have them email me their résumés and I'll set up a video chat to see how interested they are."

"Thanks, Allie, I knew you'd help." Dad got up and gave me a hug.

I was already on my feet and I noticed Mom yawning, so I decided to let them settle in. "I've got an early morning. Feel free to sleep in. Jenn's folks won't come in until ten a.m."

"Good night," my parents said.

I left them and walked the last flight of stairs to my apartment. I'd left my fur babies home tonight. I knew they missed me. Mal especially would have loved to come out for the bonfire, but I worried it would be too cold.

They both greeted me at the door and I went to the kitchen to give them treats. There were Harry's flowers. I had texted him that the wedding was taking up my time and asked for a rain check. He'd agreed. I took a moment to smell the flowers. They were so colorful and smelled so nice. I treated my pets and wondered what I was going to do about my love life. First things first, I thought. Let's get Shane cleared of any charges and Jenn happily married. Then I'd figure out what I was going to do next.

*   *   *

I was up at four a.m. to make fudge for the guests. Mal came down with me to the lobby, got her treat, and curled up in her bed beside the reception desk. On the list of fudges today were the standards, plus dark chocolate cherry, Neapolitan—which was three flavors in stripes of red, white, and chocolate—and, finally, I was trying my hand at chocolate chip cookie dough.

While I made fudge I had a lot of time to think. There had to be a way to find out what Becky had said when she woke up. It struck me that Liz had been to Cheboygan recently when her grandfather, Angus, had been in the hospital. Maybe she had connections on the nursing staff. I didn't know if they would know what Becky had said, but they might know who we could ask.

Dad was up first again and came down to get coffee from the coffee bar for himself and Mom. He stuck his head into the fudge shop. "Good morning."

"Morning, Dad," I said as I tossed the fudge. I whipped around the cold marble table, using a long-handled spatula, tossing and turning the fudge just like my grandfather and his father before him did. When it was tourist season, the turning of the fudge became a sort of theater for the people on the street to watch the magic of fudge as it cooled without sugaring until you switched to a smaller spatula and formed the loaf, then cut it into one pound pieces and finally into small bites for samples. "Did you sleep well?"

"Sure did, he said. "The new beds are fabulous."

"I'm glad you helped redesign the third floor so the suites make sense," I said. When the McMurphy had been devastated, Dad had drawn up all the new blueprints and had done a great job for the builders to follow.

He leaned against the doorjamb with his two coffees in hand. Mal sat at his feet. She didn't dare enter the fudge shop. One thing I did while training her was to be very strict about the boundaries of the shop. I didn't want her ever to be hurt by hot sugar.

"So, I hear Shane is under investigation for murder," he said. "How are you handling it? I know your mom runs hot and cold about them, but I am proud of the investigations you've helped out with. And I'll never admit that to anyone else."

I laughed. Mom was a force to be reckoned with. Dad knew it better than anyone and loved her for it. "I'm puzzling it together. The thing is, Shane won't even tell Jenn what happened that night. And if he's told Rex anything, they're not talking to me."

"So what have you found out so far?"

I explained that I had a timeline for Christopher and Becky that led to a dead end of sorts. So I was looking into Shane's timeline, but that, too, sort of dead ended with Peter taking Shane back to the cottage. "I have no idea how those three ended up in the alley with Christopher dead, Becky hurt, and Shane caught with the murder weapon in his hand. But Becky woke up from her medically induced coma yesterday. That's why Shane was in police custody all day. But I have no idea what Becky said."

"I bet you've found a way to figure that out," Dad said.

I grinned. "Yes, I think I have a way." I switched to the smaller, scraper-type spatula and quickly added ingredients like raisins and chocolate chips to the fudge. Then I folded them in and finished the loaf and cut it into one-pound slices. After you'd done this long enough, you got

HERE COMES THE FUDGE

good at eyeballing a one-pound slice. I was never off more than a half ounce or so.

"Well, good," Dad said and straightened up. "Can I use your kitchen to make breakfast?"

"Sure thing," I reached into my apron pocket and tossed him the keys to the apartment. "But make extra because Jenn got in late last night and she might need coffee and breakfast."

"Do you want me to bring you down any?"

"No, thanks, I've had my yogurt," I said. "Besides, I'm surrounded by food. Kind of makes you feel full all the time."

"Got it," Dad said. He took my key and closed the fudge shop door. Mal followed him up the stairs. One thing was for sure: Mal knew when to follow someone who would be making food.

By eight Frances and Douglas arrived. At nine my parents took a walk around the island and I had the fudge cabinet filled.

"Well, the last room is ready for the family to come in," Frances said as she came down the stairs. "I see you finished the fudge. What else is on your plate today?"

"I have an online interview set up for this afternoon," I said. "Dad has some twins who are looking for a summer internship."

"Is that for the assistant fudge maker position?" Frances asked.

"Yes, and it would be nice to get some help in here," I said.

"Agreed," she said.

"How's the hiring going for the maid service?" I asked. With the bookings we had for the summer, I had calculated we could afford one. It would free Frances up to take reservations, to check people in and out, and to work on the accounting.

"I think I've settled on Abby Blackbird's service," Frances said. "They weren't the cheapest, but not the most expensive. I checked her references and people had nothing but glowing things to say about her."

"Great," I said. "Can she start next week?"

"Yes," Frances said. "I'm paying her and her crew a flat fee, so if they finish early they can move on; then they won't feel like they have to take their time for a by-the-hour fee. I heard she was fast, efficient, and everything would sparkle when she left, including the windows."

"Sounds perfect," I said. "I'm going to run to the post office. Do you have anything I should mail?"

She pulled out a handful of bills. I added the notes I had and grabbed my jacket. "Have you seen, Mal? I thought I'd take her with me."

"I think your parents took her on their walk," Frances said.

"Oh right, okay then, I'm off," I left from the back to head down the alleyway.

Mr. Beecher was out for his daily walk. "Hello, Allie. Where's my friend Mal?"

"She went for a walk with my folks," I said.

"Ah, glad to hear your parents are here. Is it for Jenn's wedding?"

"It is," I said. "Dad thought it would be nice to come in early and get settled before the rest of the guests. How are you today?"

"I'm fine," he said. "A little older and wiser perhaps."

"I hope I can say the same thing," I said. "Say, do you walk by Jenn and Shane's fixer-upper?"

"I do," he said. "Most evenings in fact. I have a routine. I suppose that would make it easy for bad guys to stalk me." He shrugged. "But I don't tend to attract bad guys in general. Why?"

"Did you walk by there the evening Christopher Harris died?"

"I did," he said. "I believe it was around six-thirty or so. Why?"

"Did you happen to see Peter Ramfield taking Shane to the house?"

He frowned. "No, no, I don't think I did. Why do you ask?"

"Peter told me that he bought Shane a drink to talk to him about something and that Shane had been drinking previously and the drink made him drunk. So Peter took Shane to the fixer-upper to take a nap before he was to meet Jenn for dinner at eight."

"Ah, well, I can't say that I saw either fellow that night. I do circle back around that route, though, so if they had been there between six and seven, I would most likely have seen them. That said, it doesn't mean I didn't miss them if they were earlier or later."

"Hmmm," I said. "Thanks."

"How's the investigation going?"

"Not well," I said. "I've come to dead ends. It seems no one saw Shane or Christopher and Becky after eight. So I can't place their whereabouts between eight and eleven, when we found them."

"I'll see if I can discover anything. When was the last time Christopher and Becky were seen?"

"I believe it was around eight. They had finished dinner and were seen going into the art museum. Someone has to know where they went after that."

"I'll see what I can find out for you," he said. "Now, I

need to let you get where you're going before you die of heatstroke."

I laughed out loud. It was currently forty-five degrees Fahrenheit. "I'll talk to you soon."

The walk to the post office was short and I was in and out quickly. I decided to go to the newspaper office to see Liz.

I walked inside. The newspaper office had a desk in the front, where Angus sat. He was a large square man with a snow-white beard and a half-bald head.

"Well, if it isn't the bad luck girl," Angus said, his voice hoarse and slow.

"Hi, Angus," I said. "It's good to see you. How are you feeling?"

He put his lucky rabbit's foot on top of the counter in front of him. "Better now." Angus liked to tease that since I'd come to the island, old men had been dropping dead, and he used the good luck charm to chase away any of my bad juju. I figured he was mostly teasing me.

"Is Liz in?" I asked.

"She's getting us lunch," he said.

"When do you expect her back?" I asked.

"When she gets here," he said gruffly. "Now, take your bad luck out of here."

I shook my head. "Well, if you see her, let her know I stopped by."

"Why don't you just text her?" he asked. "Afraid to leave an electronic trail for whatever the two of you are up to?"

"No." I pulled out my phone and walked out. "Talk to you soon, Angus."

"Not if I have anything to say about it," he grumbled back.

I ran into Liz as she walked up with white takeout bags in hand.

"Hi," Liz said. "What's up? Where's Mal?"

"She's with my folks," I said. "Listen, I was wondering . . ."

"Why don't you come in and have some lunch with us?" Liz asked.

"Oh no, thanks," I said. "Angus gets worried whenever I get too close to him. So, really quick, do you have any connections to the nurses in Cheboygan?"

"I do have a few," she said.

"I heard Becky was awake yesterday," I said. "Any chance you can find out what she's saying about what happened to her?"

"That's a great idea," Liz said. "I'm on it. Are you sure you won't stay for lunch?"

"No, thanks," I said. "Like I said, my folks are here. I figure they'll want me to have lunch with them."

"Okay, but it's your loss. I'll let you know the minute I learn anything."

"Perfect," I said.

The day was bright and the flowers had perked up. A glance at my phone told me my parents should be back because it was after eleven now. I wondered if Jenn's parents were on the island. I'd met them once or twice when Jenn and I were in college together in Chicago. They seemed super nice and not at all as controlling as my mother was. They were outgoing and made me laugh every time. It made them easy to talk to about things. In truth, Jenn's parents held a special place in my heart.

I walked into the McMurphy and, sure enough, they had arrived. Jenn, her folks, my folks, and Mal were all sitting in the lobby, chatting and enjoying coffee and fudge.

"Allie!" Mr. Christensen said and stood to give me a hug.

"Welcome, Mr. and Mrs. Christensen," I said and gave them both a hug. "I see you've met my parents."

"We met them when we got back from our walk," Mom said. "We were talking about us all going out for lunch. Do you want to come along?"

"Can you give me about ten minutes?" I asked. "I need to wash the candy making off me and change my clothes."

"We can do that," Mr. Christensen said. "Now that we're on the island, we have no particular place to go. I like that feeling."

I checked in with Frances before I went upstairs. She and Douglas were having lunch in the back room. They were fine with me going with the families.

Now that the fudge was all made, it was time to enjoy the company of family and friends, and ensure that everything with the wedding went off without a hitch. Which meant ensuring Shane was at the altar with Jenn.

Vanilla Macadamia Nut Fudge

Ingredients:
24 ounces white chocolate
14 ounces sweetened condensed milk
2 tablespoons butter
1 tablespoon vanilla
1 cup chopped macadamia nuts

Directions:
In a medium microwave-safe bowl, combine chocolate, milk, and butter. Microwave on high, stopping every 30 seconds to stir, until chocolate and butter are melted and combined. Add vanilla and nuts.

Pour into a parchment-lined, 8 x 8-inch pan. Chill until set. Cut into one-inch pieces. Store in an airtight container in the refrigerator. Makes 32. Enjoy!

Chapter 13

Having closed the McMurphy to all guests except the wedding guests, it was a bit spooky inside. Almost as spooky as mid-January, when the place was empty except for a handful of weekends, when the ice fishermen came out.

I was in my office when my phone rang and I jumped. "Hello?"

"Hi, Allie, it's Liz," she said.

"Hi, Liz. What's up?"

"I heard back from my source in Cheboygan," she said.

"Great! Did they know what Becky said? Does she remember who did this to her?"

"That's the thing," Liz said. "It seems the trauma and the medical coma have blocked her memory."

"So, she has no idea who did it?"

"None," Liz said. "She says the last thing she remembers is holding Christopher's hand as they strolled from Market Street to Main Street. She says it was around ten-ish."

"We found them at eleven," I said. "Did she see Shane?"

"That's just it. She doesn't remember Shane being there at all."

"Well, that's the first good news I've heard," I said. "Surely she would remember if Shane attacked her."

"The doctor said that when you get a blitz attack like they suffered, your brain goes straight into fight-or-flight mode and has little time to store memories. It's why eyewitnesses are not always good at recalling the details of what happened."

"So even if she does get her memory back, it's likely it won't be correct," I said.

"Exactly," Liz said. "It's why we like to interview a lot of people and look for strands of commonality. Then we know that's most likely a real thing that happened."

"Wow, do the police do the same thing?"

"I imagine, so," Liz said. "I learned that in journalism classes. I imagine they also teach it in Cop 101."

"Then this may or may not exonerate Shane," I said.

"It does mean that they still don't have much of a case against him. It's all circumstantial."

"Will you be reporting on this?" I asked.

"I told Rex I'd wait until an arrest was made before doing anything more than putting it in the police blotter, giving the crime, the victims, and that the police were investigating."

"Okay, no wonder they brought Shane in yesterday

and kept him there all day. They had to be searching for clues."

"Doesn't Shane have a lawyer?" Liz asked.

"Yes, he does, and the lawyer was most likely with him all day. Jenn says Shane wants to appear as being co-operative with the police," I said.

"Well, with the wedding getting closer, I certainly hope we can find the killer before Rex thinks he has enough evidence to put Shane away," Liz said. "Oh, another thing . . ."

"What's that?"

"With the tourist season starting this week, the mayor is really pushing Rex to get this crime solved and out of the way."

"Which means if all he has is Shane and circumstantial evidence, the mayor might get her way and Shane will be arrested." I tapped my chin thoughtfully.

"If we can't figure out what really happened," Liz said. "That would be the most likely scenario."

"Well, darn. Thanks, Liz," I said. "See you at the bachelorette party."

"Cheers," she said and hung up.

So, Becky didn't remember anything, but they wanted the killer to think she did. And they were pointing the finger at Shane. Someone else knew what happened. I just needed to figure out who it was.

With the family coming in starting the next day, I needed to ensure I had enough breakfast food on hand. I wasn't sure how long we would be out at the bachelorette party, so I decided to make a list and head out to Doud's

Market to pick up continental breakfast food for tomorrow morning.

Dad came down the stairs. "Allie, is there any coffee left?" It was the afternoon. I couldn't drink more coffee if I wanted to sleep that night, but Dad never had that issue.

"Fresh and hot," I said. "I just made it. Also, tomorrow there'll be doughnuts and a continental-style breakfast. I'm heading out to Doud's now to pick up doughnuts and Danish and bagels, and some fruit and juice. Anything in particular you want?"

"Yes, to take your puppy home," he teased. "She's so cute and smart."

Mal wagged her stump tail and sat at his feet expectantly.

"You two have certainly become best buddies," I said. "I barely got her to go to bed with me yesterday, the little traitor."

Dad laughed. "If you don't mind, I'd like to walk her this afternoon."

"Sure, go ahead," I said. "Keep an eye out for Mr. Beecher. He likes to walk through the alley. If you see him, tell him I said hi."

"Will do," Dad said and took the coffee and Mal upstairs with him. I grabbed a tweed jacket to put over my sweater and jeans.

I walked out into the sunshine. The sky was blue and Doud's was only a few blocks from the McMurphy. I pulled open the door to the grocery store and Mary Emry nodded her hello. I grabbed a basket and headed straight to the bakery.

"Wait, you don't make your own baked goods?" It was Harry, standing near the doughnut cabinet with a box half full.

"Hi to you, too," I said. "I can make them, but I'm a bit busy today." I grabbed a box and folded it so it could hold doughnuts.

"Ah, that's right, the wedding is keeping you busy. Are your parents enjoying their vacation?"

"Yes. Mackinac Island is the best place to vacation," I said. "Or staycation. Tomorrow all the relatives and friends are coming in, so I'm taking time off from cooking." I filled my box with a dozen doughnuts and slipped it into my basket.

"That sounds like fun. I take it you're buying breakfast for tomorrow," he said and pointed to my basket, which I was quickly filling with Danish and bagels as well as the doughnuts.

"I guess I should have gotten a cart," I said. I still had to get a variety of cream cheeses for the bagels, fruits, and fruit juices.

"You can use mine." He pushed his cart toward me.

"Are you sure?"

"Positive," he said.

I took my stuff out of the overflowing basket, put it in his nearly empty cart, and handed the basket to him. He put his doughnuts in it.

"See? Problem solved," he said and smiled at me so brightly it warmed my heart.

"How's the paint job on your bed and breakfast going?"

"They're doing a great job," he said. "They should be done today. If you have time, you should stop by to see it."

"I wish I had time. Maybe next week?"

"Sounds like a plan," he said. "So, I take it you are in the wedding?"

"I am. Maid of honor," I said.

"Nice, and who's the best man?" he asked.

"Shane chose Rex Manning," I said as I picked out the best bananas and oranges. Good fruit could be left out all day as a snack.

"Ah, so he's your date for the wedding?" Harry asked casually.

"Yes," I said as I moved toward the cream cheeses. "It's traditional."

"Right," he said and absently put some cream cheese in his basket. "So, do you like him?"

"Who?" I asked as I filled my basket.

"This Rex Manning," Harry said.

I turned to look Harry in the eye. "I do. Rex and I have this kind of . . . I don't know. Thing? Anyway, we try to date and then something happens."

"Like what?" Harry asked.

"Like somebody dies, or one of his ex-wives show up."

Harry winced. "Ex-wives?"

"He has two," I said. "Right now Melonie, wife number two, is on the island and making a play for him."

"Sounds like a guy who can't commit," Harry said. "If I found a beautiful woman who was interested in me, I would thank my lucky stars and do whatever it took to let her know she was the one for me."

I felt the tension rise between us.

He broke it by shrugging. "But that's just me."

He let me go first in line to pay for my stuff. We didn't talk as Mary Emry rang us up. "See you tonight, Mary," I said and waited for Harry to pay for his things so we could walk out together.

"What's tonight?" he asked.

"Bachelorette party," Mary said.

"Sounds like fun," he said.

"I planned it to be," I said.

"Where's it at?" he asked.

"Why?"

"So I can stop by and see what a party looks like here on the island," he said.

"You can't come," I said. "It's only for women."

"Right," he said as he paid for his stuff and gathered up his bags. "Until the stripper gets there."

"There isn't going to be a stripper," I said and shook my head at Mary, who looked slightly horrified. "I promised Jenn that I wouldn't do it. We're going to try to be more dignified."

"Try?" he teased with a grin that made my heart melt.

"Well, there will be an open bar," I said. "After three hours, all bets are off."

"Too bad I won't get to see it," he teased again.

"Oh, I'm sure someone will be gossiping the blow by blow," I said. "Mackinac Island is a small town."

"That it is." He tipped the bill of his baseball cap. "Have a great day, Allie."

"You, too," I said and opened the door to the McMurphy as he strolled down the street.

"Who is that?" Mom asked as she watched him out the window.

"Harry Winston," I said. "He just bought a bed and breakfast and is trying to make a go of it."

"I see," Mom said. "He seems nice."

"He is." I went over to the coffee bar and pulled out a folding table, covered it with a white tablecloth, and put the fruit on it, along with some cookies I'd picked up while I was in the bakery section at Doud's. The other baked goods went under the bar, waiting for their morning debut.

"This is nice," Jenn's dad said as he picked up a paper plate and helped himself to a plate and some fruit and cookies.

"Oh, can we get yogurt tomorrow?" Jenn's mom asked. "I like to limit my carbs." The woman was tall and slender, just like Jenn. I couldn't understand why she might need to limit her carbs.

"Sure," I said. "I can pick up some low carb yogurt and some hard-boiled eggs for tomorrow."

"Don't get too good at this," Jenn's dad said and winked. "We might not ever want to leave."

"Keep eating like that and you won't fit into your tux for the wedding," Jenn's mom teased. They both walked over to the couch to sit with my mom and dad, who were enjoying their coffee.

Jenn came downstairs looking perfect in a flowy, midi-length, flowery dress with puffed sleeves and espadrilles. "Hi all," Jenn said. She grabbed some tea and sat in a wing-backed chair next to her parents.

Frances had finished her paperwork—being general manager, she was also my accountant—grabbed a coffee, and went over to join the group. I decided we needed more chairs and went to the basement door only to have Douglas come through it with extra folding chairs in hand.

"Hey, you read my mind," I said.

"You might want to give these a once-over with a clean cloth. They've been downstairs for months," he said.

"Good idea," I said. "Help yourself to a snack."

I went upstairs and grabbed some cleaning supplies for the chairs. Mal bounced after me and hurried down the stairs to see if anyone would slip her a bit of food. Mella came out of her closet and I scratched her head. Then opened the door to see if she wanted to go downstairs, too. She put her nose and tail in the air and went back to her closet. "Too many guests for your taste?" I asked her with a chuckle. Then I closed and locked the apartment.

It looked like the parents were getting along fine. Tomorrow Shane's mom and dad would join us. Then the hotel would be full of Jenn and Shane's friends and relatives. I loved the energy.

"We're all going to take a walk around the island," Mom said. "I want Frances and Douglas to come."

"That's fine," I said. "I can handle things here on my own." I waved them all off. Jenn went with them. Dad even leashed up Mal and took her, too. My pup was loving all the company. Even with only a few guests there was still work to do. The cleaning service didn't start until next week. So it was up to me to clean my parents' suite and Jenn's parents suite, too.

I started there. I opened the door and was surprised to see that someone had slept on the couch. I quietly refolded the blanket and added extra clean sheets, folded neatly on the couch. I cleaned the bathroom and vacuumed and made the queen-size bed. Then I dusted and left a candy on the pillow of the bed and on the stack of sheets and blankets for the couch.

Next I cleaned my folks' room. Lucky for me, no one was sleeping on that couch. Maybe I would mention it to Jenn. Perhaps it was simply that one of her parents snored, so they slept apart. I certainly hoped it didn't mean anything like separation or divorce. On second thought, maybe I wouldn't mention it to Jenn until after the wedding. I vacuumed the hallway and then checked to see that the rooms for Shane's folks and the others coming in Friday were clean and ready.

A trip downstairs showed me that no one had arrived. Now that I had cameras everywhere but in the guest rooms and my apartment, it was easy to tell if anyone had entered. I figured they wouldn't because I had a big sign declaring the hotel was full.

Next, I went upstairs and baked sugar cookies for after-dinner snacking. Finally, it was time for my video interview with the twins. I sat down at my computer and hopped onto the video meeting site. They were both there, eager and ready.

"Hi, guys," I said. "I'm Allie McMurphy, the owner of the Historic McMurphy Hotel and Fudge Shop. How are you?"

They answered that they were well. The twins' names were Kent and Kelly. Both had thick blond hair and a cheery demeanor. We went over the requirements and both seemed to think it would be a great place to work.

"Now, I can't supply housing," I said. "But there are a lot of places needing roommates. Plus, you'll get to meet other young people like yourselves, on the island for the season. How does that sound?"

"Sounds great to us," they said in unison.

"Perfect. I'll send you a link with more information and where to go to look for roommates. Do you have any other questions?"

"Yes," Kelly said. "What was it like taping the fudge-off show?"

"It was a little crazy," I said. "But a whole lot of fun."

"Are they coming back to the island to film again?" Kent asked.

"I don't know," I admitted. "After the murder, I think they were put off by the island as a good place for production."

"Okay," Kent said, looking a little downhearted.

"I can say that the tourism bureau is always working to get more productions on the island. So you never know. Are you up for the challenge?"

"We are," they said in unison. The unison stuff was a little spooky, but I thought I could handle it for the summer.

"Great. Can you start next week?"

"Sure!" they said in unison again. "Can we have half days our first week so we can get set with housing and such?"

"Sure, why not," I said. "Take care and I look forward to you coming. Oh, and I'll send you a link to discounted ferry tickets. It's one of the perks to working on the island."

"Cool," they said. Their voices blended in perfect harmony.

I ended the call and sat back. Mella had come out of her closet to see what I was doing. She crawled across my keyboard and onto my lap. I petted her until she purred. "You are a very good girl," I told her. "I'm glad I have you because it's going to be lonely when Jenn moves out to her new home with Shane."

The downstairs doorbell rang, letting me know someone had walked in. I hurried downstairs to find Rex looking at the fudge counter.

"Hi, Rex," I said. "What can I do for you?"

He wore his uniform and had his hat in his hands. His impossibly blue gaze moved slowly from the empty fudge shop to me. "Hi, Allie," he said. "I heard you didn't do any shipping today. Is there a problem with the fudge making?"

"Oh no, I'm just taking time off from making fudge

for the wedding. My parents, Jenn's parents, and soon Shane's parents will be here, along with friends and relatives. I wanted to focus on that. Besides, I'm in charge of keeping Jenn on track. Don't you have to keep Shane bolstered and ready?"

"I'm not very good at weddings," he admitted. "You would think I would be because I've had two, but it's not my forte. Listen, I was wondering if you had time to talk about what you know about Christopher's death."

"Sure. Can I get you a cup of coffee?" I asked. "We have some baked goods and fruit if you want any."

"Coffee will be fine. Black."

I poured us both a cup. He pulled a chair away from the window, swung it around, and sat so he could lean on the back of it. I handed him a coffee and remained standing. He took a sip. "I heard you had Liz look into what Becky knew about that night."

"I can neither confirm nor deny it," I said.

"Becky has no recall of that night," he said and studied my face. "But she does remember that she talked to Shane that day."

"What did they talk about?" I asked.

"She's not sure," he said. "The stabbing plus the trauma of seeing Christopher killed, plus pain meds, etc., has her memory shaky. So I asked Shane what she called him for. He said he doesn't remember."

"He doesn't remember?" I sat down. "Why doesn't he remember?"

"Shane tested positive for roofies in his system from that night," Rex said. "That drug will erase a few memories."

"Who would do that?" I asked. "Why would they do that?"

"He doesn't know, which is why we haven't said anything. Listen, Shane is embarrassed that he got roofied. It has a stigma of being a date rape drug and he's a guy."

My eyes widened. "Is he okay?"

"As far as we can tell. It seems someone simply wanted Shane out of the way," he said.

"Well, I know he had drinks with Annie Hawthorne and Peter Ramfield," I said.

"But it could have been anyone from a server to a bartender," Rex said. "I'm telling you this because we're down to the wire. I'm getting pressure from the mayor to close the case, but so far no one really knows what happened."

"And all the circumstantial evidence points to Shane," I said. "But he's getting married. Please don't haul him off in handcuffs during the reception."

Rex rubbed a hand over his face. "I'm doing my best not to let that happen. So if you find out anything more, promise me you'll come see me right away."

"I promise," I said.

"Good, thank you." He finished his coffee and stood, handing me the empty cup. "I hear you have a bachelorette party tonight."

"Yes," I said.

"Have fun, but stay safe, okay? There's a killer on the loose." For a brief moment I saw concern in his gaze and then he went back to the flat cop stare.

"I won't forget," I said.

Chapter 14

The girls gathered in the lobby at about eight p.m. We were all dressed to the nines in body-hugging short dresses and spiky high heels. My hair was tamed by a wide curling iron into fat curls. Even Liz wore a dress and spike-heeled ankle boots. The team consisted of me, Jenn, Liz, Sophie, Sandy Everheart, Paige, and Mary Emry.

I poured us all a glass of champagne before we left. "A toast," I said, "to get the party started. To Jenn, may she be happily married for the rest of her life and make us all envy her happiness."

"Hear, hear," the other girls said. We clinked glasses and downed the champagne. Then we linked arms and walked outside, where I had a horse and carriage ready for us. The party room was a few blocks away, but I thought it would be fun to ride in a carriage. The driver climbed down and held our hands as we scrambled into the carriage in our short skirts. Laughing and chattering, we were off down the street. I let streamers fly behind us and made Jenn wear a sash that said *Bride*.

She looked gorgeous in a gold body hugging gown, sparkly hose, and gold shoes. I hadn't seen her face that happy in a long time. We arrived shortly at the bar where I had reserved the back room. The guys inside hooted and hollered at us as we walked past them. The whole place clapped and applauded Jenn. She raised her hand and waved like the Queen of England. Probably because I'd bought her a tiara and made her wear it.

The back room was decorated with gold, blush, and pink balloons. There was a dance floor and a deejay playing all our favorite dance tunes. Without guys, we felt free to leave our drinks on the table and dance our hearts out. The wine and cocktails flowed and I was feeling no pain as I grabbed Jenn.

"You are the best, most beautiful friend a girl could have," I said. "I'm so lucky to have you. Now that you're getting married, please don't forget about me."

"Oh, honey, I won't," she promised. "I'll still be working out of the McMurphy. We'll see each other every day."

"Good." I swayed. "That's just how I want it."

About ten-thirty the men crashed the party. Shane took Jenn by the hand and ordered a slow dance. Rex put his hand on my waist and took me out to the dance floor. The other girls grabbed partners from Shane's friends.

I leaned into Rex to keep from falling over. "Aren't they cute together?" I asked. I knew my voice sounded sloppy, but I didn't care. Sometimes you had to let go of being perfect and just have fun.

"They are," he said. "I couldn't keep Shane from crashing your party. He said he didn't want to be single another night." Rex looked into my eyes. "I feel the same way."

"Are you going to ask Melonie to marry you again?" I teased, deflecting his advance. I wasn't going to commit to anything when I was drinking.

"No," he said sharply. "I think we should go on another date."

"We have a date during the wedding," I pointed out.

"It's not the same and you know it," he said and tucked a long piece of my hair behind my ear. The gentle brush of his finger sent chills down my spine. "We've been dancing around this thing for over a year. Let's make it official."

"Official that we should go on a few dates?" I pressed.

"Official that we're in an exclusive relationship to see where it goes," he said.

I bit my bottom lip. "Exclusive?"

"Yes," he said.

"I had dinner with Harry Winston the other night," I blurted out. "He sent flowers after."

"I heard," Rex said. "I might not be a start-up millionaire who is playing at being an innkeeper, but I'm here. I'll always be here. I'm not playing and I won't be gone in two years when I get bored."

"You can't predict that," I said.

"I know it."

"I mean, you can't predict that Harry will be gone in two years," I said.

"Allie, you are the most frustrating woman I've ever met," Rex said.

"That's no way to ask a girl to go steady," I quipped and did a twirl.

He pulled me back into his arms. "Will you at least think about it?"

"I'll think about it," I said and rested my head on his warm chest.

"When will you let me know?"

"I'll let you know after the wedding," I said. Then I looked into his eyes. "Even if we go steady, be prepared for me to investigate anytime someone I love is in trouble with the law. Can you do that?"

"Do I have a choice?" he asked, his blue gaze sincere. Rex Manning looked like an action hero, but he had the most amazing blue eyes ringed with long black lashes. It made my heart sing.

I put my head back on his shoulder so I wouldn't lose my head. There always seemed to be people or circumstances keeping us apart. Maybe if we were exclusive we could see where this thing between us went. Maybe that would be the most honest thing to do. Maybe.

Next morning, Jenn and I were nursing hangovers and prepping for the afternoon ladies' tea.

"Whose idea was it to invite the female relatives and friends to a tea?" Jenn asked. She popped two more aspirin and drank from her second bottle of water with electrolytes.

"I'd forgotten what a hangover feels like," I said and tried to keep my head from turning too fast. "I haven't had one since I aced my candy class freshman year of college."

"Lucky for you, we catered this affair. Can you imagine having to make all the tea cakes and sandwiches this morning?"

My stomach churned at the idea. We put the round tables up in the lobby near the elevators and placed chairs around them and along the walls. It seemed the entire group of women from the senior center were coming, as well as my mom, Jenn's mom, and Shane's mom.

Sandy Everheart came in, the doorbells jarring in my head.

"Oh good, you're here," I said. "Was it hard to make the centerpieces?"

"Not terribly," she said and put her box on the nearest table. The centerpieces were multitiered cake and sandwich stands made completely of white and dark chocolate. She pulled the first one out.

"Wow, those are spectacular," I said.

"They are perfect for the little cakes and scones and such," Jenn said.

"We'll let you place them," I said. "I wouldn't want to be responsible for breaking them."

"How are you feeling today?" I asked Sandy, who was with us last night. "Jenn and I are hurting."

"I'm fine," Sandy said with a shrug. "I didn't drink anything but soda with a twist of lemon."

"Lucky you," Jenn said and rubbed her temples.

"Smart," I said with a smile.

"I learned from my grandmother never to drink. Alcoholism runs in the family."

"Oh," I said. "I'm sorry to hear that."

Frances walked in from the back door with a box from the florist. "I picked up the flower parts of the centerpieces."

"Thanks," I said and took the box from her. The entire centerpiece consisted of the chocolate stands to put the treats on, with a ring of pink and blush flowers around the bottom to match Jenn's wedding colors. Then there was a rose for every plate in pink. One lucky person at the table would win the chocolate and the rest would all go home with flowers.

The doorbells jangled again. This time it didn't hurt as much, so the aspirin and water were helping. It was Terra Reeves, a local caterer who had worked for us before when we hosted a senior center meetup.

"Hi, Terra," I said. "Thanks for doing this."

She pulled a cart behind her filled with cooler boxes to keep things cold and other boxes for the things that didn't need to be kept cold. "The place looks gorgeous," she said. "I've got a tier of sweets, a tier of scone and tea cakes, and a tier of bite-size sandwiches, including the infamous cucumber sandwich."

"Sounds yummy," Jenn said. "Can we help you place them on the chocolate trays?"

"Sure," she said. "I've got extra gloves." She handed us both plastic gloves made specifically for food prep.

I put on the gloves and grabbed a box, set it on one of the tables, and started to fill up the stands. We followed Terra's lead on what to put where and soon all the food was out on display.

We finished just in time for the ladies to start arriving. My mom and Jenn's mom were first and made themselves cups of tea. Jenn stationed herself at the door to welcome everyone inside. I stationed myself at the teapot table to ensure the little flame pots under the teapots remained lit and the teapots didn't run out of water.

"Mrs. Carpenter," Jenn said and hugged a thin woman with Shane's brown hair and thick glasses. Her hair was styled in a clean modern bob, her makeup perfect. The thick glasses made her pretty eyes seem larger than life.

She wore bright red lipstick. Beside her was a much smaller and older woman with white hair who looked just like Shane's mom. I assumed it was his grandmother.

Jenn introduced the moms. After Mrs. Carpenter got herself and her mother tea, the four women moved to the fireplace to keep an eye on everyone who entered next.

I had invited all the ladies from the senior center. They arrived in droves wearing flowered dresses and lovely hats. It was starting to look like Easter or a meeting of church women. I laughed to myself at the analogy before grabbing an empty teapot and going to the back room to refill it with water.

By the time I came back the lobby was buzzing with ladies talking. Most of the seniors found seats and started serving themselves the treats from the stands. I put the pot on the burner to heat and then went to the group of moms and pointed to the reserved table nearest the elevator. They went and sat.

Then I picked up a teacup and a spoon and tapped them together to make enough noise for people to know I wanted their attention. "Attention, ladies," I said. "Thank you all for coming. We're here today to celebrate friendship. Jenn has been my best friend for over five years. Ever since we met in college. I don't know how different my life would be right now if I didn't have her. So I would like to make a toast. To Jenn, may her marriage be filled with joy and sunshine, and when it's not, may she come to me so I can support her as women have supported each other through the ages.

"To Jenn." I lifted my teacup and everyone drank a tea toast. Then Jenn and I went to sit with the moms and Frances. From the level of chatter in the room, the tea was a hit.

What I loved about it was that it gave the moms a chance to get to know one another better in a neutral setting. At the end of an hour, I stood again and asked the ladies to look under their chairs, explaining that one chair at each table was marked with an X. That person got to take home the chocolate centerpiece.

This went over well. The ladies were having so much fun, they lingered for another hour. Jenn and I made our way from table to table, thanking everyone for coming and sharing their day with us in our celebration of friendship and Jenn's wedding. Not everyone was invited to the wedding—we only had so much space on the roof—but this gave the seniors a chance to congratulate Jenn.

Finally, everyone left. Frances was busy checking in more family members who'd arrived early so they could explore the island and all its treasures.

"Allie, have you heard from Shane?" Jenn asked me after we folded chairs and put the tables back in storage.

"No," I said. "Why?"

She frowned. "I've texted him three times in the last hour and he hasn't replied."

"I'll text Rex to see if he knows where Shane is," I said.

"It's not as if he's in the lab," Jenn said. "He's suspended until they catch Christopher's killer."

I texted Rex asking if he'd heard from Shane today. The answer was no and why? So I let him know that Shane wasn't answering Jenn's texts. The first thing Rex did was ask if Jenn had called Shane. Maybe he was busy and a phone call would alert him.

"Jenn, Rex says to try calling Shane," I said.

"Okay," Jenn replied. She dialed and then frowned. "It went straight to voice mail, as if the phone is turned off."

"When was the last time you saw him?" I asked her.

"Last night," she said. "When he walked me to our door and kissed me good night."

"Let's ask his mom if she's heard from him," I said. "Surely he met his parents at the dock when they came in this morning."

Jenn texted Shane's mom. "She says he didn't meet them as planned. They figured he was busy working on the house and lost track of time."

"Well, that might explain everything," I said. "Let's go to the house. He's probably working and didn't hear his phone ring." I put my arm through hers and steered her toward the door. "Frances, we're going to run out to Jenn's house to talk to Shane. We'll be back in about an hour."

"Okay," Frances said. "You need to be back by six. We have the dress rehearsal and dinner tonight."

"Sure thing," I said and looked at my phone. It was three-thirty in the afternoon. I was sure we could wrap this up in fifteen minutes.

Jenn and I walked arm in arm to her new fixer-upper. "I'm probably worrying for nothing," Jenn said. "I mean, the tea was for the ladies. He's probably getting some finishing touches done on the bedroom and bath so we can move in after we get married on Saturday."

"Wait, don't you want the kitchen and living room done, too?" I asked.

"We decided to do most of the work ourselves, so I knew when we purchased the house it would take a few months of living in construction to make it the perfect place for us to grow our family. In the meantime, all we really need is the roof, plumbing, and wiring done. The heater and air conditioner are already in and brand-new."

"Air conditioner?" I asked. Usually it didn't get hot enough long enough for anyone to be in need of air conditioning on the island. We loved to open the windows and let the lake breezes cool off the rooms. The McMurphy had air conditioning, of course; guests expected it.

"The previous owner put it in for his grandmother, who had a lung condition, which meant she couldn't live in any unfiltered air."

"Well, there you go," I said. We rounded the corner to the house. It appeared to be quiet. The door was locked, so Jenn opened it with her key.

"Hello?" she called. "Shane?"

There was no answer. We moved from the stripped-bare kitchen and living room area to the hall with three bedrooms, a Jack-and-Jill bath, and the master suite. The door to the suite was closed.

"Shane?" Jenn called and pushed the door open. The bedroom was huge, with soft gray walls and white trim. There was a bed made with paisley-patterned gray bedding and striped sheets. Two gray chairs and a small table sat in front of the windows. There was an open closet that was deep enough to walk in and then the door to the bathroom. Jenn pushed that door open.

Shane was inside, wiping down the jetted bathtub. He had big round earphones on and was humming to the music. Jenn went up and touched his shoulder. Startled, he looked up and pushed off his earphones. "Hey."

"You scared me to death," Jenn said and kissed his cheek. "You weren't answering my texts or my calls."

"You called?" he asked and looked around. "Where's my phone?"

"We wouldn't know, silly," Jenn said. "You also missed

meeting your parents on the dock. You need to call your mom to apologize.

"Well, shoot," he said and stood. "I guess I got caught up in finishing tiling around the tub and the floor. What do you think?"

The master bath was huge, with a two-person shower and rain shower heads along with body jets. Then there was the jetted tub, which was big enough for two, double sinks across from that, and a separate doored area for the toilet. The floors were tiled with small, old-fashioned black-and-white tiles that carried into the shower floor. The sides of the shower were tiled in white subway tiles with a black tile chair rail. Around the bottom of the tub was tiled in white subway tiles to hide the electricals that allowed the tub to have jets.

"This is gorgeous," I said and did a three-sixty turn. "I'm so jealous."

"It looks great," she said. "You did a lot of work."

He put his arm around her. "I want it to be perfect for Monday."

The couple was staying at the Grander Hotel in the honeymoon suite Saturday and Sunday nights. I'd offered the McMurphy, but knowing all the relatives and friends were there wouldn't give them the privacy they were looking for. We didn't tell anyone where they were honeymooning. That way they could keep things peaceful.

"It would be more perfect if Christopher's death wasn't hanging over us," Jenn said with a sigh.

"Shane," I said gently. "Rex told me you were drugged and woke up in the alleyway. Is that why you didn't tell us what happened? Because you don't know?"

"Is that true?" Jenn asked.

Shane turned three shades of red. "I didn't want you to

know. I feel stupid for not watching my drinks. They tested me for rohypnol and it came back positive."

"That's the date rape drug, right?" Jenn said.

Shane took off his glasses and wiped his right hand across his face. "Yes," he admitted.

"Were you hurt?" Jenn asked and put her hands on his forearms.

"No," he said and shook his head. "It appears whoever slipped the roofies in my drink just wanted me knocked out."

"Why?" Jenn asked.

"That's the three-million-dollar question," Shane said. "I woke up groggy and saw someone in a black hoodie stabbing Christopher. I raced over there as fast as I could, given that I still felt sluggish. I managed to wrestle the knife away, but the killer ran, and then . . ."

"Then we found you with it in your hand," I said. "And you didn't see their face while you were wrestling them?"

"No," he said and took a deep breath. "My glasses got knocked off in the fight and I was concentrating on not getting stabbed."

"Shane is practically blind without his glasses," Jenn said.

"I can only see about a foot in front of my face," he said.

"Why did you spend the day at the police station, then?" Jenn asked.

"Rex had a hypnotist come in. We were trying to see if I could remember anything distinguishing about the person—height, size, a glimpse of their hands? But it didn't work. It seems I'm not great at being hypnotized."

"I heard Becky doesn't remember anything about the stabbing," I said.

"It's troubling," Shane said. "So Rex wanted to make it look like I was his suspect in hopes the real killer would get comfortable and make a mistake."

"Well, that's the first thing I've heard about this case that makes sense," I said. "What's the last thing you remember?"

"I remember having drinks with Annie Hawthorne," he said.

"You also had drinks with Peter Ramfield," I said. "Peter said you were drunk, so he walked you here so you could sober up before your date."

"Well, there you go," Shane said. "It could have been Annie or Peter. Did you tell Rex that?"

"I did," I said, "and he's looking into it." I glanced at my phone. "Oh darn, the time is slipping away. I'm glad you're safe. Please don't disappear again until after we find the killer, okay?"

"Got it," Shane said.

Jenn walked me to the door. "Why didn't you tell me earlier about Shane being drugged?"

"We had the tea party to get through, and I didn't want to upset you," I said. "But now you can talk freely with Shane, so I'm glad you both know what I knew."

"I'm glad, too," Jenn said. "I'm going to stay here a while and help Shane with the finishing touches. I'll see you later."

"Don't forget we have the rehearsal and dinner at eight," I said. "But otherwise, take your time. I can entertain the guests."

She gave me a hug. "You're the best!"

"Bye."

Chapter 15

The rest of the day was busy for the McMurphy as guests arrived and the rooms filled up. We were busy into the late afternoon, handing out extra towels, offering advice on the best way to see the island, and telling people how to get to the rooftop deck. Also, we set up round tables and chairs on the roof in anticipation of the reception. People liked to take coffee and cookies up there and sit. The views of the lake were amazing, the weather perfect for relaxing.

When Jenn didn't show up by six p.m., I didn't think much of it. I knew she and Shane were working on their house. But when she wasn't at the McMurphy to greet her family and friends by seven p.m., when they were all checked in, I grew worried.

"Frances, I'm going to take Mal for a walk," I said. "Are you good to hold down the fort?"

"I think I'll be fine," she said. "Go get a dose of that sunshine."

We went out the back door and down the alley. I phoned Rex, who I knew was working.

"Manning," he said.

"Hi, Rex. It's Allie," I said. "I hate to bother you while you're working."

"You're not a bother," he said. "What's up?"

"Have you seen or heard from Shane this afternoon?"

"No," he said. "I figure he's getting ready for tonight."

"Well, I haven't heard from Jenn lately, either," I said. "And that's concerning because she was planning on being at the hotel by six to greet her family and friends. Rehearsal starts at eight. I'm on my way over to the house to check on them."

"Keep me posted," he said and ended the call.

"Come on, Mal, let's go get Jenn," I said. We walked the few blocks to the fixer-upper. The house was quiet. I knocked, but there was no answer. I knocked again. "Jenn, it's Allie. You're late for greeting your guests."

Still no answer, so I tried the door, but it was locked. I went around to the back door and knocked again. This time the door sprung open at my knock. Mal barked and pulled me inside. The kitchen and open living room were dark and smelled of sawdust and construction. Both spaces were gutted. Only a few miscellaneous contractor tools could be seen. There was a ladder leaning against the wall, a couple of buckets of primer, some tools, an extension cord, and very little else.

"Hello? It's Allie." I walked to the back three bedrooms. The first two were open and empty, as they were earlier. "Hello?"

Mal barked twice, but nothing stirred. I went to the

master bedroom and knocked. "Jenn? Shane? Anyone home?" I listened but heard nothing. "I hope you're decent because I'm coming in." I gently opened the door, giving them enough time to holler if I was opening into a compromising situation. But the room was empty. The bed looked mussed. The window was wide open and so was the dresser. Someone had gone through it and pulled out all the clothes.

"Jenn? Shane?" I moved toward the closed bathroom door. Opening it, I saw that it, too, was empty. That was when I noticed Mal sniffing daintily at blood drops on the bedroom floor. They looked to start near the bed or at the window. Either way, it didn't mean anything good. I pulled out my phone.

"Manning," he said.

"Rex, I'm inside their house and there's no sign of Jenn or Shane. Their clothes are in a pile on the floor. It looks like someone went through the dresser and the bedside tables. Also, there are blood drops. I can't tell if they are going toward the window or toward the bed."

"Okay, Allie, I'm on my way. I'm going to ask you to slowly and carefully leave the bedroom and go outside."

"Got it," I said. My heart rate was up as Mal and I carefully left the bedroom and went out the back door. I walked around the opposite side of the house toward the open window. The window sill looked as if someone had used a crowbar on it. There were several sets of footprints. Some looked large enough to be a man's.

"Allie?" It was Rex.

"I'm on the side of the house," I called and walked around the back to the other side of the house and toward the front.

"Are you okay?" he asked when he saw us.

"Yes, we're fine," I said.

Officers Brown and Lasko bicycled up to the yard and got off, leaving their helmets on the bike handles.

"What's going on?" Officer Brown asked.

"I came to check on Jenn," I said. "She didn't show up to greet her guests. The front door was locked, so I went around back. The back door was open. So I went in, and it looks like someone took them."

"Who?" Officer Lasko asked.

"Jenn and Shane," I said. "Check out the outside of the open window. It looks like it was forced open. There are drops of blood on the bedroom floor."

All three police officers pulled out their guns.

"Stay here," Rex ordered.

"Okay," I said.

"Brown, try the front; Lasko and I will take the back," Rex said. I watched them go to work, carefully checking out the yard as they approached the house. Officer Brown couldn't open the front door. So he hurried around to the back and entered. I could hear them holler, "Clear, clear."

After long tense moments, Officer Brown came out to talk to me. "You did the right thing calling us," he said. "Rex wants you to go home and wait. He'll be there to ask you questions. We're going to call out the Cheboygan Crime Scene Unit to process this. It could take a while."

"What about Jenn and Shane?" I asked. "They have their wedding rehearsal and dinner tonight."

"We'll find them," he said with a nod. "Trust us."

"Okay," I said and glanced inside the house from the now-open front door. There wasn't anything to see. Mal and I turned toward the sidewalk. I wondered if whoever took Jenn and Shane went this way. I saw the footprints. The blood meant someone was hurt. Was the kidnapper going to kill Shane and hurt Jenn just like they did Christopher and Becky?

It was something I didn't want to think about. Instead of going straight home, I knocked on the neighbor's door. Mrs. Summer answered. She sometimes came into the shop to buy fudge to send to her granddaughter in college.

"Oh, Hello, Allie," she said and then spotted Mal. "Hello, little dog. To what do I owe the honor of your visit?"

"Hi, Mrs. Summer. Can we come in?" I glanced toward Jenn's house to make sure Rex didn't see me.

"Sure. Come in, come in. Can I get you some tea?"

"That would be nice," I said. Mal and I sat on her flower print couch. Her house was warm and cozy, stuffed with bits and pieces of a long life well lived.

"I've got Earl Grey and some orange zest," she said as she brought out a tray with a teapot in a cozy and two cups.

I made myself a cup of tea and we chatted a bit about the weather and the wedding to come. Mrs. Summer had come to the tea to meet the moms the day before.

Glancing at my phone, I realized I didn't have much time before the police would be knocking on the door. I wanted to get ahead of them. "Actually, I'm here to ask if you saw or heard anything unusual today," I said.

"Why?" she asked.

"It looks as if someone broke into Shane and Jenn's home after I left this afternoon," I said, downplaying that they were missing and there was blood at the scene.

"Did I hear anything? Well, I wear hearing aids and sometimes I turn them off because they squeal." She winced. "I'm afraid I had them off for my afternoon nap."

"Did you happen to look out the window to see anyone around who isn't normally here?" I asked.

"No, dear," she said and patted Mal's fluffy head. "I don't notice much during naptime."

"Okay," I said. "Thank you." My phone dinged and I saw I had a text from Frances.

Rex is here asking for you.

"Oh dear," I said. "I have to go. Thank you for the tea and the visit," I said and brushed a kiss on her cheek as I let myself and Mal out.

So, the next-door neighbor didn't hear or see anything. I suspected this break-in had something to do with Christopher's murder.

We hurried back to the McMurphy. I walked in through the back door, pulled Mal's leash and halter off her, and she went running to the front.

I followed close behind. Rex was in the lobby talking to my parents. I was pretty private about the men I dated. I didn't want my mom to get any ideas about grandchildren. I didn't want my father to think he needed to protect me.

"Hi, Rex," I said. "You wanted to talk to me?"

"Yeah," he said. He was in full uniform with his hat under his arm.

"Let's talk in my office," I said.

"Allie, don't forget we have the rehearsal in an hour," Mom called. "Wear something nice."

"I won't forget," I said. Rex followed me up the stairs while Mal stayed with Dad, begging for his attention.

When we got to the office I unlocked it and stepped inside. Rex followed me, closing the door behind him. "Allie, have a seat," he said.

"I thought I was supposed to say that," I said as I took a seat at my desk and he paced in front of me.

"Where were you?" he asked. "Remember, you said we need honesty if we want to build a relationship."

"I was at Mrs. Summer's house," I said.

"The next-door neighbor?"

"Yes," I admitted. "We had tea and caught up on chit-chat. She loves Mal."

"And you asked her questions about Jenn and Shane, didn't you?" he said with a soft voice, his face carefully set.

"I did," I said. "But she told me she had her hearing aids out and didn't see anything unusual. So it was a dead end."

"You just couldn't leave that to the professionals?" He blew out a long breath.

"If you remember from my mom's pointed comment, the wedding rehearsal is in an hour. How can we do it if the bride and groom are missing—possibly kidnapped? I wanted to get a head start on finding them."

"You think this is connected to Christopher's murder," he said. "And now we know the killer definitely isn't Shane."

"Right, because why would he break into his own home and stage a kidnapping?"

"Okay," he said. "Tell me your working theory."

"I think Peter Ramfield roofied Shane and killed Christopher," I said. "He was the last one to have a drink with Shane and he lied to me about taking Shane back to the house."

"Okay, so he had opportunity," Rex said. "What's his motive?"

"I haven't figured it out yet," I said. "But no money was taken, so it wasn't a mugging gone wrong. And with all those stab wounds . . . it appeared to be a crime of passion."

"So you think Peter put Shane in the alley, lured Becky and Christopher there, killed Christopher, stabbed Becky, and then ran off, leaving Shane to wake up with the knife in his hand?"

"Yes," I said. "I bet Peter thought Shane was remembering stuff. Word got out that you tried hypnosis on him. If Shane remembered something, Peter would have to remove the threat."

"So why take them?" Rex asked. "Why not just stab them and leave them for dead?"

"I don't know." I shrugged. "Maybe Peter couldn't do it. So he took them somewhere to let them die of exposure or something."

"Let's say you're right," Rex said. "I'll send some guys out to Peter's home."

"There was blood at the scene, which makes me think someone was hurt. So Peter dumped them somewhere where he could seal it up and then ran home, showered, and burned his clothes. Then he's just going to go about his day naturally. With Shane out of the way, there's no worry of anyone exposing him."

"Except Becky," Rex said. "I'm going to call the Cheboygan Police and ask that they put a guard on her room."

"Sounds good," I said. "But we really need to find the bride and groom before their parents and relatives discover they are gone and start to panic."

"Yes," he said. "I called in a handler with his cadaver dog. He's going to search the island."

I swallowed. "A cadaver dog? Do you think they're dead?"

"I've also called in a search and rescue dog to find them if they are alive," he said. "Both are best just in case."

"They can't be dead," I said. "I won't let them be dead. They're getting married tomorrow." I took a deep breath to calm my racing heart. "I want to be there when you pick up Peter," I said. "I want to watch the interrogation with my own eyes."

"I'm sorry," Rex said. "That's not going to happen. What you need to do now is to gather the family and let them know what's going on. Tell them we are doing everything possible to find them and bring them safely home."

"Okay," I said. "But they may storm the police station to find out what's going on."

"Ask them to stay at the McMurphy until further notice. We need them safe."

"What about the rehearsal dinner at the Oak's? I asked.

"See if they can bring it to the hotel, serve it on the roof. Just don't let anyone in or out until I say it's safe."

"Yes, sir," I said and stood.

Rex took me by the hand and gave me a hug. "It's going to be all right," he murmured against my hair. "We're going to find them and catch the guy who did it."

I rested my cheek against his shoulder and took a moment to collect his warmth, the scent of cologne and starch. Then I stepped back. "I'll go make the announcement." First, I went to my apartment to pick up five or six board games. Maybe having something to do would help them feel less isolated. I walked into the lobby with my hands full of games to find people laughing and catching up.

"Hey, Allie," Frances said. "Have you seen Jenn? She's supposed to be here."

"I have an announcement to make." I put down the games and stood by the fireplace mantel and shouted, "Excuse me, everyone. I need a moment of your time." The crowd noise died down as they turned to me.

"I just came from Shane and Jenn's home. They weren't there. The back door was broken into and there was blood on the floor. We suspect foul play."

The murmur of the crowd became a roar.

"Everyone, please, stay calm," I shouted until they quieted down. "The police are on the case. I have been asked to keep you all in the McMurphy for the time being. It's your safest bet. We have a coffee bar, tea, and water. I've brought down some board games if you need something to do. As you know, there are also televisions in your rooms."

"What about the rehearsal?" Shane's mom asked. "Are we canceling it?"

"We can and should postpone it. The dinner is going to be brought here. We can eat it buffet style on the rooftop deck. Remember, this is for your own safety." I stepped down and handed out board games.

Then I went to Frances. "Rex said to lock the door and not let anyone in or out," I said. "Do we have a room for Shane's parents?"

"I'm sure I can figure out something," Frances said.

"Good, because I'm sure they'll want to stay on the island until we find Shane and Jenn."

"Got it," Frances said.

"I need to go to Doud's really quick to pick up snacks for everyone to keep them busy."

"I'll let you out the back," Frances said. "Go straight there and back. We don't need you missing, too."

"Okay," I said. I grabbed my purse from the hook near the door and stepped out into the waning sunlight. I hurried along the alley and around the corner to the street beside Doud's. Then I came face-to-face with Peter Ramfield.

Chapter 16

"Peter!"

"Hi, Allie," he said. "How are the wedding details going?"

I shook my head. "What are you doing?"

"Going to the pub to play snooker," he said.

Feeling like I was in a strange dream, I asked him. "Do you know where Jenn and Shane are?"

"No, why? Are they missing?" he asked.

"I heard Rex Manning was looking for you," I said and took two steps back away from him. "You should go to the police station."

"Why?" he asked and cocked his head, looking strangely confused.

I hit the button that dialed Rex's phone. "Hang on," I said to Peter, holding up my hand like a stop sign.

"Manning," Rex answered.

"Rex, I'm standing beside Doud's and Peter Ramfield is here."

"How close are you to him?" Rex asked.

"Close enough," I answered. "I told him you were looking for him and he should go to the police station."

"Don't move, Allie. I'm on my way." Rex hung up. I pretended to stay on the line.

"Yes, that's right, he helped paint Harry's bed and breakfast," I said and then put my hand on the receiver end of the phone. "Peter, I think he wants you to paint one of his properties."

"Then he should call the boss," Peter said. "I didn't have to go to the police station to tell him that."

"Do you have the boss's number?" I asked.

Peter gave it to me and I repeated it into my phone.

"Right," I said to the soundless phone. "Um, he still wants to see you in person. Do you mind going to the station? I can walk with you if you'd like."

"Naw, I'm good," he said. "I'll head over there if you think I must."

"I'll go with you," I said. "That way if it's nothing, I can buy you an apology drink."

"But you looked like you were going somewhere," he said.

"It's no trouble," I said and casually eyed his gray T-shirt, work jeans, and heavy work boots, which were spattered with a variety of paint.

We walked in step for a few minutes and then Rex came ripping toward us on his bike. We stopped on the corner of Market. Rex got off his bike.

"Peter Ramfield," he said. "I need you to come to the station. I have some questions for you."

"Sure thing," he said, still seeming confused.

Rex took Peter by the arm and escorted him down Market. I rolled the bike behind them. Any excuse to hear what Peter had to say about the missing couple.

"What's this about?" Peter asked.

"We'll talk inside," Rex said as they crossed the street.

I crossed behind and then kickstanded the bike just outside the station. Then I made my way inside, but the duty cop wouldn't let me follow Rex to the back. "Allie, you need to go home. I'll take care of this," Rex said, stopping at the door to the back.

"I just have one question for Peter," I said. "Where are Shane and Jenn?"

"Huh?" Peter said and acted confused.

"What did you do with them?" I asked, stepping close to him.

"I told you I didn't do anything to them," he protested.

"Allie—"Rex said, warning me off, but I refused to be pushed away so easily.

"We know you were the last person to see Shane before the murders and we know you lied about taking him home. Why? Were you looking for a scapegoat?"

"Allie, enough," Rex said and pulled Peter toward the door.

"All right, so I lied about taking Shane home," Peter admitted. "He was heavy and it was late."

"So you left him in the alley," I said.

"Allie," Rex said. "Go home!" Then he dragged Peter into the police station and closed the door in my face.

I blew out a long breath. My phone dinged. It was Frances, wondering what was taking so long with the snacks.

I got delayed, I texted back. **Going to Doud's now. Any preferences?**

None, she texted back. **Be safe**.

* * *

I walked into the back of the McMurphy with four grocery bags of snacks, two in each hand. "Hi, all. How's it going?" I asked Frances, who met me at the door. I locked the door behind me and hung up my purse. Mal came racing to greet me. I patted her head awkwardly. My hands were full of bag handles.

"Let me help with that," Frances said. She took two of the bags. "Douglas, we're going to need some platters. Can you get them?"

"Sure thing," he said and hurried upstairs. I kept decorations and platters and other things in a closet on the second floor.

"Where were you?" Frances whispered.

"I ran into Peter Ramfield," I said. "So I called Rex. Peter lied about taking Shane home the night Christopher died. I think he knows where Shane and Jenn are. Anyway, he's the prime suspect."

"That was not at all safe," Frances chided me.

My mother arrived in the hall. "What's going on? Do you need help with the snacks?"

"Just a bit of local gossip," I said. "You can take one of my bags. We need to put the snacks on platters so people feel festive. I bought two cheese plates plus crackers, chips and dip, two veggie plates, and pretzels and corn chips."

We unpacked the snacks on a table Douglas set up next to the coffee bar. He came back with platters and we set out the chips and crackers and such. I'd also bought a bag of assorted pops.

I turned to Douglas. "Can you bring up a tub of ice?"

"On it," he said.

After a few minutes he came back with an old-fashioned

washtub filled with ice. I put in the pops, then announced the snacks were ready. Some of the guests were embroiled in board games. Others were watching a movie. I did a quick head count.

"Are the others in their rooms?" I asked Frances.

"Some went up to the rooftop deck," she replied.

"I'll go up to let them know we have snacks," I said. As I walked up the steps I thought about Peter admitting he'd left Shane in the alleyway. But he'd claimed he didn't know where Shane and Jenn were. Why?

The rooftop deck was accessed through a staircase that came off the far side of the third floor. It meant if I wanted to go to the roof, I had to go up to the third floor, but I didn't mind.

I came out on the roof and found people sitting in lounge chairs or standing at the railing watching events unfolding beneath them.

"You guys," I said. "We have snacks and pop downstairs. Go help yourselves and, as always, there's coffee available."

"What, no liquor?" Jenn's cousin Paul asked with a grin.

"Sorry," I said. "We don't have a liquor license, so we can't serve it."

"What about the open bar at the reception?" he asked.

"The caterer is licensed. It counts as BYOB," I said. "So don't worry."

Paul laughed and patted me on the back and went down with everyone else to get snacks. When the rooftop was empty, I pulled out my phone and called Liz.

"This is Liz," she answered.

"Hi, Liz. It's Allie."

"What's up?" she asked.

"Shane and Jenn are missing," I said.

"What? They have rehearsal in less than an hour," she said.

"I don't think they're going to make it," I said. "I went to their house to check on them and their bedroom was trashed, the window open, and blood on the floor. I think someone took them."

"Who? Why?"

"Good questions," I replied. "I told Rex that Peter Ramfield was the last person to see Shane the night of the murder. He has to be the murderer and he most likely took Jenn and Shane because they were figuring it out."

"Do we know where Peter is?" she asked.

"Strangely, I ran into him on Main Street and called Rex. Peter is currently at the police station, but he claims not to know anything about Shane and Jenn's disappearance, although he did admit to lying to me about taking Shane home the night Christopher was murdered. He said he left him in the alley because he was too heavy to carry."

"So he lied once," Liz said. "How do we know he's not lying now?"

"He looked confused when I asked him where Jenn and Shane were," I said. "Who else would take them? I mean, it has to be the killer. They must think Shane is remembering things."

"I'll do some digging," Liz said. "Where are you?"

"I'm at the McMurphy, trying to keep everyone occupied. Rex asked us to stay locked down so no one else would go missing."

"Are people worried?" Liz asked.

"The parents, of course," I said. "But others seem to

think it's some kind of prank because Jenn helps me with investigations."

"Well, let's keep them thinking that," Liz said. "What about the rehearsal?"

"It's off. I'm having the caterer bring the dinner food here. We'll set up a buffet for everyone."

"Make sure you have enough food," she said. "The last thing we need is a riot on our hands."

"Good thinking." I told her goodbye and hit END. Then I dialed the caterer.

"This is Reeves Catering, Terra speaking."

"Hi, Terra," I said. "We have a last-minute change of plans for tonight's dinner. Shane and Jenn are moving their rehearsal to tomorrow morning."

"Oh dear," she said. "What can I do to help?"

"We have a hotel full of friends and family. I was wondering if you could bring some dishes to augment what the Oak's is serving. There are about eighty people here and we only planned on the wedding party eating at the Oak's tonight. I thought we could eat buffet style."

"Well, I usually make up a lot of the food in advance, so I don't know about feeding all the guests . . ."

"Oh okay," I said with a sigh.

"Most caterers do," she said. "But you know what? I had a cancelation yesterday, so I have some extra food I can bring and we can do a mixed menu buffet."

"Sounds perfect," I said with some relief. "Can you be here at eight?"

"Sure thing," she said.

"Thanks. You can coordinate with the Oak's on what they are bringing, and let me know if you need anything else," I said and hit END on my phone. I looked out across the island. "Where are you, Jenn? What clue did you leave me?"

People were coming back to the roof with plates in hand and pops. I went back downstairs and found my parents talking to Jenn's folks. Shane's parents were there, too. I hoped Frances had found a room for them. They were from St. Ignace, so they hadn't reserved a room.

"Allie, what's happening?" Mom asked me.

"Well, as I said, it appears Jenn and Shane are missing. It looks like they are most likely still alive. I saw several sets of footprints walking away from the house."

"Oh dear," Shane's mother said and covered her mouth with her hand. "Are the police working on it?"

"Yes," I said and gave her a big hug. "We think we know who did it and that man is in police custody."

"So this should all be resolved in the next few hours," Jenn's dad said as he rubbed his wife's back.

"I certainly think so," I said, putting up a brave front. "In the meantime, I'm going to call the pastor to let him know the rehearsal has been moved to tomorrow morning. The caterer to coming here to set up a mixed menu buffet so everyone can eat."

"Okay," Jenn's dad said.

"But a lot of people have come to see the island," Mom said. "You're spoiling their vacation."

I looked around as family members played board games and talked. "They don't look like we've ruined anything," I said. "Besides, finding Jenn and Shane is the police department's top priority. Heaven help us if more relatives went missing."

Jenn's mom started crying and I handed her a tissue. "I'm sorry," she said. "I tried to put on a brave face."

"She's been crying in her room," Shane's mom told me.

"Well, I would be, too," I said. "But you have to know the police are doing their best."

"Do you think the kidnapper is going to ask for a ransom?" Shane's dad asked. "We'll pay whatever."

"Yes," Jenn's dad said. "We will pay."

"I don't think you need to worry about that just yet," I said.

"Don't they usually set up a phone recorder or something?" Jenn's mom asked.

"Rex has the suspect in custody," I said. "It's just a matter of time before he gives them up."

"All I can do is pace," Jenn's mom said. "I don't know what to do with the family."

"Don't you worry about anything," I said. "Frances and I will take care of the guests." I handed my dad the key to my apartment. "Dad, can you take the Christensens and the Carpenters up to the apartment? You all should stay there. If I hear anything, I'll let you know."

"Come on," Dad said and guided them up the stairs. "Let's make you comfortable."

Frances came over. "Where are they going?"

"I sent them up to the apartment. They don't need to be down here worrying everyone."

"The rest don't seem that worried," Frances said and frowned.

"I think they think this is all a setup," I said. "A prank Jenn pulled."

"Hmmm, that makes sense," Frances said. "She does like her jokes."

"I don't want them to think anything else right now," I said. "We don't want the whole place pacing and crying."

My phone rang. "Excuse me," I said and went to the back room. "Rex?"

"Allie," he said. "How's everyone holding up?"

"Jenn and Shane's parents are a mess, of course," I said. "I sent them to my apartment with my folks. The rest seem to think it's part of a mystery dinner or something."

"Let's keep it that way," Rex said.

"Did Peter tell you where they are? Or why he took them?" I asked.

"Peter isn't telling us much beyond what he told you," Rex said and I could hear what sounded like him wiping a hand over his face. "I'm thinking this is a dead end."

"Did the other cops find anything else at the scene?" I asked. "Any clues? Any reasons why?"

"I've got guys sifting through stuff now," he said.

"What can I do? I canceled the rehearsal, of course, told everyone it will be tomorrow morning."

"Just hang out there and make sure no one leaves."

"Jenn's mom wanted to know if there was going to be a ransom demand and if you'd be tracing her cell phone." I rolled my shoulders to help ease the tension that was building.

"She's not wrong," he said. "Has anyone gotten a call?"

"Not that I've heard," I said. "My mom and dad have been with Jenn and Shane's folks ever since I announced it."

"Good," he said. "I'll send over Officers Brown and Lasko to relay the cell phones in case the kidnappers call."

"What if they're in the woods somewhere?" I asked.

"We've got people scouring the island," he said. "I called in some help from Mackinaw City. They're working their way from Main Street across the island. If they are out there, we'll find them."

"Whoever took them must know the island well," I said. "It has to be a local or you would have found them by now."

"Just do me a favor," he said, "and stay at the McMurphy. I promise we'll get this figured out."

"I'll do my best," I said. "Stay safe."

"Stay safe," he replied.

No ransom calls came in. Jenn and Shane's parents were beside themselves. My mom did a great job of ensuring that Mrs. Christensen and Mrs. Carpenter had warm tea and blankets. Mr. Christensen paced back and forth. I excused myself when the door buzzer rang.

Terra was there with the food. "I stopped at the Oak's and picked up the meal you all had planned for tonight. It's quite a bit."

I helped her unload it from her cart and set up the buffet in the lobby. Most of the guests had gone to their rooms or up on the roof. A few seniors had stayed and continued playing board games.

"How are Jenn and Shane's parents holding up?" Terra asked.

"Not well," I said. "It's been hours and no ransom call. That could be a good sign or a bad one." We set up aluminum pans filled with potatoes, roasted veggies, and salad. Terra set the warm foods on top of kerosene burners. There were rolls and then a pan filled with beef and another one with chicken. She had brought cold cuts and cheese also in case anyone wanted a sandwich.

"This looks terrific," Frances said. "Thank you for feeding so many so quickly."

"Anything for Jenn's family," Terra said. She looked around. "Is this all?"

"No," I said. "Most are either in their rooms resting or on the rooftop."

"It's amazing you've been able to keep them all inside," Terra said.

"It's for their own safety," I said. "Rex doesn't want them to be kidnapped as well."

"Any idea who would kidnap the bride and groom?" Terra asked. "Is this some kind of bad prank? I can't imagine anyone who would want bad things to happen to Jenn and Shane. They are the nicest people."

"Rex is working on figuring it out," I said. "Do I need to get any of this back to you?"

"No, it's all disposable, even the plates and utensils. I know it's bad for the environment, but sometimes you have to go that way. You have better things to do than wash dishes."

"Thanks, Terra," I said and patted her shoulder. "Frances, can you let all the guests know there is food?"

"Will do," Frances said and started toward the seniors first.

"I'll walk you out," I said to Terra and we went out the back. "Be safe on your way home. Things are crazy right now."

"I will," she said and grabbed her cart and walked down the alley.

"Hey, Allie!"

I turned to see Liz walking quickly toward me. "Liz, what's going on?"

"I've got some news," she said. "It seems Becky remembered something."

"What? Really? Do you think that's why Shane and Jenn are gone?"

"It could be," Liz said. "The killer has to be getting nervous."

"Do you think they're on the island or are they going after Becky?"

"Who?"

"The killer," I said.

"I think he went after Shane first," she said. "My guess is Jenn just got caught up in it."

"Which means they are probably all on the island," I said. "Rex has Peter in custody, but he swears he didn't do it."

"Becky remembered that she has a stalker," Liz said. "She wasn't sure if it was related to Christopher's murder, but I think it is."

"Who's the stalker? Do they live on the island?"

"Becky said it was one of the painters on the island," Liz said. "He has brown hair that is receding fast. He always stayed just outside of her line of sight, but she noticed he wore painter's pants and a shirt and cap splattered with color."

"Sounds like Peter," I said.

"Becky remembers telling Christopher and Shane about it," Liz said. "Shane said he might know who the stalker was and would talk to him."

"So maybe Shane was roofied before he could talk to the stalker," I said. "Maybe the stalker had plans to tell Becky how he feels. Wait, did she say how he stalked her? Was there anything unusual or did she just notice him following her?"

"She said he would leave flowers on the front porch of

her subleased rental. She just assumed they were sent to someone else who lived there before her. Then one time she came home to find someone had gone through her dresser and laid on her bed. It was creepy."

"Sounds creepy," I said and made a face.

"Not only that but they left flowers inside the house with a love note," Liz said.

"Okay, now I have goose bumps," I said.

"She told Shane to look over the apartment like a crime scene. He did and picked up fingerprints."

"So Shane knew who it was?"

"The fingerprints weren't in any database," Liz said. "Well, that's when Becky moved in with Christopher."

"Smart girl," I said.

"But the stalking didn't stop. She spotted the cap and the outfit on the man following her." Liz rubbed her arms. "I'm sure whoever did this was the one who killed Christopher and has now taken Jenn and Shane."

"I know a painter, Mike Hangleford. He painted the McMurphy. We can go talk to him. He's a nice guy and has lived here all his life. Maybe he knows who the stalker is and can point us to Jenn and Shane."

"Let's go now," Liz said.

"I'll leave a text for Frances so she won't worry." I pulled out my phone and texted where we were going.

Frances replied with **OK, stay safe, call Rex if you find anything out.**

"It's always best to have someone know where you're going," I said. We hurried off in the direction of Mike Hangleford's house.

Super Easy Fudge

Ingredients:
1 16-ounce can vanilla frosting
12 ounces chocolate chips

Directions:
Combine frosting and chocolate in a glass bowl. Microwave on high for 1 minute, then stir and microwave 30 seconds more, stir, and repeat as needed until melted and combined. Grease an 8 x 8-inch pan. Pour fudge into pan and let cool. Cut into one-inch pieces. Makes 32. Enjoy!

Note: You can have fun with this by selecting any frosting and substituting white chocolate chips for birthday cake fudge, pink strawberry fudge, etc. This is a great activity for older kids. Might be too hot for kids under eight.

Chapter 17

Mike lived on top of the hill in a neighborhood that looked out toward St. Ignace. His home was a beautiful bungalow that looked as if it was built in the 1930s. The house was painted white with blue trim on the shutters. Liz opened the gate to the picket fence and we walked up onto the front porch. The roof of the porch was the same sky blue as the trim.

Liz rang the doorbell, waited five seconds, and knocked on the door with the side of her fist.

"Mike, it's Allie McMurphy and Liz McElroy," I said.

The door opened suddenly. "Allie, Liz," Mike greeted us. "What brings you here?"

"Can we come in?" I asked.

"Sure," he said, and we stepped into hardwood floors, lots of wood trim, and a long open living and dining area with a kitchen at the back. Mike glanced both ways before he closed the door. "Sit, ladies, sit," he said. "Can I get you two a beverage? Tea maybe?"

"Tea would be great," I said and we both sat on the couch. The room was painted a pale blue. The area rug in the living room was a deeper blue and white with a Persian motif. The couch was comfortable, but you could tell Mike was a bachelor. The room was missing the touches that a woman usually added, like pillows and curtains.

He came out with two mugs with tea bags and hot water in them. Steam rose from the top. "Sorry. I don't have a tray, so I'll have to hand these to you. Do either of you want milk or sugar?"

"I'm good," I said.

"Sugar please," Liz said.

"Be right back," he said and hurried off. Mike was not wearing his painter's clothes and instead wore jeans, heavy boots, and a gray T-shirt.

"Sugar," he said and handed Liz two tiny paper sugars he must have picked up from a diner.

"Thanks," she said and tore them both open and put them in her tea. She swirled her mug, then took a sip. "This tastes great. Thanks."

I wrapped my hands around mine to keep them warm. "Listen, Mike, you know all the painters on the island, right?"

"Sure," he said. "If they haven't worked for me, they've worked with me. Why?"

"Apparently, Becky Langford had a stalker. She saw him once or twice watching her. He wore a painter's outfit."

"Really?" he said and sipped his tea.

I mirrored him, lifting my cup, but then putting it down. "We want to know if maybe you heard anything. Or if you know who was crushing on Becky. I'm sure guys talk. Did you hear any gossip?"

He just looked at me for a moment. Liz took another sip of her tea.

"Did you hear anything at all?" I asked.

"Well, most guys had a crush on Becky at one time or the other. She is a beautiful woman. Sad to hear what happened to her. Are you sure she said it was a painter?" He sipped his tea and I did, too.

"I'm sure," Liz said.

"We need to know now," I said. "Because someone took Jenn and Shane. We figure it might be whoever is stalking Becky."

"Well, now, Peter liked her," he said.

"Peter is in police custody and doesn't have any idea who took them," Liz said. Her words were starting to slur.

"Liz?" I asked and tried to stand up but felt dizzy. "Wow, that's weird," I said.

Mike put his cup on the end table and stood. "Are you two all right?"

"I feel tipsy," Liz said and wiped her mouth with her hand. "Can't feel my face."

"Liz," I said. "Are you okay?"

"Just want to close my eyes a minute," she said.

Mike caught her cup as she closed her eyes and went limp.

It dawned on me that we'd been drugged. I still had most of my faculties because I'd only taken one sip. But I didn't want him to know that. "Mike?" I slurred and closed my eyes, pretending to go limp. He gently took my cup from me.

"Well, ladies," I heard him say. "Sorry to have to do this to you, but you were getting too close to the truth."

It was hard not to try to run. Relaxing and pretending to be out of it was the best thing to do at this point. Mike must be the killer. Most likely he had my friends somewhere. With any luck, he would take us there and we could all get out of this.

I felt him reach into my pocket and retrieve my phone. I wished he'd left it, but even without a phone, there had to be a way for me to figure things out.

"All right, you first," I heard him say to Liz. Through the slits of my eyes I saw him pick her up and toss her over his shoulder. He then strode with purpose to the second door from the back porch. It must be his basement. When he disappeared down the stairs I knew I didn't have a lot of time. I opened my eyes and looked for something, anything, that might help us.

My phone was on the end table. If I took it back, would he miss it? I grabbed it quickly and placed it in the pocket he'd taken it from. That way if he did notice, he might just think he hadn't removed it in the first place. Next, I grabbed the spoon from Liz's cup and stuffed it in my shoe. Finally, I poured some of my tea into Liz's cup so it looked like we drank the same amount. I didn't want him to get suspicious. His footsteps were loud coming up the stairs and I quickly went back to my limp pose.

"Now, you, Allie," he said and threw me over his shoulder. It was hard and pushed my diaphragm, making me say, "Ouf!" He moved his head at the sound, and I stayed as limp as I could. "Are you awake?"

I just moaned and let my arms dangle.

He didn't say another word, just took me down the

stairs into his basement. He went across it and through a small door into what once must have been a coal bin. I closed my eyes as he flopped me down on the concrete floor. It was so difficult not to wince at the pain it caused. I let my head roll to the side.

"Troublemakers, all of you," he muttered. "I should have known. I should have known. Well, now you've gone and done it. Stay here and rot for all I care. Ain't nobody going to find you."

I heard him kick someone, who cried out. Was that Jenn? As tempting as it was, I had to keep my eyes closed and my jaw slack until he left. I felt him hovering over me for a moment. His breathing was uneven.

"This is all you guys' fault," he shouted. "Now you have to pay."

Then he stormed out and slammed the door. I held my breath and counted to ten. Then I heard him moving some heavy things in front of the door. Like a dresser or a cabinet? It struck me then that we were well and truly stuck. Even if the police did manage to search his basement, they wouldn't see us in the coal shoot behind a set of shelves.

I opened my eyes. It was pitch-black. I stood. "Who's here?"

I heard mumbling, as if mouths were gagged. Reaching into my pocket, I wrapped my hand around my phone and breathed a sigh of relief. I hit the flashlight app on the phone and looked around.

There were no windows and no lights. I suppose that wouldn't be needed. After all, the basement light was all you needed to see inside the bin. I shone my flashlight toward where the mumbles came from. "Jenn!" I raced to my friend and pulled the gag from her face.

"Allie," she whispered hoarsely. "Shane is hurt . . . bad."

I went over to where Shane sat and took note of the pool of blood that was mirrored in the blood on his shirt. I took off his gag, but he didn't speak. He barely opened his eyes.

Pulling off my shirt, I folded it up and pressed it against his wound. That made him cry out.

"Untie me," Jenn said. "Then I can take care of him."

"Hang on, I don't want to lose this pressure." I untied Shane's hands and pulled one of his hands over my shirt. "Press on this," I ordered in a voice strong enough that it got a response from him. He pressed. Not hard, because he was weak, but he pressed.

Then I raced back to Jenn and untied her. She stood and rubbed her wrists. "I've been trying to get out of those ties for hours." She rushed over to Shane and pressed down on my shirt until he moaned. "Sorry, baby," she said. "I've got to stop the blood."

I ran my light around the room and saw Liz unconscious on the floor a few feet away. I went over and checked for a pulse. She was breathing and had a heartbeat, although it was slow.

"What happened?" I asked Jenn as I tried to get cell service. The coal shoot was lined with some sort of metal.

"He broke in through the window when we were working," Jenn said. "He stabbed Shane once before I struggled with him. But he got the best of me. Then he thought he heard someone coming, so he pushed us out the back door. I have a few scraps and cuts from him pushing us around, but Shane fell in the grass, making the stab wound worse. He got us down here and had me tie up Shane, and then he tied me up.

"I rolled closer to Shane, but I wasn't able to stop the bleeding. He's lost a lot of blood," she said. "I don't know if he's going to make it."

"Don't worry," I said. "I managed to hang on to my phone, but there's no signal down here."

"What time is it? Does anyone know where you are?"

"It was seven p.m. when we left the McMurphy. I texted Frances where we were going," I said. "We came to ask Mike if he had any idea what painter might have been stalking Becky. I had no idea it was him. I trusted him. He was in and out of the McMurphy and did a great job painting it. I recommended him to Harry."

"Then Frances should come knocking soon, right?" Jenn asked.

"Rex will," I said. "But Mike can send them on a wild-goose chase. It could be days before they figure it out."

"Shane doesn't have days," Jenn said, tears running down her cheeks.

"Let me think," I said. I went over and tried the door. It was locked and didn't budge. Then I ran my flashlight over each wall, looking for anything—a crack, anything. That's when I found it, hidden behind a bunch of shelves. The coal chute. In the early twentieth century some furnaces ran on coal. The delivery man would open the shoot and pour the coal into the bin, then send a bill. Once the coal was in the basement, the homeowners would shovel it into their furnace.

I pushed and pulled, but the shelves wouldn't budge. Were they that heavy or were they bolted to the floor? I shone my light down. Oh no, they were bolted. I didn't have time to try to remove the bolts, so I climbed the shelves and squeezed myself through them to the coal chute. I tried to open it, but it was meant to be opened from the outside. My fingers couldn't pull it open.

That was when I remembered the spoon in my shoe. Would that work? I pulled out the spoon and tried wedging the handle into the cracks of the chute. It started to budge. But every time I tried to catch it with my fingers, it slammed shut.

At every slam I would turn off my flashlight and we would hold our breath, praying Mike didn't hear it and come down. On the third try I managed to get my fingers in the crack as it tried to spring closed. Pain radiated down my arms. Tears burst from my eyes, but I could smell fresh air. Once I could push through the pain, I was able to pull the chute open. It opened about six inches—enough for coal to slide down, but not enough for a person to climb through. I wedged myself far enough up the shelves to get my elbows to hold the trapdoor open. Then I texted Rex and Frances. **Mike is the killer. We are trapped in his basement in the coal shoot behind some furniture. Come quick. Shane is losing blood.**

It took a while, but finally the phone said the text had been delivered. I didn't want to call in case Mike heard me talking. I hid my phone in the chute and tried to close it carefully, but it snapped shut. I held my breath and listened. There were big footsteps marching across the house toward the basement door.

"He's coming," I said and scrambled down the shelves, tearing the skin on my knees and elbows. It was difficult because my fingers still hurt so much. It was pitch-black in the coal room. I stumbled over Liz on my way to the door. What was I going to do? Hit him if he walked in? With what? My smashed hands? When I was able to look around the room I'd seen there was nothing in it but us and the shelves. There was nothing to hit him with. The basement door slammed and I heard him coming down the stairs. I stumbled toward the door. I was either going to jump on his back and try to hurt him or distract him by jumping out at him from the front. I waited with the cold metal wall at my back.

"What's going on in there?" he called, not yet moving the things he'd put in front of the door. "No one can hear you but me. So just be quiet, or I'll come in there and make sure you're quiet." Then it sounded like he cocked a rifle.

Jenn and I held our breath. He hit or kicked whatever he put against the door so hard I jumped. I didn't think my adrenaline could get any worse, but I felt like a trapped rabbit who wanted nothing to do but run. Except there was nowhere to run. I had to trust that the text messages went through or, at the very least, Rex could follow my phone's GPS to the coal chute.

Mike hit whatever it was again for good measure and I covered my mouth to keep from crying out. I was shaking from head to toe. Then silence came and after what seemed like forever, he walked back up the stairs and closed the door.

I crawled my way, bumbling through the dark, to Jenn. She was shaking, too.

"What if they don't get the text?" she asked. I could hear tears in her voice. "What if Shane dies?"

"He's not going to die," I said and hugged her. "Do you need me to relieve you for a while?"

"No," she said. "I'm not letting him go. You hear me, Shane? I'm not letting you go."

After what felt like days but could have been hours,

Liz started to wake up. I crawled to her and wrapped my arms around her to help her sit up.

"What's going on? Where am I?" she asked. "It's so dark."

"You were drugged," I said. "It was in the tea."

"Mike?" she asked.

"Yes. Jenn and Shane are here, too. We're in the coal room of Mike's house."

"How long have I been out?" she asked. "I have such a headache."

"I have no idea how long," I said.

"I hear breathing. Who else is here?"

"Jenn and Shane," I repeated. Liz seemed so groggy. "Mike brought them here. He's the painter who was stalking Becky."

"Mike's the killer?" Liz sounded confused. "But he's a nice guy. He's lived his whole life on the island."

Suddenly, she straightened away from me. "How do we get out of here? Do you have your phone? Where's my phone?"

"He took your phone," I said. "After I saw you start to crash, I pretended to be drugged, too. He took both our phones and keys."

"That means he has the keys to the McMurphy," Jenn said. "That's not good."

"I don't think he's going to hurt anyone else," I said.

"How do we get out?" She stood and stumbled to find a wall.

"We have to wait until someone finds us," I said. "I managed to get my phone back when he was bringing you down here. I sent a text and Frances knows we were coming here. We have to wait."

"Why didn't you call?" Her tone was slightly elevated as panic set in.

"Because there is no cell reception," I said.

"Then how did you text?"

I rubbed my forehead and explained everything I had done. She crumpled to the floor. "I feel like I'm going to be sick."

"Oh please don't," Jenn said. "Or I will, too, and how are we going to clean it up?"

"Come here," I said and crawled to her. "You're still processing the drug. Let me hug you. Body heat might help."

After a while she stopped shivering. My own trembling slowed down. Jenn was quietly sobbing.

Then we heard a scrape and a screech. "Hello?" came a whisper from the coal shoot.

"Hello," I shouted and stood. "We're here!"

"Help us! Jenn shouted

"Hurry!" Liz said.

The chute banged closed and everything went silent. Then, suddenly, we heard the door upstairs crash open, and what sounded like a herd of men in boots came rushing in.

I stumbled toward the door and began pounding on it. "We're here! We're here!"

Liz was beside me beating the door, while Jenn joined us as we yelled and made a fuss.

We could hear them storm down the basement stairs, shouting. Then whatever was pushed in front of the doorway was dragged away.

"Stand away from the door," someone shouted. I grabbed Liz and hunkered down near Shane and Jenn and we covered our heads with our hands.

BAM! There was a loud crash and dust and smoke. Policemen in tactical gear rushed in, shouting. Someone turned on a light. It was total chaos and confusion. I raised my hands and so did Liz. Jenn refused to give up her pressure on Shane's wound.

When everything cleared, Rex was there. Tears filled my eyes as he hugged me. I hugged him back and then pulled away. "It's Shane—he's been stabbed and bleeding for hours," I cried.

Rex pushed past me. My ears were ringing from the blast. Someone took my arm and led me out of the coal room. They passed me to someone else who guided me up the stairs. Another person was at the top of the steps and they guided me out into the yard. Another person put a blanket around my shoulders. I watched as George Marron and Jacob Psik rushed into the house with their medical kits and a stretcher.

"Here," Marcy Wentz said and handed me a steaming cup of tea. "This will help. It's cold out here." Marcy lived nearby and had a thermos in her hand.

"I don't want tea," I said. "It's how he drugged us to get us down there."

"Okay, then." She took the tea away. "Can I get you something else warm? Coffee?"

"I'm fine," I said, and then my knees gave out and I sat down hard.

"I'm sure you are," she said. "Come on," She pulled me up. "Let's go over to where the EMT is looking at Liz."

I walked with Marcy until she handed me over to an EMT I didn't know. Her name tag read Smithfield. I sat down on the ambulance bay beside Liz.

"She was drugged," I said. "I don't know what with,

but Mike roofied Shane last week before killing Christopher Harris."

"We're going to take blood and urine samples when we get her to the clinic," EMT Smithfield said. She was an older woman with short gray hair and wide shoulders. "You, too."

"I only sipped the tea once," I said. "I think I'm okay."

"Right," she said and bundled us both up in the ambulance. "As soon as Rex releases you, we'll go to the clinic and have them check you out."

She took my blood pressure and gave me a side eye. "It's very high," she said. "I'm going to want you to take a few breaths for me."

I did and she listened to my heart and lungs.

Rex showed up at the ambulance, and in the distance I could see George and Jacob carrying Shane on a stretcher. Jenn was beside them, trembling and covered in blood.

"Is he going to live?" I asked with tears welling up in my eyes.

"He lost a lot of blood," Rex said. "They're going to life-flight him to Cheboygan. He needs surgery and intensive care."

"Did you find Mike?" Liz asked.

Rex frowned. "He wasn't here when we got here."

"So he's still on the loose?" I felt my eyes widen. "That's . . ."

"Not ideal," Rex said. "But we have people scouring the island for him. He won't get away."

"That's eight miles of coastland. What if he has a boat?" I said, my voice rising, on the edge of panic.

"Let me worry about that," he said firmly. "Smithfield, take them to the clinic and get them checked out. Officer

Bedichek will ride with you. I've got officers at the clinic. He won't get near you again."

A young officer with the name tag Bedichek climbed into the ambulance. He was about six foot tall and built like a brick wall. It was reassuring to know he stood between us and Mike. Rex closed the ambulance doors and pounded on them twice, and we pulled away from the crime scene. My thoughts raced as I tried to figure out where Mike might be and prayed that everyone at the McMurphy stayed locked down tight.

Chapter 18

The police recovered my cell phone and it to me at the clinic, where Liz and I were given IV drips of saline and carefully monitored for any lasting effects. The staff had orders to keep us until Rex said otherwise.

Our protection detail was stationed outside our room with a gun.

"Well, that didn't go as planned," Liz said.

"But now you know what it feels like to be roofied," I said. "It will make a good article for the paper."

She ran a hand over her curly hair and winced. "He dropped me hard. There's a knot on the back of my head the size of a goose egg."

"They took you away for a CT scan," I said. "Did they say if you had a concussion?"

"They haven't said yet," she said. "But I have a splitting headache."

The nurse came into the room. "Here's an ice pack for your head," she said and handed it to Liz. "Looks like you have a mild a concussion." She checked Liz's IV and then moved to check mine. "You two ladies are pretty bruised up."

Dr. Prost came into the room with X-rays in his hand. He held them up for me to see. "Looks like you broke all four of your fingers on your right hand. The breaks are near the tips, so we'll get those splinted. Do you need anything for the pain?"

"I can't feel any pain," I said. "They're numb and swollen."

"That's probably a good thing," he said. "I'll splint your fingers. You're not going to be able to use that hand for about six weeks. Then come back for another X-ray to see how they are healing."

"So much for fudge making," I said with a sigh. "It really is something you can't do with only one hand."

"How's the search for an assistant coming?" Liz asked.

"I hired twins to intern over the summer," I said. "They'll be here next week."

"So, see, all is not lost," Liz said.

I tried to text from my phone with the new splits. I could barely hold it with my splinted right hand and texting with my left thumb was more hunt and peck.

"Who are you trying to text?" Liz asked.

"My parents. I need to let them know we're all right, and then Frances and Douglas to keep all the friends and family corralled until we find Mike," I said.

"Let me do it," she said and winced when she reached for my phone.

"You've got a concussion," I protested.

"And you are broken," she countered. "Let me use my hands." She took the phone and texted my parents. **Hi Mom and Dad, I'm fine just need a splint on my right hand. I'll be home soon. Please keep everyone safe.** She showed it to me.

"Thanks," I said. "I heard they are flying Jenn's parents to Cheboygan to keep her company while Shane is in surgery."

"So everyone at the McMurphy knows what happened?"

"I'm not sure," I said. "My parents were keeping Jenn's parents company in my apartment, away from the rest. They might have gone down the back stairs instead of through the hotel."

"Hmmm, that makes sense," she said. "Do you want me to text Frances?"

"Yes, please," I said. "Tell her that we are safe and that the killer is still on the loose, so please don't let anyone leave the McMurphy."

Liz's thumbs clicked as she quickly texted. "People aren't going to like it," she said. "Especially now that tomorrow's wedding is off."

I winced at the thought. But there was no way Shane would be healed enough to go through with the wedding. "It's not off, it's just postponed," I said. "We'll deal with that later."

She showed me what she wrote and I nodded. "You can hit send."

The phone made the whoosh sound that it was delivered. Then dinged, letting me know that I got a text.

"Your parents want to know when you'll be back."

"Oh gosh," I said. "Tell them . . . what should we tell them? I mean, we still have to talk to Rex."

Liz typed, **I'm safe but it's going to be a long night. Please stay safe at the McMurphy, go to bed and get some sleep. I will see you in the morning.** "How's that?" she asked and showed me the text.

"Perfect," I said. "Hopefully, Frances will keep them from trying to see me. The last thing I want is for Mike to hurt my parents. He seems truly unhinged."

"Yeah. I had no idea he was the stalker," Liz said. "What a story I'm going to have when I get out of here."

"You have to stay the night," the nurse said. "We need to ensure your concussion doesn't get worse."

"So Saturday's edition," Liz said and then looked me over. I had scrapes and bruises from climbing the wooden shelves. I had stitches and a splinted hand. "Good thing they aren't getting married tomorrow. Can you imagine the wedding pictures?"

I laughed, but it hurt. "Ow, don't make me laugh. I'm sure my hair is standing up all over the place."

"Hey, at least you don't have my hair," she said and patted her head. While Liz had soft ringlet curls, I had frizzy ends that tended to stick out like I put my finger into a light socket.

The nurse left and Rex arrived. He spoke softly to our bodyguard for a moment and then came into the room. "Well, aren't you two a sight for sore eyes," he said.

I reached up with my left hand and tried to flatten my frizzy hair to no avail. "Hi, Rex," I said. "Any word on Mike?"

"No," he said. "We're searching the island and have the coast guard watching the docks, but without being able to go into every building on the island, the search has been slow."

"You can't go into every building?" I asked.

"Not without warrants," He said.

"Have you deployed the search and rescue dogs?" Liz asked. "The ones you were bringing in for Jenn and Shane?"

"My guys are on it," he said and pulled out his notebook. "Now, ladies, why don't you tell me what you were doing at Mike Hangleford's house in the first place?" His scowl was probably appropriate but didn't last long.

We repeated the story of learning about the stalker who wore painter's clothes and how we trusted Mike, so we went to ask him who he thought it was.

"And that's how we ended up in the coal room," I said.

"How did you break your fingers?" he asked.

"The chute isn't made to be opened from the inside," I said.

"By the way, that was a smart move, leaving your phone in the chute. We were able to track your phone's GPS," he said.

"Did you get my text?" I asked. "And we told Frances where we were going before we left the hotel. I would have called, but I would have had to shout into the chute and that wasn't the best thing to do. As it was, Mike heard me trying to open the chute and nearly caught us."

"I didn't get the text," Rex said. "But Frances did and called me. Luckily, we had a SWAT team deploying to look for Jenn and Shane. I used them to get to you."

"How come Mike wasn't there?" Liz asked.

"He must have heard us coming," Rex said. "I saw a police radio on the counter in his kitchen. Don't worry, we'll get him."

"Liz has to stay the night," I said. "She has a concussion, but I can go home, right?"

"That's what I heard," Rex said.

"I want to see my parents and talk to the family members staying at the McMurphy. We need to have a plan for them to go home and be safe," I said. "We can't keep them locked up in the hotel all weekend."

"I'll walk you home when your IV is done and the doctor says it's okay," Rex said. "We can work out a meeting in the morning. By then we'll have a plan to get them safely off the island."

"Darn. I don't want to stay here all night by myself," Liz said.

"I'll have a police officer stationed outside your door. Don't worry, Mike can't get to you." Rex straightened up. "I've got some work to do, but I'll be back in an hour to walk you home."

We watched him go.

"He is so stuck on you," Liz said.

"Sometimes I think it's true," I said, "and sometimes I'm not so sure. Melonie is still living on the island. I heard she was working for the mayor. Which means she works in the same building as Rex. And you know she told me she set her cap for him and no one was going to get in her way."

"Melonie was always a drama queen," Liz said.

I looked at Liz. "I have real feelings for Rex, but I also have so many doubts."

"What kind of doubts?"

"I don't know. I have to ask myself if I want to be someone's third wife. I mean, his track record isn't so good. Then, we both know I'm not going to stop investigating if my friends are in trouble. That would be a conflict of interest for him. I mean, that could really mess up his cases in court."

"Pish," she said. "You two are perfect together."

"Yes, but if we ever get married and then end up divorced, it's going to really be a mess because I'm not leaving the McMurphy and he's not leaving the island police."

"Girl, why are you thinking divorce? Are you even dating?"

"Maybe," I said. "He wants to be exclusive, but I'm not ready for that yet. We only had the one date before Melonie showed up."

"Well, of course you're not ready if you've already got yourself married and divorced in your head. You know you can't predict the future, right?"

"I know that," I said and messed with the blanket that had been thrown over me before they put the IV in.

"And the past is the past. You can't change it. So I think you're nuts if you don't live in the present. Seriously, take a deep breath and relax. That's a whole lot of handsome, hunky, protective man."

"You know I've never been scared of anything as much as I'm scared of what could happen if I give my heart to Rex," I admitted and felt the heat of a blush rush up my cheeks.

"Ah, there's the actual truth," Liz said. "Listen, you don't have to go there yet. Just take it slow and enjoy the moments you actually have."

"Sounds like good advice to me," the nurse said as she came in to check my IV.

"Okay, fine," I said. "I can do one day at a time."

"There's my smart girl," Liz said.

The nurse pulled out my IV and took my vitals one

more time. "The doctor will be in in a few to check on you and sign you out."

"Thanks," I said.

"Try to stay safe this time. I see you in here far too often." The nurse shook her head at me.

"I'm not doing it on purpose," I grumbled.

"To be fair," Liz said. "we walked into this one blind."

"I wonder how Shane is," I said. "Can you text Jenn to see if she's heard anything?"

"Sure," Liz said and used my phone to text Jenn. "She says he's still in surgery. He lost a lot of blood."

"I know," I said. "It makes me so mad we didn't find him sooner."

The doctor came in and checked my vitals, waved a light in front of my eyes, and handed me a prescription for pain meds. "I wish there was more we could do for your fingers, but a splint is the best thing at this time. Keep them as immobile as you can. Now go home and get some rest."

"Thanks, Doc," I said and slid off the hospital bed, slipped on my shoes, and gathered my purse while he checked on Liz. "Does she have to stay the night?"

"It's safest," he said. "Don't worry, we'll take good care of her."

Rex appeared at the door. "Are you good to go?"

"The doctor says yes," I said.

"Here are her discharge papers." The doctor gave them to Rex. Rex nodded as he motioned for me to leave.

"Hold on," I said and went over and gave Liz a hug. "I owe you a drink when this is over."

"And a story," she said as she handed me my phone. I slipped it into my purse.

"And a story," I repeated. Then I walked out, letting

Rex guide me to the nurses' station, where I paid my deductible and we left.

We walked in silence for a few blocks. The clinic wasn't too far from the McMurphy. I had no sense of time. The stars filled the sky and the sounds of the lake waves breaking filled my ears.

"Are you going to say 'I told you so' about leaving the McMurphy?" I asked.

"No," he said.

"Because if I hadn't gone to Mike's, we likely wouldn't have found Shane in time, or Jenn," I said.

"That's most likely true. Mike was not on my suspect list. Even Peter didn't say anything about Mike stalking Becky."

"But Peter did admit to lying about taking Shane home," I said. "So he could have roofied Shane."

"He swears he didn't. And after we rescued you from Mike's place I went in to see him and asked him if Mike was in the pub when he and Shane had that drink," Rex said. "Peter said he was. That he stopped by to say hi and then went home. The encounter was short, so he didn't think anything of it. But Peter swears he didn't see Mike put any drugs in Shane's drink."

"But he must have," I said. "Now he's still on the island." I glanced around and moved closer to Rex. "Thanks for walking me home."

"I would do anything to keep you safe," Rex said and put his arm around my waist and drew me closer. "You know that, right?"

"I thought you didn't like PDA while you were in uniform," I teased.

He kissed me hard. Then continued to walk. "You scare the daylights out of me. What is it with you and getting kidnapped anyway?"

"Well, it seems as I get closer to the truth, the bad guys get more desperate."

"One of these days you aren't going to come back from something like this," he warned.

"You couldn't have stopped it even if you were there with me," I said. "You would have been roofied just like Liz was."

"Why weren't you?"

"I don't like tea that tastes funny," I said.

"What do you mean, funny?" he asked.

"It tasted a bit bitter," I said. "Liz puts sugar in her tea, so she didn't notice. As soon as I noticed, I didn't let it go between my lips. When Liz went down I pretended to go down too—that way he assumed I drank the same amount."

"Be careful with that," Rex said. "You probably didn't have the same amount of liquid in your cups. He could have noticed that."

"I poured it out to match Liz's before I grabbed my phone and he came up the stairs to get me."

"Smart move," he said.

We arrived at the back door to the McMurphy. I noticed the back light was on and the cameras picked us up. I waved to the camera with my splinted hand and then used the key with my left one. We went inside and locked the door behind us.

The lobby was empty. A quick glance at the clock on the wall told me it was nearly one a.m. Frances met us in the hall. "Oh good, you're home." She gave me a hug.

"Why are you still here?" I asked. "Is Douglas, too?"

"I told them to stay the night," Rex said. "That way I have full control of everyone connected to the McMurphy."

"Wait." I turned to him. "I just remembered, Mike took my key. He has a key to the McMurphy."

"It's okay," Rex said. "We found your key in Mike's house. That's the one you're holding."

"Oh." I put my hand to my chest. "Good. Did you find Liz's phone?"

"No," Rex said. "It's another reason to keep you all together here."

"We're in room two-thirteen," Frances said. "It was empty because the shower was leaking and Douglas didn't get to it in time for a guest."

"Are you okay with staying?" I asked and tried to stifle a yawn.

"Yes, of course," Frances said. "I've locked the downstairs and the doors. The cameras are all on. We've been watching the screen, but there hasn't been any activity besides the hourly patrol who comes by the front and the back."

"Good," Rex said. "That means he's not trying anything right now. Hopefully, Mike is hunkered down in a shed somewhere, trying to wait us out."

"Well, I'm glad you're home," Frances said and gave me a kiss on the cheek. "Why don't you go up and check on your folks?"

"I want you to go to bed, too," I said. "Rex wants us to meet with everyone about nine a.m. I'm glad I thought to cater breakfast goodies for everyone in the morning. How did dinner go?"

"It was a smashing success. Terra does a good job." Frances urged me up the stairs. "Don't you worry, she'll do a bang-up job on breakfast, too."

"Thanks, Frances," I said. Rex accompanied me up the stairs. We left Frances at the second floor and went up to the fourth. This floor didn't have any cameras in the hall; I had to have some privacy. There were cameras at my back door and in the stairwells. That was good enough.

I unlocked my door to find my parents half asleep on the couch in their pajamas. Mal came running up to me and wagged her stump tail, happy to see me home. I picked her up and gave her pets. She sniffed my broken fingers.

"What's the latest news on Shane?" Dad asked Rex.

"The surgery went well, but he lost a lot of blood, so they will put him in the ICU when he comes out of recovery."

I hadn't thought to ask about Shane and felt a little guilty. "Can I make everyone some tea? I have chamomile for those of us going to bed and Earl Grey for Rex."

"Sounds good," Mom said. She came to the kitchen and gave me a hug. "How are you, baby?" she asked and touched the bandages on my forehead and tsked at my broken right-hand fingers. "Oh, let me make the tea," she said and took the teapot from me.

I scooted out of the kitchen and onto one of the barstools. Rex and Dad came over to watch Mom make tea.

"How did that happen?" Dad asked and pointed at my fingers.

"I was trying to open the coal chute from the inside and it snapped back on my fingers."

"Ouch," Dad said. "Did they give you good pain pills?"

"Just a few," I said.

Rex stood behind me with his hand on the small of my back. His thumb brushed circles there.

"Did Jenn's folks and Shane's folks get to Cheboygan okay?" I asked my dad.

"They did," Dad said. "They said to thank you for the hotel room, but both sets of parents are spending the night in Cheboygan."

"No wedding tomorrow," I said with a sigh, "unless they get married in the hospital. Either way, we have to come up with a plan to keep the guests safe. I'm sure they don't want to waste their entire weekend locked up in the McMurphy."

"Well, surely they don't want to go until they see that Jenn and Shane are well," Mom said as she poured hot water into four mugs and put tea bags in them.

"Some may want to go home," I said. "It's natural when a suspected killer is on the loose."

"When the ferry boats run in the morning will this killer be able to get off the island?"

"No," Rex said. "We have alerted the ferry operators to keep an eye out for him and we have the coast guard circling the island."

"Why did he do this terrible thing?" Mom asked.

"We can't talk about the investigation while it's ongoing," Rex said and took his Earl Grey and sipped it.

I just let my tea steep. After today, I really didn't want any tea, I just wanted something to do.

"Oh, Allie, you didn't get anything to eat tonight, did you?" Mom said as she hovered. "We have leftovers in the fridge. It won't take but a minute or two to reheat them."

"I'm not hungry," I said. "I'm surprised you had any leftovers with a full house of guests unable to go out to eat."

"Well, with all the snacks you bought, there was plenty of food," Mom said.

"By the way, the rooftop deck is a big hit," Dad said. "Most people took their dinner up there to eat. Douglas put out the heating lamps and people grouped around and enjoyed the view and company."

"Wonderful," I said. "I had a gas line installed. Next year I plan on putting two firepits up there. Dad, I need you to think about the space and how we can have weddings and receptions without firepits getting in the way."

"Do you have the footprint of the gas lines?" he asked.

"Let's not talk about that tonight," Mom said with a frown. "Come on, dear, let's go to bed and leave these two kids alone."

"Right," my dad said and gave me a kiss and a hug. "Good night, dear." He shook Rex's hand. "Thanks for bringing Allie safely back to us."

Mom gave me a kiss and a hug and waved at Rex as she took Dad's hand and walked him to the bedroom.

We waited for them to close the door before we spoke.

"I have something stronger than tea, if you're off duty," I said.

He sent me a straight-line smile. "I'm not off duty until we get this guy."

"Well, then, just wine for me." I took a bottle out of the fridge, uncorked it, and poured a glass a quarter full. Any more and I wouldn't sleep.

"You shouldn't drink when you're taking pain pills," he said.

"I didn't take any pain pills," I said and took a sip.

"I want to walk through the hotel to make sure you're locked up tight and the security cameras are working."

"I'll go with you," I said. "The last thing I need is another encounter with a killer."

Chapter 19

Saturday

The next morning, I was up early due to the pain in my hand. I swallowed some aspirin and went downstairs to start coffee before people got up. Mal needed her walk, so I put a jacket over my T-shirt and jeans and leashed her up to go out. I took my phone with me just to be safe.

Outside, the weather was perfect for a spring wedding. The sky was blue and the sun rose a lovely pink and pastel orange. The lake wind was gentle and flowers were blooming everywhere. It made me sad to think that Jenn and Shane were in the hospital. I wanted to go be with her, but I had guests and a killer on the loose.

Mal and I walked down by the beach. The sound of the lake waves calmed me. My hand throbbed. My fingers were swollen under the splint. A fine maid of honor I was going to make. The doctor said the splint needed to be on for at least six weeks. I had to wonder when Jenn would reschedule her wedding. Next weekend might be too soon for Shane, and she had the Wilkins wedding to think about.

A glance at my phone told me it was only seven a.m. Too early to call Jenn. I turned and moved back toward the McMurphy. Terra would show up with breakfast at eight. I wanted to set up tables and such on the roof. It was perfect weather for outdoor breakfast.

Mal started barking and caught my attention. A figure stood off in the distance as we walked down an empty Main Street. It was a man, and he stared at us as he stood three blocks away. I stopped and used my left hand to hit the button to dial Rex.

"Manning," he said, his voice sounding gravelly with sleep.

"Rex, it's Allie," I said, my heartbeat pounding so fast I heard it in my voice. "I'm walking Mal and there's a male figure on Main Street just staring at us."

Mal barked and barked.

"Is that Mal?" Rex said. "I've never heard her bark like that. Can you see who it is? Is it Mike?"

"I would need to get closer to tell," I said. "He's shaped like Mike and wearing a baseball cap. Oh wait, he's turned toward Market Street and is walking away. Maybe it was nothing."

"I'm glad you called me," he said, and I could hear him getting dressed. "Is he between you and the McMurphy?"

"I don't know; he ducked down Astor Street toward Market and I'm not close enough to tell if he's hiding in wait or walking away."

"Mal's still barking," he observed. "I don't like you out in the open like that."

"I have to walk Mal," I said. "Maybe if I cross the street? I mean, it could just be a fudgie."

"Okay, cross the street and stay on the line with me. I'm coming your way." I could hear his door open and close.

"I'm crossing now," I said. "I'm about a block away from the street he turned up."

"I'm coming down the other way," he said.

"Great," I said. I slowed down when I hit Astor. I realized it was the same street that fed the alley where Christopher was killed. Did Mike's family have a home near here?

"Okay, I'm at Astor," I said. "He's not here." There was relief in my voice. "He must have gotten to Market. Maybe he was just going for coffee."

"Maybe," Rex said. "I'm nearly to Main. There's no one on Market."

I crossed the street to the McMurphy side of Main and turned up the road that led to the alley and the stairs to my apartment. Rex was within sight when I hung up the phone. Mal barked again, startling me. A man jumped out from behind a dumpster and put a knife to my throat.

"Don't say a word," he whispered near my ear, sending fear spiking down my spine. I dropped Mal's leash and she growled and bit at the man's pant leg. He kicked her and she cried out as she tumbled away from me.

The knife was cold and razor-sharp against my skin. The edge stung like a long paper cut on my throat.

Rex had pulled out his gun. "Put down the knife," he ordered.

"No," Mike said. "You put down the gun or I'll slit her throat. I'll do it."

"Rex, don't," I said.

"What do you want?" Rex asked Mike.

"Put down the gun and get me a boat off this darned island," Mike said.

"I can get you the boat, but you have to put down the knife."

"No," Mike said and grabbed my arm, wrenching it behind me. I made a noise at the pain that radiated up my arm. The knife pressed harder into my throat. My left hand grabbed his arm, trying to pull him away from me, but he tugged on my right arm, bringing tears to my eyes.

"Okay," Rex said. "I'm putting down my gun."

"No, Rex, don't," I said.

But he slowly lowered the gun. I tried desperately to remember my self-defense class. I knew my left arm couldn't reach anything vital. Maybe my elbow could connect with his solar plexus. My foot could stamp his insole.

I burst into action, jamming my elbow. It hit his side ribs, making a cracking sound. I stomped on his foot as hard as I could. The knife jerked off my neck. I bent from the waist, trying to flip him, and heard a crack in my arm. Tears of pain flooded my eyes. Then a gunshot, and Mike dropped behind me. The knife dropped to the ground. Once I realized I was free, I stumbled toward Rex as fast as I could. He rushed forward and grabbed me, putting me behind him, and held the gun on Mike.

Mal was at my feet and I reached down with my good hand and grabbed her by the collar, lifting her into my arm and behind Rex. Rex was the wall between me and the man who wanted to kill me.

"You shot me!" Mike sounded astonished as he held his shoulder. Blood pooled on his shirt.

"I'll do it again if you move," Rex said. He moved me a safe distance away, keeping his gun trained on Mike. "Stay here," he ordered me. Then he left me and moved closer to Mike. Police came running from the administration building down the street. I couldn't hear what was happening. My arm throbbed and my body shook. I slid down the side of the building and put my head to my knees, Mal in my lap licking my face.

"Allie?" It was Officer Lasko's voice.

I lifted my head. My arm throbbed horribly and tears filled my eyes.

"It's okay," she said. "Rex has him. Can you stand?"

I nodded and she tried to help me up with my right elbow, but I winced.

"Sorry," she said. "We need an ambulance here," she said over her radio. "How's your left arm?"

"Okay," I said and she helped me up with my left elbow. I had Mal tucked firmly against my body. My left hand cradled her and I clung to the warmth and weight of her body.

"Did he kill Mike?" I asked, shaking violently, not remembering everything that had happened.

"No," she said. "Rex shot him, but it's not life-threatening." The sound of the ambulance siren could be heard coming toward us. We were only a few blocks from the police station and the clinic. The ambulance was parked at the mouth of the alley and the sirens stopped. George hopped out and came toward me.

"Allie, are you all right?" he asked and studied the odd bend in my right arm. "She has a broken arm." He took a look at my neck. "Get me my kit," he called the other EMT. The kit was brought and he opened it up and grabbed fresh gauze, pressing it to my neck. "Come on, let's get you to the ambulance where you can sit down before you fall down."

One hand on my neck and the other around my waist, he walked me gently to the ambulance.

"Can you put Mal down?" he asked.

"No," I said firmly. "No."

"Okay, okay," he said and hoisted me up on the back of the ambulance.

I gritted my teeth at the pain. The other EMT was Billy Raven. He wrapped a blanket around my shoulders. Mal sat calmly in my lap. Her little head against my chest.

Rex came over. "Is she okay?"

"I'm fine," I said and tried to smile, but tears spilled down my face.

"She has a broken arm and we need to take care of the cut on her neck. Luckily, it's not very deep."

The shaking had slowed down. "What about Mike?" I asked. "Shouldn't someone look after him?"

"You first," Rex said. "There's someone with pressure on Mike's wound. Raven is heading over there now." He looked straight at George. "Take her to the clinic and come back for Hangleford. I don't want them in the same ambulance."

The island only had one ambulance. It usually was enough for the population.

"Will do," George said. "Lasko, can you help me get her inside and stay with us on the way to the clinic?"

She glanced at Rex and he nodded, so she climbed up into the ambulance and she and George got me seated and buckled in. We took off.

"How badly is Mike hurt?" I asked. "Rex didn't seem worried."

"The bullet pierced his shoulder below the collar-bone," Lasko said. "It didn't hit anything vital. They've stopped the bleeding. He'll be fine until they can clean him up and repair the wound."

"Good, good," I said and hugged Mal. "I don't want to be the cause of his death."

"You aren't," Lasko said and patted my knee. "You aren't."

I arrived at the clinic to find Liz shaking her head at me. "Back again so soon?"

"They just can't keep a good investigator down," I said. "When do you get out of here?"

"I'm waiting for the doctor's orders, but they said in an hour or two," she said and yawned. "It's a good thing because they don't let you sleep around here."

"We have to check your pupils every hour," the nurse said. "You don't want a brain bleed." She took my vitals and tsked at my arm. "Looks like you really wanted a cast on that arm." Then she lifted the gauze on my neck. "Lucky for you this is shallow. Some surgical glue should take care of it. The doctor is on his way."

I nodded and clung to Mal. She covered me with a blanket.

"Okay, doggie visit time is over," the nurse said and pulled Mal from me. "Aren't you just the cutest thing?" she said in a sweet baby voice. Mal, of course, loved the attention, her stump tail wagging.

"What are you going to do with her?" I asked.

"Your parents are in the waiting room," the nurse said. "They'll take good care of her."

Dr. Prost came in as the nurse left. He frowned at me.

"You're back too soon, young lady." He picked up my chart, glanced at it, and then looked at my neck. "I can fix this right up, but right now the priority is your arm. We need to get you down to the X-ray room so I can see how bad it is."

My arm was swollen and purple, but no bone showed. He shone a light in my eyes to check my pupils. "We need to get you in a gown so I can see where else you might be hurt. Cara," he called.

"I'm here," she said.

"Take her down to X-ray and then get her in a gown. I'll also need a kit for the neck wound."

"I've got that ready," she said and put a sterile kit still wrapped in packaging on the rolling table by my bed. She left for a moment and came back with a wheelchair. Then helped me in as the doctor looked at Liz one final time.

As I was wheeled off to the X-ray room, I heard him pronounce Liz ready to go home. At least there was one happy thing happening this morning.

It was two hours before they let anyone come see me. I had a spiral fracture in my humerus. The doctor had finished gluing my neck wound and then cast my arm from the shoulder down to the forearm with my elbow at a ninety-degree bend. Apparently, I had contusions and scrapes as well. He told me sleeping was going to be fun. Then ordered me an IV painkiller and let me have guests.

Mom and Dad and Mal were the first to come in.

Mom gasped. "Oh, my poor baby! You look terrible."

"I hope they throw the book at that guy," Dad said and held my good hand.

"How did this happen?" Mom asked. "Did you go

looking for him again? Did you learn nothing yesterday? That man is dangerous. We should've never let you go out by yourself." She patted my shoulder.

"First off," I said, "I did not go looking for him. He was looking for a way off the island and thought a hostage would help. Secondly, I'm a grown adult and am fully capable of taking my dog for a walk."

"Honey, tell her that it's pretty obvious from the cast and the splints that she is not fully capable of keeping herself safe," Mom said.

I gave my father a look and he raised his hands. "I'm not getting in the middle of this. Allie," he took my good hand, "are you okay?"

"I'm fine. They have me on some really good pain drugs," I said.

"Oh no, she needs pain meds," Mom said. "What if she gets addicted?"

"She's not going to get addicted," Dad said.

"Have you heard from Jenn's parents today?" I asked. "How is Shane? How is Jenn?"

"Jenn's dad called me," Dad said. "Shane is doing much better and is being moved out of the ICU. Jenn's good. She could come here, but she's staying in a hotel with her parents until Shane is allowed to come home."

"What did you tell the relatives?" I asked. "Did Terra come with breakfast?"

"Douglas said breakfast went off without a hitch. He and Frances set up the rooftop with tables covered with white tablecloths and the buffet was brought up to the roof. They explained to the relatives what Jenn's dad said about the kids. Rex stopped in and told them that they were free to come out of lockdown after you took the killer down."

"Did you guys get any breakfast?" I asked.

"We're not going to leave you for some breakfast," Mom said.

"I'm fine," I said. "Really. Why don't you two go get something to eat? It's after noon."

"Are you sure you want us to leave you?" Mom asked.

The nurse came into the curtained area. "She's fine if you want to leave for a while. Doctor said he was going to let her go home in a couple of hours. She just needs to rest a bit and get through her IV. Then she'll be released by the doctor. It will be about six p.m. when we let her go."

"All right," Dad said, ever the pragmatist. "Come on, dear, let's go get something to eat."

Mom gave me a hug and I bit my lip not to wince out loud. Then they left with Mal.

Exhausted, I closed my eyes, and when I opened them time had passed. Rex was sitting in a chair nearby. "How long have you been here?" I asked. My throat sounded hoarse. He poured me a glass of water and handed it to me.

"About an hour," he said. "Those pain meds really knocked you out."

"What did I miss?" My voice was clearer after a sip or two of water.

"Hangleford is in Cheboygan to get the bullet wound repaired. It was a through and through and didn't hit any major arteries."

"Did he say anything about why he did it? Oh, what about Becky and Shane? They're in Cheboygan, too. That has to be scary for them."

"I've got police stationed in front of Shane's room. Becky went home today to her parents' house in Detroit."

Rex took the glass of water from me and put it on the bed table. "Jenn is okay. She's a bit black and blue, but you and Shane took the most punishment."

"Is Shane awake?" I asked. "Dad said they moved him out of the ICU."

"He's awake," Rex said. "I'm going to go to Cheboygan tomorrow to see him. Then I'm going to see that the Cheboygan PD takes good care of Hangleford. Once he's well enough for transport, we'll drag him back to Mackinac County for trial."

"Good," I said and sat up. It was hard to do with only one hand. Rex helped me. "I can't wait to get out of this bed. I've got so much to do. We're going to have to cancel the wedding vendors and reschedule them."

"Frances told me to tell you not to worry, she's taken care of it. Jenn and Shane's new date is the weekend after the Wilkins wedding. Frances has rescheduled anyone who had reservations that weekend and offered all the friends and relatives to come back."

"Are they going to?" I asked.

"Frances seems to think so," he said. Rex took hold of my left hand and rubbed his thumb along it, caressing it. "Can you tell me what happened this morning?"

"I was up early, worried about Jenn and Shane. Mal needed her morning walk and there wasn't anyone around. I knew you'd have a patrol coming by soon, so I thought it was safe. We wandered over to the shore for a bit. I was on my way back when I spotted him and called you. The rest you know."

"Any idea how he knew where you were?"

"I don't," I said. "I didn't tell anyone where I was going. Heck, even I didn't know. I was lost in thought and ended up at the shore." I shrugged. "He had to just be looking for someone, anyone, to take as a hostage to get him off the island."

"Or he could have known you would walk Mal and lain in wait for you to do just that," Rex said. "You shouldn't have gone alone."

"No one else was up and you have to sleep sometime," I said and squeezed his hand. "I'm glad the wedding is rescheduled for two weeks from now. At least most of the bruises will be gone and my neck should be healed. I'd hate to look like Frankenstein's monster in Jenn's wedding photos."

"You'll always be beautiful to me," he said and kissed my fingers

There was a sound of a man clearing his voice. I looked up to see Harry.

"Hi," he said. "I heard you got hurt." He lifted the flowers in a mug that he had in his hand. "Thought I'd bring you something to cheer you up." He stepped into the curtained area and put the flowers on the bed table, then planted a kiss on my cheek. I felt Rex's fingers tighten around mine.

"Hi, Harry," I said. "Thank you, the flowers are beautiful."

"You look . . . amazing," he said with a sideways grin.

"Amazingly messed up," I said and smiled at him. The pressure on my left fingers grew. "Harry, you know Rex, right?"

"Sure," Harry said and stuck out his hand. "Nice to see you, Officer Manning. Glad you're taking such good care of our girl, here." There was an underlying current of sarcasm.

"He is," I said. "He saved me from the killer."

"Mike Hangleford." Harry's face clouded. "The very guy who painted my bed and breakfast."

"I had no idea when I recommended him," I said.

"Not your fault," he said and went to pat my hand, but I was covered in cast and splints. "Right, so, how long are you staying in the clinic?"

"Not long," I said. "My parents are coming at around six and the doc said I could go home if I was a good girl and got some rest."

"That's good to hear," Harry said. "Looks like the fudge shop will be out of commission for a few months."

"My dad introduced me to two assistants. They're going to intern for the summer. They're coming in next Monday. Hopefully, if they're good enough, they can take over while I'm sidelined."

"My guess is the fudge won't taste the same," Harry said with a wink. Then he glanced at Rex, who was still holding my hand, and sent me a sexy grin. "I don't want to wear you out. Doctor's orders to rest and all." He brushed another kiss on my cheek. Winked at Rex and walked out, throwing a "Talk to you soon," over his shoulder.

"That man has a lot of—"

I cut him off before he could say anything more. "Harry is my friend and you and I are not yet exclusive. Not that I am dating him or anything, but I'm not some piece of property to be fought over."

This time it was Rex's turn to grin. "I like you when you get all riled up." He kissed my hand and stood. "I'm going to let you get some rest. Enjoy your flowers." He kissed me on the mouth, soft and sensuous. "See you soon," he whispered against my lips. Then he left, whistling a jaunty tune.

The doctor and nurse came in to do a final check. My parents were back, my mother still horrified about how I looked. She brought me fresh clothes to wear and bagged up what I had on this morning. "You don't want to look at that," she said.

I was released and thanked Dr. Prost. The walk home was a bit shaky with the pain medication still in my system. Cara offered a wheelchair to get me home, but I refused. It was only a few blocks.

When I arrived at the McMurphy, Frances ran up and gave me a big hug. People from the wedding party swarmed me, asking questions, wanting a good story. So I gave it to them. Then I was bundled off to my apartment, which was filled with flowers.

"What? Where did all these come from?" I asked as I sat on my couch and looked at how many bouquets were there. There was barely any room to move. The scent of flowers perfumed the air.

"They're all from Rex," Mom said. "They just kept coming and coming. I think he bought out every florist in town."

I shook my head. No wondering he was whistling. His bouquets made Harry's look small in comparison. I tried to roll my eyes but couldn't. My heart warmed. Maybe this time Rex and I would grow even closer.

Hazelnut Spread Fudge

Ingredients:

2 cups hazelnut spread
½ cup of butter, melted
1¾ cups powdered sugar
1 tablespoon vanilla
1 cup chocolate chips
1 tablespoon butter

Directions:

In a mixing bowl, mix hazelnut spread and ½ cup butter until smooth. Sift powdered sugar into bowl with spread and butter. Add vanilla and blend. This should be thick but smooth. Place in a parchment-paper-lined 8 x 8-inch pan. Microwave chocolate chips and 1 tablespoon butter together, stirring every 30 seconds until melted and smooth. Pour over hazelnut fudge. Chill for ten minutes. Remove from refrigerator and cut into one-inch pieces. Return to refrigerator and chill until firm. Remove pieces from pan. Store in an airtight container and enjoy! Makes 32.

Chapter 20

M y new assistants arrived on Monday. They stopped by the McMurphy first before going to their temporary quarters, with many of the other seasonal workers.

"Hi, I'm Allie," I said. "I'd shake your hand, but . . ." I showed them my sling and cast. "Welcome to the Mc-Murphy."

Mal barked and came running, then slid into them.

"I'm Kent," the brother introduced them, "this is Kelly." They were both blond and beautiful, with wide smiles and blue eyes.

"What a cutie," Kelly said as she picked up Mal and scratched behind her ears.

"That's Mal," I said. "Short for Marshmallow. The McMurphy also has a cat, Caramella, or Mella for short. She's a calico. You'll see her around. Let me give you the grand tour." I took them around and showed them everything and then we returned to the lobby, where their suitcases rested beside Frances's desk. "So that's it. Frances will give you directions to your apartment. I hate to rush you, but if you could be back here by two p.m., we can make some fudge for the online orders today. I'd do it myself, but I'm a little . . ."

"Slinged up?" Kent said with a grin. "Do you find that humorous?"

"Very punny," Kelly said and rolled her eyes. "We'll be back by two."

They left and Frances looked up from her work station. "Those two are young."

"Just finished their senior year in college," I said. "Great time for an internship."

"You might have your hands full," she said. "Pun unintended."

I shook my head. "So, I heard from Jenn that Shane is coming home today. I'm going to go over to the house to make sure it's all fixed up." Jenn had been juggling a lot, ensuring the Wilkins wedding was ready to go off without hitch and spending her remaining hours at the hospital with Shane.

"Sounds like a good way to spend the day," Frances said. "Just don't do too much or stay too long. Remember, the doctor said not to use your arm and to get plenty of rest."

"I have to be back by two to supervise the interns, but I promise I'll just supervise at the house," I said. "The police station employees pooled enough money to repair the window and the locks. So, there should be very little left to do." With any luck, I'd see Rex there.

The walk to the house seemed to take forever. I was still recovering after my injuries. I can't lie; I'm sure the pain and exhaustion showed on my face.

"Allie, what are you doing here?" Liz asked as she came out the front door. "Did you walk? Seriously, you need to sit down. Come on, there's a chair in the bedroom."

I let her bundle me off until I sat and caught my breath. "I wanted to be here when Shane and Jenn came home."

"Well, you should have at least taken a carriage."

"I can't climb into one," I said and pointed my chin at my right arm and hand cast. My arm throbbed and I wished I had thought to bring a pain pill.

"Which tells me you shouldn't be here," she scolded me and brought me a glass of water with a straw. "Drink this."

I took a few sips. "The place looks wonderful," I said. "Like nothing happened. Did you get the blood off the floor?"

"All the blood is gone," Liz said. "Our friend Franklin came in with a hand sander, sanded, and then touched up the floor stain and replaced the broken window. I'm sure you can smell the paint."

"The window's open," I said as I watched the curtains flutter.

"It's only until they get here," Liz said. "I'm trying to get as much of the paint and stain smell out as possible. As soon as they arrive, I'm going to close the window and light a candle."

"Have you heard how Shane's doing?" I asked.

"He's recovered enough to come home," Rex said as he walked into the room.

I blushed at the sight of him, remembering the flowers. "Great news," I said. "Thanks again for the flowers."

He came over and kissed me. "You're welcome."

Liz watched us with a lifted eyebrow.

"I'll tell you later," I mouthed to her as Rex crossed the room to inspect the window.

"The guys did a great job," Liz said. "They even brought in a minifridge." She pointed to the dorm-sized fridge beside the dresser. "That way they can keep drinks cold and any food they get."

"Oh right, their kitchen is hollowed out and people are going to be stopping by with food," I said. "How are they going to store all that?"

"The guys brought in a chest freezer," Rex said. "It's plugged in and waiting in the carriage house."

I'd forgotten about the little carriage house that was behind the fixer-upper.

"We were going to put it in the basement, but we didn't want either of them going up or down stairs."

"How's Jenn?" I asked Liz. "She's been too busy to talk."

"She's good, like me: bumps and bruises and sore in places she didn't know could get sore."

"Sorry for not asking about you," I said.

"I'm okay," she said. "A little shell-shocked, but wow, do I have a firsthand experience to talk about. It really gave me perspective on what victims go through."

There was a lot of commotion at the door and I got up and followed Liz out of the bedroom. It was Jenn and Shane. Charles had Shane's arm around his shoulder and helped him into the house. He made his way to the bedroom with Jenn at his side. They got him in bed, sitting up and covered with a blanket.

I gave Jenn a huge hug. She took a step back and stared at my cast. "Feeling any better?"

"I'm fine," I said. "I'm going to supervise my new assistants making fudge this afternoon. You look good."

"I'm doing okay," she said and took a seat on the bed next to Shane and held his hand. "We're doing okay."

I gave Shane an awkward hug. His knife wound was on the same side as my arm, so we both winced.

"I'm so sorry we missed your wedding date," I said. "But I'm so glad you are both alive and healing."

"I think we're doing better than you," he said and pushed his glasses up on his nose.

"It looks worse than it is," I said.

"What happened?" Shane asked.

Rex filled them in on Mike's capture. "So, piecing it all together, Mike roofied you to frame you. Then he lured Becky and Christopher into the alley. He attacked Christopher and Becky tried to fight him, so she was knocked out and cut. Then he killed Christopher. But you woke up too soon and fought Mike, grabbing the knife. Mike ran off, and that's when the ladies found Shane."

"Was Peter in on it?" I asked. "He lied about taking Shane here."

"As far as we can tell, Peter didn't know anything except that Mike told him not to worry about taking Shane here. He could leave him in the alley and he'd be fine."

"So he did," I concluded. "He should still be charged as an accessory to the crime."

"I'm leaving that up to the DA," Rex said.

There was a knock on the door. Frances and Douglas came in with a casserole in hand. "We brought you food," Frances said.

"Smells wonderful," Jenn said.

"But you have no counters to put it on," Frances pointed out.

"Just leave it on the dresser," Jenn said and then stood to give Frances a hug.

Frances pulled up a chair next to the bed and asked how they were feeling. Then she went into all the arrangements she'd made to have the wedding go off without a hitch a week from Saturday. "Hopefully, Shane will be good to stand for the ceremony."

"Oh, he will be. If we had it our way, we'd get married today," Jenn said. "But I'm thinking about our families. So, thank you, Frances for doing all that."

More people started to come in bringing food, from desserts to meals. Douglas and Rex started taking it all out to the carriage house and putting it in the freezer.

It was time to go to train my new assistants. I kissed Jenn and Shane and Rex walked me back to the McMurphy.

"The flowers are beautiful," I said. "It was a grand gesture."

"I wanted you to know I'm capable of grand gestures, too, you know," he said.

"I can see that." I smiled.

We got to the McMurphy and my new assistants were in the kitchen with Sandy Everheart, making fudge.

"What's this?" I asked as I stuck my head into the shop.

"Frances called me," Sandy said. "I'm not working at the Grander tonight, so I'm here."

"Thank you!"

Rex left me at the door and I went upstairs. The apartment was quiet since the family had gone home. But it would be busy again starting Friday. I looked at the flowers again and pulled out my phone and texted Rex. **Are you busy?**

Just getting home, why? he texted back.

Want to come over for dinner?

My phone rang. "Hello?"

"Yes, I'd like to have dinner with you," Rex said. "What time and what can I bring?"

I felt a warm glow in my chest. "Say seven and bring what you're drinking because all I have right now is wine."

"On it," he said. "See you then." He hung up, and I realized that the prospect of having drinks with Rex sounded like a perfect way to spend the night. Having a few hours alone with a handsome man would help relieve the pressure of having to entertain a full hotel.

I relieved Frances at the registration desk and she and Douglas went home. After checking that all the guests coming in today had arrived, I closed up the desk and left the buzzer that rang in my apartment on the desktop with a note to buzz if anyone needed anything. With my staff gone for the night, I was the one left to bring more towels, more toiletries, or answer questions. It didn't mean I couldn't spend time with Rex.

I made chicken breasts in cream of mushroom sauce and some rice as best I could with one hand in a sling. I was dumping a bagged salad in a bowl when there was a knock at my back door. I peeked out to see it was Rex and opened the door. "Come on in," I said.

Rex had his hands full of whiskey, flowers, and a pink box. He was out of his uniform, dressed in black jeans, a skintight black Police T-shirt, and a gray sweatshirt. "Thanks for having me," he said. "The flowers are for you. I brought cheesecake for dessert. It's a sampler because I didn't know what kind you liked, so I figured you must like something in it."

"Oh, thanks," I said. I tried to take the flowers, but it was awkward with only one hand.

"Let me," Rex said. He put the cheesecake box on the counter.

"There's a vase here," I said and opened a cupboard.

He took out the vase, clipped the bottoms from the flowers, added sugar and water to the vase, and then put the flowers in.

"So pretty," I said as he put them on the bar top. "There are highball glasses in the cupboard to the right of the sink," I said. "The fridge has an icemaker in the door."

"Fancy," he said, noting the water and ice dispenser on the front of my fridge. "But I drink my whiskey neat."

The kitchen was small and Rex seemed to take up a lot of it. I brushed past him to pull out a cheese plate from the fridge. I turned with the plate in hand to find him looking at me with his warm blue gaze. "What?" I asked as heat rushed over my cheeks.

"You are a beautiful, talented woman, Allie," he said and took the plate from me. "Don't let anyone tell you otherwise."

I swallowed my embarrassment and said, "Thank you." My mother had always told me not to say a compliment wasn't true. Instead of arguing, I was to say, "Thank you." Now it came naturally to me.

He stood very close to me, cheese plate in hand. "Why did you invite me here tonight?"

"I had free time and needed to have some downtime from thinking about the wedding and Christopher's murder," I said. "You said you wanted me to think about being exclusive with you. I need more than one partial date before I make a decision that momentous."

"So, this is a date," he said.

I looked at his clean clothes, smelled his aftershave

and soap. He'd showered and dressed up. I'd done the same, showering and wearing a strapless sundress. "Well, I'd be sad if it isn't a date because I fixed my hair and makeup one-handed and put on a cute dress." I twirled for him.

"You're not wearing shoes," he said. "So it's more of a casual date."

"Feel free to take off your shoes. I don't like wearing them in the house." I brushed past him to pick up my glass of wine and sat on the couch. "Are you going to stay in the kitchen all night?"

He slipped out of his shoes and walked over in stockinged feet to put down the cheese plate on the coffee table. "Here's to having enough dates for you to be exclusively mine."

I tapped my wineglass on his whiskey glass. I had music playing soft and low from my iPod. There were candles on the side table, the flames were dancing and let off the scent of peonies. It mingled well with the scent of chicken on the stove.

We talked and laughed about nonsensical things. I finished my wine and got up to pour myself another glass and to pop the rice into a pot of boiling water. He brought the cheese plate to the counter, poured another two fingers of whiskey in his glass, and sat on the barstool, watching me cook. He snagged bites from the cheese plate. I joined him.

"I understand Melonie hasn't left the island yet," I said. "You know, she practically threatened me this winter."

"What do you mean, threatened?" he asked, his expression darkening.

"She said she had every intention of marrying you again and would harm anyone who got in her way."

"She's bluffing," he said. "Harming someone takes forethought and hard work. Melonie is lacking in both areas. Now, if it was *you* threatening someone, I'd take that seriously."

"Thank you for the compliment . . . I think."

"I asked Melonie to move out in March," he said.

"But she hasn't left the island," I pointed out. "I hear she's renting a room from the Fastwells. You know, in their carriage house."

"What does that have to do with us? I promise you, I'm a free man. You're free right now. We should continue to be free together." He sent me a look that warmed my heart.

"Just checking to see if that's over. I don't take other women's men. It's a thing with me," I said. "Also, lying. I'm not a fan of lying or hedging."

"I couldn't tell from the way you manage your little investigations," he said, his right eyebrow cocked, sipping his whiskey.

"Okay," I said. "As we're dating, I'll tell you anything you ask me," I teased. "But it doesn't mean I'll do what you want and not what I deem necessary."

"You are a hard woman," Rex said. "Complicated and whip smart as you are beautiful."

"Is that a problem?"

"Not for me," he said.

"Good."

The rest of the evening was filled with talk of the people on the island, how we grew up, where we want to be in the future, and maybe some hot snuggling.

We took Mal out for her late-night walk under the clear sky. Stars sparkled above. We wandered by Jenn and Shane's fixer-upper, but the lights were off, so we didn't knock. Rex left me at my back door with a promising kiss that curled my toes.

"How'm I doing?" he asked, his voice low and husky. "Are you ready to be exclusive?"

"After one and a half dates? A girl would be crazy to commit so early," I whispered back.

"Challenge accepted," he said. "The next date is on me."

"No, the next date is the wedding," I reminded him.

"Good night, Allie."

"Good night."

Jenn was back at the McMurphy by Wednesday, drumming up business for her next wedding planning event. She worked half days and worried over Shane the other half. Shane grew stronger every day.

The Wilkins wedding went off without a hitch. Everyone gushed at how great the rooftop deck was for the views and an outdoor reception. We were able to reschedule the people who had booked the McMurphy for the following weekend and Jenn's family and friends returned. This time we didn't have a bachelorette party, or a tea, but we did get in the rehearsal out at Arch Rock Park on Friday night.

Carriages took us all to the park, and Jenn had timed it so that they brought us around the island and back to the McMurphy in time to watch the sun set from the rooftop deck.

The rehearsal dinner was full of joy and stories exchanged about the happy couple. Shane was mostly recovered and would go back to work after their honey-moon.

I woke up the day of the wedding to a bright sunny sky. Jenn had stayed with me the night before and her dress hung in the closet of my spare room. I took Mal for a short walk—no farther than the end of the alley and back. Poor pup missed our long walks, but until my arm was better and Rex deemed it safe, our walks were short.

Mella greeted us as we entered the apartment. She was not happy with the full hotel and all the hustle and bustle, and spent most of her time in her box in the closet. As I fed my fur babies breakfast, I was amazed at how well I was getting along using only my left hand.

We had a bridesmaids brunch planned for ten a.m. That was when Liz was coming over for the day. We planned on pampering Jenn all day. Frances and our moms were also invited. I was going to cook, but Liz thought it was better if she did.

I poured myself a cup of coffee, added cream, and sipped it to enjoy the last few minutes of quiet. Jenn came in dressed in a slip and a robe.

"Good morning," I said. "Happy wedding day!"

"Finally," she said with sleep still in her voice. She poured herself coffee. "How's the weather looking? Are we going to need canopies?"

I checked my phone, which was sitting on the counter-top. "According to the Weather Channel, it's supposed to be clear skies all day, sunny with a high of seventy-eight. Perfect day for a wedding."

"Thank goodness," she said, sipping her coffee and sighing as she leaned on the counter. "I think there's been enough drama where my wedding is concerned."

"I'm glad we are doing it now. It gave the seamstress time to fit my dress around my cast."

"And for your neck to heal. A little makeup and no one will notice," Jenn said. "It would have been quite some look for my wedding pictures."

"Memorable to say the least," I said. "My cast will be bad enough. I can't fix your train or anything else a maid of honor is supposed to do for you."

"It's okay," Jenn said. "I'm just glad to have everyone alive."

There was a knock at the door, and Liz and my friend Sophie, the pilot, came in. Then Frances and our moms appeared fifteen minutes later. It was a sunshine-filled day of laughter, champagne, and joy. We had a mani-pedi setup after brunch, followed by the hair and makeup artists. By three p.m. we were dressed and posing for pictures.

The seamstress had cleverly turned my three-quarter-length sleeved dress into a one shoulder. Liz and I had the lace overskirt attached to our dresses and I felt as much a princess as Jenn looked in her hoop-skirted, off-the-shoulder, Victorian-inspired gown.

At four the carriages arrived to take the guests to Arch Rock. Then the moms left together. Finally, we stuffed Jenn and her dress into the elevator to the lobby. The florist had transformed the lobby with flower garlands going up the twin staircases. Douglas had been busy all day, helping the caterer and florist set up the reception area on the rooftop deck.

The most elaborate carriage arrived. I was helped in first, then Jenn in the opposite side by herself, and finally Liz beside me.

"I feel like it's a royal wedding," I said with a laugh.

Jenn's eyes sparkled and her veil flew about as we took off toward the rock. "That was my plan."

"Everyone should feel like a princess on their wedding day," Liz said.

We arrived at the park and helped Jenn out, adjusting her veil and dress. My mom and dad and the guests were already seated. We remained out of sight behind a large tree as a harp played and the men took their places beside the flower-covered trellis Douglas had built.

The usher came for Jenn's mom first. Then, as soon as she was seated, the harp began to play *Arioso from Cantata 156* by Bach. Liz headed down the white rice paper carpet. White chairs were set out and flowers decorated the ends of the aisles. I was next. Holding my bouquet in my left hand, I carefully walked down the aisle. I looked at Rex and he looked at me, and happiness slid down my spine. I sent him a smile. Taking my place at the front, everyone stood as Jenn and her father came around the trees to walk up the rice paper carpet.

Tears filled my eyes. Jenn was so beautiful. I glanced at Shane, who looked at once stunned and amazed. Tears glistened in his eyes, too.

The ceremony took about thirty minutes. Tears trickled down my cheeks at the love that was so palpable between the bride and groom.

"By the power vested in me, I now pronounce you husband and wife. You may kiss the bride." The minister was female and looked as happy as the rest of us as Shane kissed Jenn.

The newlyweds hurried down the aisle as we showered them with rose petals. The reception line formed as we finished walking back up the aisle. Rex had his hand on my back because he couldn't offer me his arm. I hugged Jenn tight.

"I'm so happy for you! Congrats," I said.

Then I hugged Shane and got into the line. The guests flowed out of their chairs with joy. Once everyone had congratulated them, they were taken away in carriages as we stayed for more pictures. Then the bridal party was put in carriages and given a trip around the island, turning down Market to the fort and then down Main Street as people clapped and hooted.

We stopped in front of the McMurphy. After entering the lobby, Liz and I removed our lace overskirts and then helped button up Jenn's train before getting her and Shane into the elevator. We all met on the third floor in front of the steps to the roof. Bridesmaids and groomsmen went up first and, finally, the bride and groom appeared.

The rooftop was transformed into a fairy light wonderland as dusk descended on the lake. We laughed, we ate a sumptuous meal, and when the meal was done we danced. Rex put his arm around the back of my chair as we watched Jenn dance with her father and Shane dance with his mother.

I sighed. "It's so romantic," I said. "Seeing families begin."

Next up was the bridal party slow dance. Rex stood, pulled out my chair, and held out his hand. "Shall we?"

I took his right hand with my left. And let him guide me to the dance floor. We slow danced as best we could with my cast between us. I looked up at him. "I seem to remember dancing with you at another wedding," I said.

"I'll never forget it," he replied. "It was our first kiss." He pulled me in gently.

"I think you are hiding a true romantic under all your cop-who-serves-and-protects persona," I said softly.

"Why do you say that?" he asked, leaning toward me until our breath mingled.

"You like weddings," I teased. "You've had two."

His face grew solemn. "Does that bother you?"

"Maybe a little," I said. "But only because I want to be your one and only." I rested my cheek on his chest.

We danced in silence for a few moments. I could feel his heart pounding. Then he gently turned my face toward his. "You are my one and only and have been ever since the night we first met."

"When Mr. Jessop was dead in my closet, if I recall."

"Just kiss me, woman," he said.

And I did.

Tonight there was no more talk of murder as we celebrated family and friends. The killer was caught. Justice was done, and I would heal with Rex by my side.

Acknowledgments

I'd like to thank Mackinac Island's tourism bureau and The Island Bookstore for all their help in researching Mackinac. Any mistakes are my own. Thanks also to the wonderful staff at Kensington for all their hard work and dedication to quality books.

Don't miss the next delightful Candy-Coated mystery by
acclaimed mystery writer Nancy Coco

A Midsummer Night's Fudge

Coming soon from Kensington Publishing Corp.

Keep reading to enjoy a sample excerpt . . .

Chapter 1

I'd much rather make fudge and celebrate festivals with my friends than find murder victims. But finding victims seems to be my luck these days. Of course, murder victims were the last thing on my mind as we celebrated the very first Midsummer Night's Festival. The festival celebrated summer on the island and opened with an outdoor masquerade ball, a bonfire on the beach, and the crowning of the Midsummer Night's Queen.

"Mrs. Higer really outdid herself with this ball," I said as Jenn and I exited the dance floor. Jenn was my best friend and sometimes partner in sleuthing. Recently married, Jenn was gorgeously slim, wearing a black jumpsuit and large blue butterfly wings. Her beautiful eyes were half hidden behind a black lace eye mask.

"I think Mayor Boatman is trying to take some credit

for the event," Jenn said and pointed to where the mayor stood beside Mrs. Higer as people congratulated her.

"Well, she was on the committee," I said.

"She's on all the committees," Jenn reminded me. "But she's really good at delegating all the work."

The dance floor was a ten-by-ten-foot deck that rested on the sandy beach. A live band played behind it. There were cash bars on either side of the event area and a large bonfire to the left, where people sat in grouped lawn chairs while others put out picnic blankets and coolers.

There was a long buffet table and Porter's Meats had roasted a pig. Little kids dressed as fairies and unicorns ran through the sand, laughing and squealing as they chased one another around the beach.

I wore a floaty green dress with a kerchief hem, flutter sleeves, and huge fairy wings. My bichonpoo pup, Mal, was dressed as a dragon. She loved festivals and people. Thankfully, my boyfriend, Rex Manning, didn't mind watching her while I danced.

We returned to our spot, where Rex and Jenn's new husband, Shane Carpenter, sat drinking beer and watching the flames grow and pop as people added fuel to the bonfire.

Mal barked and jumped up on me and I picked her up, giving her a quick squeeze as she licked my face.

"Hurry up and take a seat," Shane said. "They're about to announce the winner of the Midsummer Night's Queen contest."

I sat down in a lawn chair next to Rex. My boyfriend was a police officer and, with his shaved head and gorgeous eyes, had that action-hero look about him. Shane, on the other hand, was lanky, with thick glasses and caramel-colored hair. Both men had indulged us by wearing black T-shirts, jeans, and black eye masks. After all, the event was a masquerade.

"Ladies and gentlemen, your attention, please," Mrs. Higer said, her voice loud through the microphone in her hand. We all turned to look at the main stage. Five young ladies stood there wearing long, flowing evening gowns, fairy wings, and pointed ears. Mrs. Higer herself was dressed as a unicorn, complete with a rainbow wig, a tutu, and a rainbow tail. "As you know, these girls have been competing for the last three days in various portions of the contest: talent, health, and interview. Now the scores have been calculated and are currently being verified by the local firm of Bradford Accounting. Mr. Bradford, could you please bring up the results?"

Everyone clapped as the accountant, in black tie attire and a black eye mask, walked up and handed her an envelope. He then motioned for her to bend down and whispered something in her ear.

"I see," Mrs. Higer said. "Thank you. Tonight, ladies and gentlemen, you see five girls before you, but unfortunately, due to a disqualification, there will only be four places awarded for the queen and her court. Your queen will receive a five-hundred-dollar scholarship to the school of her choice and she and her court will ride in the queen's float in tomorrow's parade."

The crowd clapped. The girls looked at one another, puzzled. Who was disqualified?

"The third runner up is . . . Amy Newhouse." Everyone clapped as she received flowers and a sash. "The second runner up is . . . Lakesha Smith." A beautiful girl with chocolate-colored skin stepped up and received her sash. "There are three girls left," Mrs. Higer said. "And only one winner. The first runner up is . . . Pamela Oustand." Everyone clapped as she received her flowers and sash and the two remaining girls stood together holding hands.

"Two girls stand before us. Each one lovely. Each one receiving high marks for community service, health, and interview. Unfortunately, only one will be queen. The other is disqualified for not meeting the criteria to compete. And the winner is . . . . Julie Rodriquez!" Everyone clapped as a lovely brunette clasped her hands over her mouth and cried. "Unfortunately, that means Natasha Alpine has been disqualified. She may leave the stage."

"There must be some kind of mistake," Natasha said. "Why would I be disqualified?"

"We can talk about it backstage," Mrs. Higer said. "Now, let's crown our queen." She shooed Natasha off the stage and took the tiara from the hands of her assistant, Michele Bell, and pinned it to Julie's head. Then she placed a sash around Julie's dress and handed her roses. With a flourish, Mrs. Higer waved the crowd to clap for their queen as she pushed Natasha out of the way.

Natasha continued to argue that the crown should be hers, but Bill Blankensmith grabbed her by the waist and pulled her off the stage.

"Now it's time for the fireworks," Mrs. Higer said.

"Seems like there were a lot of fireworks already," Jenn said with a laugh. "Poor Natasha is not a good loser."

"She was already Lilac Queen and Fudge Festival Queen," I said. "It's time for some of the other girls to win."

"I wonder what she did to be disqualified?" Jenn asked.

"I don't know," I said. "But I bet the reason will come

out pretty quickly. Natasha's mom looks hot under the collar."

We both watched as Mrs. Alpine stormed the stage.

There was a boom, a zinging noise, and the whoosh of fireworks. We turned to the sky as the fireworks shot up over the straits of Mackinac and exploded into the air with loud booms. Mal was not a fan and jumped into my lap. I wrapped her tightly in a blanket, but she shivered and tried to hide her head.

"I'm going to run Mal home," I said. "I'll be right back."

"Do you want me to come with you?" Rex asked.

"No, I'll be fine."

I lived at the top of the Historic McMurphy Hotel and Fudge Shop. It was on Main Street, just a few blocks from the beach. Hugging Mal as the fireworks exploded and people oohed and aahed, I scurried through the crowd. Mrs. Higer was busy arguing with Natasha and what appeared to be her mother and her grandmother. They looked livid over the disqualification.

I shook my head at the silliness of it all and walked up from the beach onto the sidewalk, past the school, and onto Main Street.

The festival drew most of the island residents, so Main Street was unusually quiet. I unbundled Mal and let her walk/run back to the McMurphy with me. Hurrying down the alley around the back of the building, I saw that Mal was better because we were no longer right near the fireworks.

I took her upstairs, gave her a chew bone, checked on my kitty, and then locked the door. The fireworks were slowing down as I left Main Street and walked the footpath toward the beach.

Then, just as the last fireworks exploded, I saw something in the water. It looked like a person and they were facedown. Glancing around, I didn't see anyone nearby to help, so I hurried to the water's edge and waded into the waves.

It was a woman wearing a unicorn costume. The white tutu and long, rainbow hair flowed in and out with the waves.

I dove into the water, came up next to the woman, and turned her so that her face was out of the water. I dragged her to shore as I was taught in my high school lifeguard class. I got maybe a yard onto dry sand when I heard someone approach.

"Allie, are you okay?" It was Mrs. Tunisian. She was a dear friend and one of a handful of senior citizens who'd retired on the island. She was dressed as a dragonfly with her hair in a mohawk and a headband with twin antennae.

"I'm fine," I said, "but she isn't. She was in the water." I set down the woman and gasped as I saw it was Mrs. Higer, the head of the Midsummer's Night Festival. I got on my knees to push water from her lungs when I noticed a dark round hole in the center of her forehead.

Grabbing my phone, I turned on the flashlight.

"Oh, that's not good," Mrs. Tunisian said.

Indeed, it was not. Mrs. Higer had been shot right between the eyes. I didn't think there was anything I could do to save her life.

"Run to the bonfire and get Rex," I ordered Mrs. Tunisian. Then I dialed 9-1-1.

"Nine-one-one, what is your emergency?" Charlene, the dispatch operator, asked.

"Hi, Charlene," I said, my voice breathless.

"Oh my goodness, Allie, who's dead?" It seemed to be a growing theme between Charlene and me.

"It's Mrs. Higer," I said. "She's been shot."

"Is she alive?"

"No, I don't think so," I said. "I found her in the water and when I pulled her out I saw that she had a bullet hole in the center of her forehead."

"Where are you?"

"I'm at the beach, just at the bottom of the path from Main Street."

"I've got police arriving soon," Charlene said. "Are you okay? Did you see the shooter?"

"No," I said, looking around. "I didn't see the shooter, but her body is still warm, so it had to have happened not too long ago."

"Does she have a heartbeat?"

I placed my fingers on the side of her neck. "No," I confirmed. "She's definitely dead."

I heard the sirens from the ambulance coming my way. Mackinac Island had banned motor vehicles nearly a century ago. That meant most people got around by bicycle or horse and carriage. I liked to walk everywhere. But when it came to safety, we had a modern firetruck and a modern ambulance. They were the only vehicles allowed on the island.

Rex and Mrs. Tunisian came running, followed by Jenn and Shane.

"Allie, what happened? You're soaked!" Rex said.

"I was coming back down the path when I saw someone in the water. She was facedown, so I swam out to get her and bring her in," I said.

"That's when we saw the bullet hole in her forehead," Mrs. Tunisian told Rex. "So I went to get you."

"Did anyone hear a shot?" I asked.

"The fireworks must have covered up the sound," Rex said.

Two bikes approached. It was Officer Lasko and Officer Brown. Rex waved them down.

"It's Mrs. Higer," I said and pointed toward the body. I walked a good distance away from the body so they could take care of things. "Someone shot her in the head."

"Were you here when she was found?" Officer Charles Brown asked Rex. Charles was a handsome man with a strong chin and short brown hair.

"No," Rex said. "Allie found her in the water."

"I pulled her out and dragged her to where she is now," I explained.

"I went and got Rex," Mrs. Tunisian said. A crowd had begun to form behind Jenn.

"I'm going to go get my kit," Shane said. He was our local crime scene investigator. He and Jenn had bought a small bungalow not far from the McMurphy. That was where he kept his kit.

"How did you find her?" Officer Megan Lasko asked. She pulled a notebook out of her pocket to take my statement.

I went over what happened. I knew from experience that I would be asked the same questions over and over to ensure I didn't change my story or to help me remember something I might have forgotten.

"Did you see anyone else?" Officer Lasko asked.

"No." I shook my head. "The fireworks must have covered up the sound of the gunshot."

"What was she doing way over here?" Tracy mused.

"I don't know," I said. "I found her in the water, so she could have drifted here."

"Did you see her at the bonfire?"

"I did."

"Did you see her leave?" Megan asked.

"No," I said. "Last I saw her, she was talking with the Alpines about the pageant. It seems Natasha Alpine was disqualified, and her mother and grandmother weren't too happy about it."

The ambulance arrived and George Marron stepped out. He was dressed in a blue EMT's outfit, his hair pulled back into a long single braid. His cheekbones were high and strong in his thin face. His copper-colored skin shone in the light from my phone.

"Hello, Allie," he said.

"Hi, George," I greeted him.

"What do we have?" he asked, his voice smooth as sanded wood.

"Mrs. Higer, shot in the middle of her forehead," I said and pointed toward the body. "I don't think she needs you. You'd better call the coroner."

"You're wet," he said. "Are you okay?"

"I'm fine," I said. "Just a little chilled."

"Is Shane on duty?"

"He went home to get his kit," I said.

Jenn came over with a beach towel for me. I hadn't seen her leave, but there was a lot going on and it was dark. "Here," she said. "You're shivering."

I huddled into the warmth of the beach towel. My wings were soggy lace.

"I'll tape off the crime scene," Megan said. "The crowds are growing, and we don't need them trampling evidence."

"Thanks, Lasko," Rex said. He and George squatted down to take a good look at the body.

Jenn hugged me. "Are you okay?"

"Yes," I said, hugging her back. "I'm just chilled from the water. How did this happen without anyone seeing anything?"

"Did you see anyone nearby when you found her?" Rex asked as he stood, leaving the body to George.

"No." I shook my head. "I didn't hear anything, either. I think the shot was covered up by the fireworks."

"Last I saw her, she was talking to the Alpines at the festival," Jenn said.

"I know," I said. "That's when I saw her."

"We were on the beach and didn't hear the shot. But that doesn't mean others didn't. We're going to have to interview the people at the festival to see if anyone saw her leave," Rex said.

"Well, then, you'd better hurry, because people are leaving already," I said.

"I'm sure that anyone with information will come forward," Rex said with confidence. He turned to give me a glimpse of the crowd formed outside the tape lines. "It looks like everyone showed up for this crime scene."

"Maybe even the killer," Mrs. Tunisian said.

If only things were that easy.